"A fresh and engaging take on the mysterious death of Jane Stanford, Sara Ackerman's *The Guest in Room 120* offers grief, intrigue, and romance set against the lush backdrop of Hawai'i, both present and past. I devoured this novel!"

—Bryn Turnbull,
internationally bestselling author of *The Berlin Apartment*

"A real historical mystery sets a struggling writer on a 'path of discovery as she untangles the threads of the past in this elegantly braided narrative. Touched with gothic suspense and a hint of the supernatural, *The Guest in Room 120* will hold readers in thrall with its blend of mystery, romantic intrigue, and atmosphere."

—Paulette Kennedy,
bestselling author of *The Devil and Mrs. Davenport*

"For fans of Fiona Davis who love braided historical fiction and contemporary narratives that are set against backdrops where setting becomes character, *The Guest in Room 120* is a page-turner that crackles with suspense, romance and mystery."

—Bianca Marais,
author of *A Most Puzzling Murder*

THE GUEST IN ROOM 120

A NOVEL

SARA ACKERMAN

/||MIRA

//|MIRA™

ISBN-13: 978-0-7783-8722-0

The Guest in Room 120

MIRA
22 Adelaide St. West, 41st Floor
Toronto, Ontario M5H 4E3, Canada
MIRABooks.com

HarperCollins Publishers
Macken House, 39/40 Mayor Street Upper,
Dublin 1, D01 C9W8, Ireland
www.HarperCollins.com

Printed in U.S.A.

Recycling programs
for this product may ·
not exist in your area.

THE GUEST IN ROOM 120

It is not all of life to live, yet nor all of death to die.

—EDGAR CAYCE

FROM THE JOURNAL OF
ʻILIAHI BALDWIN, 1901

At our school in Waikīkī, there were two camps. Those whose families were invited to the grand opening of the Moana Hotel, and those who weren't. Ours wasn't, but I don't care because I think it was a foolish idea to build a hotel right on the beach. Ma agrees, but I can tell Pa wishes he would have made the cut since he helped build the thing. Sometimes after school, Max and Liko and I would walk down and swim, and he would wave to us from the unfinished peepholes just below the roof. White and four stories high, the structure has more windows and arches and columns than leaves on a tree. I have not been inside yet, but I hear the hallways are double wide and the rooms plush as a palace.

At dinner, Pa would tell us all about Mr. Price's plans to attract wealthy people from Europe. But I see foreigners on the beach all the time in front of the San Souci or Castle's house, and I tell you this: They are nothing to write home about. Most of them can't swim, and they are the color of fresh cow's milk and burn like boiled lobster.

Yesterday afternoon the big gala finally happened, and I have to admit, I was curious. We all were. So much so that Ma packed a picnic of rice balls, kūlolo and dried aku, and we did what we often do. We walked down and set up under the big old kamani tree just down from where the hotel now sits. Pa refused to go any farther, not wanting to be seen gawking, but my brothers and I had no shame. We marched over to the beach in front of the Moana, where we could see a big crowd had formed, all in suits and high-necked dresses, fanning themselves in the unseasonable March heat. An orchestra was set up on the veranda, and their music caught in the wind and traveled out over the water, causing its own ripples. *Moana* means open sea, a fitting name when you look at the expanse of blue out front.

No one noticed us. They were too busy conversing. We were invisible. And then Liko decided he wanted to go inside and take a tour. We were dressed in swimming attire, and barefoot, but once Liko makes up his mind, there is no swaying him. I glanced back at our parents, and Pa waved as though calling us back. I acted as if I hadn't seen and followed Liko up the beach and into the crowd. We garnered a few looks from the guests, but we wove through so quickly no one had a chance to stop us. On the deck, I almost collided with Ma's friend Kui, carrying a tray the size of a giant lily pad, full of colorful drinks. I could tell she was surprised to see me, and I nodded and then ducked away.

Inside the lobby, people were smashed together, and it was loud and smoky and smelled like burnt meat. In the center were tables full of food. We stopped and gaped. There was enough food here to last us through summer, maybe longer. I looked at Liko with a heavy feeling. Sure enough, he grabbed a plate, shoveled it full of food, and then slinked away toward the stairs. Max and I both followed. By no means are we beggars, and we always have enough to eat, but the tangy and smoky smells were too tempting for Liko. He has never been one to control his impulses, and I worried we would soon be thrown out, but we found a bench in an empty hallway and devoured the most delicious food I have ever tasted. He wanted to go back for more, but I knew that would be pushing our fortune. Thankfully, Liko listened, and we went back out the way we came; this time, I was in the lead. As the older sister, I try to have some command over my wild brothers. Still, no one seemed to notice us. The shiny new building, with its polished wood floors, luminous chandeliers and thick carpets, was far more appealing than three Hawaiian scoundrels testing their luck.

Ma and Pa made like they were angry, but since we hadn't gotten caught, no harm, no foul.

A CURIOUS INCIDENT

Jane

January 14, 1905

THE JANUARY COLD bit savagely into her, gnawing on her old bones like a pack of winter wolves. Jane was alone and yet not alone in the sprawling mansion on Nob Hill that more resembled a palace than a house. Fifty rooms and just one member of the Stanford family in residence. Husband and son, Leland and Leland Jr., both long gone. But still close by—always close by. When she closed her eyes, she could see that thin-lipped smile on her son's soft face. Or those red-topped boots he loved so much he had worn them to bed more than once. And feel her husband's warm breath skimming her neck as he whispered in her ear, *My dearest Jennie*—his nickname for her.

They took turns visiting her, their spirits filling her with contentment and advising her in all matters of life. Some people thought she was not of sound mind, but that was their concern, not hers.

Now, although Ah Wing and the servants were supposed to keep all the doors closed tight, Jane swore she felt an icy breeze scraping against her cheek. At precisely 8:00 p.m., she walked down the hallway, checking the windows on the second floor to be sure. She was already sick with a cold. Catching a chill in this dreadful weather would be the death of her. But she wasn't ready yet. At only seventy-six, she still had plenty of work to do in the world.

The university needed her, and there was no one else who could run it like she could. No one who could protect the Farm like she could—*Farm* being the affectionate nickname of the university, though quite honestly Jane was not a big fan of the term. Everyone wanted a piece of the Farm, it seemed—some to line their pockets, others for the heady power that came with a tenured position, and others for their own personal glory. But these men—yes, they were all men—had lost sight of Jane and Leland's original mission: forming an institution to meet the challenges of a new world, and turning out useful men and women who would positively influence humanity.

Jane was the voice of the place. The voice of her late husband now too. Voice of God, even. And that didn't sit well with some. Starting a school had been her husband's idea—to honor their departed son. In the beginning, Jane had gone along with it as a dutiful wife, as she'd done with his mercantile business, his stint as governor of California, and his role as head of the Central Pacific Railroad Company. But this time felt different, as though a new life's mission was unfolding. She could still remember standing under an oak tree with Harvard's president as he offhandedly mentioned they would likely need five million dollars to start, and it was probably a better idea to support established schools. She and Leland exchanged a look, and Leland told him, *Not a problem, we'll manage.*

That was the moment Jane realized the project had gotten under her skin. For the first time, she and Leland were on equal footing, building a university from the ground up, on dusty farmlands in Palo Alto. The thought titillated her now as it had then. Because the sad truth was, even when Leland Jr. had been around, Jane's life had lacked any purpose. She'd been fat and bored and pathetic, and then with the school, she became a woman on a mission. A brighter version of herself.

The door to the sewing room adjacent her opened, and her maid, Eliza, stuck her head out. "Is everything all right, Mrs. Stanford?"

"It's colder than the Arctic in here, and I was just checking the window at the end of the hall."

There was an echo in her own head, as though she had placed cotton balls in her ears.

"I wish you had asked me. I could have done it."

"It's fine. Nothing was amiss."

Eliza pulled her robe tight around her neck. "Shall I bring you more blankets? A cup of hot tea?"

Lately, Jane had been spending most of her time in Palo Alto, closer to the university, in the less damp air. "Perhaps I just forgot how chilly it is here this time of year. I'll be fine. Good night, Eliza."

Eliza nodded. "Good night, Mrs. Stanford."

Back in her room, she washed up and then poured herself a glass from the Poland Spring water bottle that had been uncorked and placed by her bed, as it was every evening. Her doctor swore by it as a cure for everything from dyspepsia to foul humors to peculiar fancies of the mind. And with all the undue pressures of late with the university, she was happy to try whatever means to keep herself sane and healthy. Her aging body, while kept strong from walking, had grown more prone to catching colds and other ailments.

A few gulps in, she noticed a bitter taste. The inside of her mouth began to burn, and the water came flying back up. She spit it out onto the carpet. Something was gravely amiss.

Without another thought, she stuck her finger to the back of her throat and forced herself to vomit up more of the fluid she had just imbibed. She ran to the bathroom and flushed out her mouth with tap water, spitting and gagging.

"Eliza!" she called, the stirrings of panic flapping in her chest.

A moment later, Eliza rushed in. "What is it?"

"There's something wrong with my water," Jane said.

Eliza looked down at the sink.

"Not that water, my Poland Spring. It's overly bitter and tastes off. Go tell Thelma at once and bring her here. She'll know what to do."

While she waited, Jane half stumbled back to her bedside table, opened the green bottle and sniffed. She wasn't sure what she expected, but there was no noticeable odor to the water. Her mind ran down the possibilities. Could this be a tainted batch? Had something happened to it along the way from the factory in Maine? Or could someone have added something? The last thought cast a cold shadow on her heart.

A few minutes later, Thelma rushed in barefoot, thick hair down and wearing a rather flimsy nightgown. The outline of her ample breasts was unmistakable. These periodic lapses in judgment confounded Jane. There were men in the house, and it was not proper.

Eliza called in as she passed. "I'll fetch some hot water."

"Tell me at once what has happened, Mrs. Stanford!" Thelma said.

"Taste the water and tell me if I'm wrong, but there is something foul about it. Just a drop worth, though."

Thelma dabbed some onto her finger and touched it to her tongue. Jane watched her face pucker up. "You are not wrong. Something is definitely queer with it. How much did you drink?"

Jane nodded to the half-empty glass. "A good deal, but I made myself vomit." Her neck began to heat up, and her eyes burned. Not uncommon when hysteria began to knock its way around her insides. But now she began to really fret. "Do you think someone has tampered with my water?"

Thelma grabbed hold of her wrist. "Doubtful, but just in case, we should try for another round of vomiting."

Jane didn't budge. "I have nothing left to spit up."

Every last drop of bile had already made its way out.

"We'll wait for Eliza with the hot water, then."

When Eliza returned, Jane gulped down the large cupful of warm water, and the three of them went into the bathroom as a team. Thelma held Jane's hair as Jane leaned over the sink and unceremoniously stuck her finger down her throat yet again. Only a tiny bit of thin, clear fluid came up.

Jane stood, trembling and lightheaded, though it was hard to tell if whatever was in that bottle had gotten into her system. "Get the bottle and hold it up to the light."

Thelma did as instructed. Under the glow of the washstand light, there appeared to be particles suspended in the water.

"Would you look at that," Eliza said.

Jane coughed. "What do you mean?"

Her eyes were not what they used to be.

"There's not just water in there."

Thelma shrugged. "Perhaps the glass was not cleaned?"

"The glass was clean," Jane said.

"Could it be salt?" Eliza asked.

Jane smacked her mouth, then took in some more tap water and spit it out. "Dear, I know what salt tastes like."

That something untoward was going on nudged at her, burrowing into her skin and causing even more unease than she already felt.

"Perhaps the spring water was tainted," Eliza said.

"We should get this bottle to Wakelee's. Have them check it," Jane said.

"For what?" Thelma asked, her hand shaking slightly, causing the particles to look like a flurry of snow.

"Quinine, perhaps?" Jane said. It was all she could imagine, and readily available in the medicine cabinet.

There was a moment of silence. Then Eliza nodded. "I'll go first thing in the morning."

That would simply not do. "Not in the morning. Now, dear."

THE CONFERENCE
Zoe
Oregon, 2005

E VERY YEAR IN FEBRUARY, Zoe feels herself closing off to the world, fighting a strong urge to go off to a mountain cave and hibernate with the bears. It has nothing to do with the cold. Instead, she has a heightened awareness that her best friend, Ginger, is no longer walking next to her in this world. Twelve years gone and the ache still wakes her some nights, a boulder on her chest. Certain milestones always make her wonder. *Where would Ginger be now? Who would she love? And what new memories would they have made by now?*

Not only did Ginger die in February, but they both have a birthday in February, one day apart. Zoe, February 27; Ginger, February 28. This year, they are turning thirty. At least, Zoe is. In past years, Zoe has done everything from camping in her backyard like they used to, to hiking the Oregon Trail for a week by herself, to staying home and watching their favorite movies—*The Breakfast Club, Stand by Me, When Harry Met Sally*.

The only thing Zoe hasn't done, which often haunts her, is take that trip to Hawai'i that she and Ginger were supposed to for their eighteenth birthday. But going without Ginger has always felt sacrilegious, almost like cheating, so she's never actually pulled the trigger. The trip would have been nothing short of amazing. Plane tickets in hand, hotel booked, plans hatched to learn to surf and lounge on the white sands of Waikiki while handsome beach boys frolicked nearby.

And then, a week before departure, Ginger died. Found days later at the bottom of a ravine in the hills behind her house. The authorities ruled it an accident, but Zoe has never believed that. There were too many hints and clues and a strong, lingering knowing. A sureness that lodged in the center of her abdomen and refused to budge. Friendship will do that to a person, especially one as tight as theirs. She'd told people of her suspicions, but nothing ever came of it. And now the guilt lives in her body like a parasite—for not trying harder, for not pushing for more of an investigation.

A scratch comes at her cabin door. She looks up to see Luna, the neighbor's dog, pacing outside the sliding glass. Zoe lets her in. Luna is decorated in dead leaves and goes and rolls on the rug, legs in the air, scratching her back and sniffing and snorting. Zoe has no energy to clean up after her, instead giving her a minute of belly rubs. As friendly as Luna is, Zoe is more of a cat person. It all started with Ginger's cat, Ink, who used to burrow into her side whenever she spent the night. When Ginger died, Zoe tried to adopt her, even though she is technically allergic to cats. Ginger's parents said no—they wanted to keep that last piece of their daughter for themselves—and Zoe was heartbroken all over again.

Back at the computer, she follows dead end after dead end of plot lines and is starting to feel a growing dread. Her agent needs a new book proposal from her—actually, needed it four weeks ago, and her publisher has already given her two extensions. Now she is facing down a hard deadline—next Monday. Ten days.

In the past, as a ghostwriter, there was never any problem. Turning other people's works into magic was an easier specialty. But then she'd gone and written her own novel—a romance, actually. An unexpected sensation. Now she seems unable to replicate that success. Maybe it's because just thinking about romance gives her cold sweats.

On the phone yesterday, her mother suggested a writers conference, and so this morning, desperation flapping its wings against her neck, she begins searching. Even though going off to a writers conference with a looming deadline is ludicrous, for some reason she looks anyway. So far nothing has caught her eye. Canada would be glacial this time of year; New York too much city; Greece or Paris would take days to reach.

She scrolls further along and is about to put her computer to sleep when on page four of her search, she sees the words *Waikiki Writers Conference*. Curiosity blended with something like excitement builds in her chest. She clicks the link.

Join us at the First Annual Waikiki Writers Conference, at the beautiful Moana Hotel. Learn from the finest writers of our time. Hone your craft. Write that book. Featuring top authors both literary and commercial. Meet agents and editors. February 21–27.

As her eyes take in the information, she thinks about how stuck she is, and she knows without a doubt that this is what she needs to do. There is an unexplained clarity to it, like it had already been decided by the universe. A change of scenery. Inspiration. No matter that it's in three days' time. No matter that the conference is all booked up. She will find a way. It is time to take a trip across the ocean. And maybe, somehow, convince herself that she was not in some way responsible for letting her friend die.

A SURPRISE ENCOUNTER

Jane

January 15

O N SUNDAY MORNING, Jane and Thelma went to catch the train to Palo Alto for some much-needed fresh air and sunshine. The family estate there, with its horses and tree groves and wide-open pastures, invariably stirred up memories of better times and boosted her mood. It would be at least a week until the chemical analysis of the water came back, though now the Poland Spring water fiasco felt little more than a horrid dream, and she needed to get on with things. There was certain to be a good explanation for the bitter taste. And yet, something dark tugged at her.

There was also a last-minute board meeting and business to attend to at the university. Something she had been dreading following through on, but something that needed to be done. Sometimes the weight of running the school felt almost crushing, and on many a lonely night, she sought out Leland or Leland Jr. for solace. She did not advertise her spiritualism, but people knew. Séances were as much a part of her life as breathing. When those you loved most were dead, what other choice did one have?

David Starr Jordan, the president of Leland Stanford Junior University, did not approve. Oh, he pretended to turn a blind eye, but Jane could see right through him. A man of science who cataloged dead fish, he flaunted his intellectualism as though it trumped all. In his mind, spiritualism had no place at a university, and anyone involved was a fraud or a fool. And not that he would ever say it to her face, but the fact that his job was founded on the words of a deceased teenage boy chafed at him.

She and Thelma sat in first class on cool, thick leather. Once their bags were put away, she settled into the seat and relaxed her aching back and closed her eyes. Skies were clear, but the air smelled of smokestacks and exhaust. Thelma sat across from her, reading, as she often did. Thelma preferred to stay at her family's home in Menlo Park, and it was often a struggle between the two. Jane liked to have her around, not only to help with everything from drafting letters to organizing her travels and purchases, but for her company. Because the truth was, over the years, Thelma had become a good friend, or, dared Jane say, almost family. She wasn't sure Thelma saw it that way. There were sure to be facets that Thelma kept hidden from her employer, but having her around made Jane feel cared for and safe.

Now, looking at Thelma with sunlight splashing onto her face, she was struck by the fullness of her lips and the way her high cheekbones set off her eyes. Fondness surged through Jane, as it sometimes did when the two of them were alone together. Their relationship might be complicated, but it bordered on love.

The thirty-mile train ride was one they took often, and Jane found it a good time to let her many troubles drift away, if only for the moment. She was just about to nod off when a man spoke her name.

"Mrs. Stanford?"

Her eyes flashed open, and she found herself looking up at David Starr Jordan himself, as if her thoughts had conjured him. Tall as a tree, with arms like branches, he hovered over her. It took a moment for the shock of seeing him to wear off, and she blinked a few times to make sure he wasn't just a figment of her ever-active mind.

"Dr. Jordan. What brings you to San Francisco?" she said pointedly.

"Just a quick trip for a dinner at the Palace Hotel. You've heard of Jacob Riis?"

The reporter with a book about the slums of New York, which was all the talk these days. "Everyone has, I do believe."

He stood for a moment, fiddled with his mustache. "Say, would you mind if I join you?" His eyes dashed over to Thelma, who glanced up from her book and nodded. The exchange felt almost intimate and caused Jane to pause.

Actually, she did mind, but it would have been rude to say yes. She was still furious with him over his lack of reform. Especially where women students were involved. Initially, she had thought it a good idea to have coeducation, but after recent scandals on campus, she had reversed her opinion. Throwing women into the mix had upended moral conditions and turned the school into a freewheeling fraternity.

Nonetheless, she patted the space next to her. "Please, have a seat."

A man his size really needed two seats. His broad shoulders were invading her space.

"Is this a business or pleasure visit?" he asked.

"A little bit of both," she said. "Plus, Thelma wants to visit her family, and I could use a change in climate."

He studied her face for a moment. "You look rather well to me. Have you been ill?"

"Kind of you to say. The damp cold has been sapping my strength, and, well, we had a peculiar incident Saturday night."

Jordan folded his arms. "Oh?"

Despite his nonchalance, she could tell he was curious. He never wanted to be in the dark on anything. Given that he was an ichthyologist, maybe he would have some insight. Chemical substances would be second nature to him.

"There was a very bitter taste in my Poland Spring water, and right away I knew I had better evacuate all that I had just taken in. It was not a pretty sight, I assure you, but it did the job."

"Peculiar indeed. Have you any idea what it was or how it got there?"

"No on both accounts."

"Poland Spring prides themselves on purity. It seems unlikely the water came that way," he said.

Which was precisely why she took it regularly—for indigestion and to cleanse her mind and body of lurking ailments and evils.

"Exactly. What's curious, though, is the bottle had been brought to me earlier, and I poured a glass, drank it, then recorked it. There was nothing wrong with the water in the morning."

That was the fact that kept nagging at her.

The train pulled out of the station then, rattling and rolling, and Thelma shut her book and glanced at Dr. Jordan. Her doe eyes fluttered for a few moments, remaining locked on him.

Dr. Jordan coughed. "Did swallowing the water cause any symptoms?"

"A sudden nausea, and the liquid came violently back out. Bitter bitter bitter, I tell you. What would you think it could have been, Doctor?"

"Strychnine comes to mind first. Have you been using it as a nerve tonic?"

"No."

"Have you sent it for testing, to find out?"

"Yes, but we won't get the results for a few days yet."

He turned to her and set an oversized hand on her forearm. "Mrs. Stanford, I do not like the sound of this."

Neither did she, but she refused to let on that she was afraid. If there was one thing she had learned in her position, it was never to show weakness.

"Oh, I'm sure some reasonable explanation will come up. And until then, I'm not troubling myself too much over it," she said.

"You know who all was in the house that day, and in your room?"

"I do."

She said it with conviction and was ready to move on from the conversation. But the word *strychnine*, flowing so readily off of Dr. Jordan's tongue, made her knees weak and caused a line of perspiration to prick down her spine. She was more than ready to die a natural death and join her Lelands and the afterlife. But from poisoning at the hands of some unknown adversary? Absolutely not.

THE MEN ALL sat around the massive table in various shapes and sizes, most smoking cigars. Even now, walking into these board meetings, she could feel her otherness. To combat it, Jane always imagined each of the trustees as animals—Judge Leib with his wide and bushy mustache, a walrus; Horace Davis an imposing moose; and something about Timothy Hopkins and his dark eyebrows reminded her of a bear. George Crothers, her favorite and younger than the rest, she pictured as a Labrador retriever. A sorry turnout for a board meeting. The rest were away or dead or had resigned.

The oak-paneled room went silent for a moment as she entered. Then most of them acknowledged her in one way or another—a nod or a hello—but never a handshake. Not that she wanted to shake any of their clammy hands, but it somehow made her feel lesser than. Crothers was the only one who actually rose and offered a curt bow, and she lowered herself into the empty chair next to him.

"Mrs. Stanford, we weren't expecting you," Judge Leib said.

She knew the meeting would mainly be small ticket items, which was why she hadn't planned on coming initially, but she wanted to discuss Dr. Jordan again. "No, I hadn't planned on it, but I have something important that needs resolving."

A few sideways glances shot around the room, but no one said anything. They all could guess what she was here for. She had been banging them over the head with a cast-iron skillet for a few years now about Jordan, but nothing had changed. Even Crothers had been defending him, which disappointed her tremendously, and she felt very alone in this. Alone but determined.

Once the meeting had formally begun, Judge Leib asked, "Would you like to state your business?"

She held up her chin. "I would like to discuss the matter of David Starr Jordan again, and his dismissal as president. He continues to go against our mission and sidestep all our efforts at reform."

Hopkins sighed. Davis cleared his throat into his handkerchief. It was Leib who spoke up first. "Have we not been over this already?"

"We have, and some of you have agreed with me that Dr. Jordan lacks judgment or principle. Sirs, I am sorry, but I am not going to back down on this," she said, crossing her fleshy arms. "I would lay down my life for the university, and Dr. Jordan is slowly but surely unraveling what I've built—what we've built. I don't want to just talk about him anymore. I want action."

"You chose him for a reason, did you not?" Hopkins asked.

They chose him because they could not get anyone else, but she wasn't about to say that now. And yes, Jordan might have seemed like the best option, but she had come to see that he especially excelled in being a self-serving narcissist. As in the Ross affair, when up against a wall on whether to fire the popular professor, he continually spoke out of both sides of his mouth, agreeing with her to her face and then encouraging Ross to write her a letter pleading his case. But Ross was a racist with dangerous ideas, and Jane wanted him out. To hell with academic freedom. She told Jordan in no uncertain terms to get rid of Ross, or he could also see himself to the door.

The whole thing blew up in their faces, and she still had burns from the fire that stormed through her body when she had opened the newspaper and seen Ross's words: *Well, boys, I am fired.* He placed full blame on Jane. In protest, seven of her top professors immediately resigned. Since then, her reputation had never been the same.

"I believe he has gone rogue and needs to be stopped," she said.

Crothers scribbled something on the paper in front of him, then said, "Mrs. Stanford, we all know that Jordan is not without his faults, but I worry of the backlash that will arise if we just cut him loose. It would be far worse than the Ross affair, believe you me."

Davis nodded. "No doubt Jordan's ability to hire and fire faculty at whim is hurting our reputation, but Crothers is right on this one. I think we keep him on, but mandate reform."

Jane argued. "We *have* mandated reform, and look where it's gotten us."

"How about offering him another position? Put the heat on him but also make it look like stepping down is his choice," Hopkins said.

Crothers brightened at the suggestion. "Exactly my thoughts. If we created an honorary position of some kind, where he can focus on his bloody fish and leave the running of the university to someone else."

"He'll never go for that. He likes his power too much," Jane said.

Leib pulled out a file and pushed it into the center of the table. "Here is his report on the needs and deficiencies of the university."

Crothers took up the file and read the papers aloud. The bottom line was this: Jordan said he needed more money or the school would never rise to the level of greatness they all wanted. He dug his heels in on keeping women on campus, and stated that only rich men could afford to teach there. In between the lines, even though he was trying to butter Jane up, she could smell his insincerity.

"Gentlemen, he must go. I will come up with a plan, and when we next meet, it will be implemented," Jane said.

No one said a word, but Crothers nodded.

THE ISLAND
Zoe

ON ARRIVAL AT Honolulu International Airport, the air is humid and the crowds are thick. Zoe waits for her bag amid tourists already draped in flower necklaces, and the place feels dingy. To make matters worse, the ride from the airport takes her through an industrial area that looks nothing like the Hawai'i of her imagination. Dusty roads and used car lots all underneath a wide highway overpass that opens into an even dingier neighborhood.

Rather than renting a car, she's taken a cab, and the driver has no interest in conversing, only offering up one-word answers. How far is it to the hotel? *Twenty.* Can we drive along the coastline? *No.* But she feels the pull of that turquoise-blue water they'd flown over, and is about ready to open the door and beeline it toward the ocean. She has always had this internal need for wild and open spaces, for trees or salt water or streams.

She begins her practiced self-talk for when things feel like they are spiraling out of control. *Breathe, Zoe. All is well.* Second-guessing the harebrained idea to come here, she searches for signs with the letter *Z*. A game she used to play when young that always brings her back to the moment.

When you are searching for something, the rest of the world falls away.

Ten minutes later, they pass a harbor and she gets glimpses of the ocean, and soon after that they drive past Ala Moana Center on the left and a long, park-lined beach on the right, replete with coconut trees and ribbons of white sand. It's starting to look more like Hawai'i—at least on one side of the road. Then they hit Waikiki, a bustling strip of high-end shops, jarringly out of place. Chanel, Gucci, Bottega Veneta, Miu Miu. She can still smell the salt in the air, even though the ocean is blocked by all the hotels.

At nearly the end of the strip, they pull into a columned porte cochere attached to a charming Victorian wooden building. All white and the only one of its kind in sight.

The Moana.

In the light and airy lobby, there's a long line to check in, and Zoe observes the people in front of her, guessing at which ones are here for the conference. The woman in a black suit holding a briefcase. The older gentleman reading a book while he waits. The cluster of women in bohemian dresses discussing which literary agents they've signed up to see. *I hear if she picks you up, you're guaranteed a book deal. I wouldn't want to meet with him since he only reps men. My friend said she was a real bitch.*

Zoe slides her dark glasses up so they rest on her head. She knows what it's like to be in these women's position. Wanting that book deal so badly it consumes you. Though to be honest, she'd had a head start with all the books she'd written that weren't her own. Being in the biz and having connections helped. All true crime and wildly different than her own, but at least she'd had a foot in the publishing door.

It feels weird to be here, and she wants to be stealthy, so she's decided to use an alias. Actually, that makes it sound more exciting. Just her middle name. In no way does she have the kind of fame that would allow people to recognize her, but one never knows. And she doesn't want to have to explain to anyone why she's taking classes on how to write a romance novel. Registration is at 5:00 p.m., and she's crossing her fingers she can finagle her way in.

Her room is on the first floor, which is actually the floor above the lobby, with an ocean view and a small little patio with round table and chair. The air in the room is frigid, so she turns off the air conditioner and opens the sliders, letting in the sounds of crashing waves and the rustle of coconut fronds. The woman on the phone had told her it was the last available room, and she wondered if there was a reason for that. But it seems perfect for writing, with no obvious flaws, and she feels extra lucky, as though it was meant just for her. But even with the last-minute discount, it is more than she can afford.

Her advance for *The Marriage Pact* had been sizable—three hundred thousand dollars in a two-book deal, one fifty each. But she spent the bulk of what she's been paid so far on her house. At the time, it had seemed like the right thing to do, assuming that the next book would flow right out of her. That had not happened. All the more reason she needs to get this second book proposal in: Mortgages don't pay themselves.

On the patio, a breeze ruffles up her hair as she leans on the railing under a shocking blue sky. She's almost eye level with a giant banyan tree canopy that blocks some of the beach, but it feels like the whole of the Pacific Ocean is spread out before her. So many shades of blue, and she wonders how she would describe them all—whitewashed, aqua, powder, cerulean, indigo, midnight.

After watching the waves for a while, she goes back inside and flops down onto the bed. It's soft and plush and inviting. Her eyes close, and she catches just a hint of something sweet and tart-smelling, like flowers slightly past their prime. She glances around the room to be sure, but just as she thought, there are no flowers anywhere. Only the polished nut lei she hung on a chair. Exhausted, she drifts off.

JUST BEFORE FIVE, Zoe heads upstairs to the ballroom wearing white flowing pants and a coral-colored tank top. Her best attempt at casual elegance. Her hair is down, and it's turned into ringlets in the salty air. In her author photo on the back of the book, her shoulder-length hair is pulled up in a loose bun, so she figures if anyone has read her book, they won't even think twice when they see her.

Outside the ballroom, there are tables set up stacked with books of all sizes and colors. Big windows let in a honey-colored light, giving the place a dreamy feel. Zoe hopes it will work its magic on her in the coming days, because in writing, sometimes Jedi mind tricks are precisely what you need. Along with focus and perseverance and putting your butt in the chair. By the entrance, two women with clipboards sit at a table, checking people in and handing them lanyards with name tags. Again, there's a line. Zoe waits five minutes, and when her turn comes, she gives the woman a bright smile.

"Name?"

"Bridget White," she says. "I haven't registered yet."

White is her mom's maiden name, so it's easy to remember. The woman eyes her. "The conference is closed, ma'am."

"I've flown all the way from Oregon to be here, Susan," Zoe says, reading the woman's name tag. "Can I pay a late fee? I'm happy to."

Not.

Susan ponders this, then says, "Most of our workshops are full."

"Then I'll attend the ones that are not. Please, Susan, don't make me turn around and fly back home. I *need* to be here."

Zoe holds her breath, feeling as though her whole future rests in the answer this stranger gives. The moment feels humbling and fateful and makes her skin itch.

The woman next to Susan leans over. "As long as you aren't picky, and you pay the $50 late fee, we'll accommodate you."

Zoe relaxes. "Fantastic."

She pulls out the neatly folded cash she'd brought for the occasion and counts out five crisp hundreds.

Susan hands her a folder while the other woman prints out a handwritten name tag for her lanyard. "How do you spell your first name?"

"B–r–i–d–g–e–t . . . as in Jones."

Her favorite romance novel. Her middle name. In fact, some old friends still call her Bridge.

Susan ignores the reference and pulls a schedule out, drawing a line through the workshop with Olivia Owens, *Romancing the Reader*, as well as most others. "We have morning and afternoon workshops each day. I hope you have an interest in detective stories? Because that one still has room, though I'm surprised."

At this point, she'll take anything, and smiles. "I love them." Once in, she knows she can finagle her way into relevant workshops. Nothing is ever set in stone at these things—she's been to several, and people are always moving around, changing their minds.

Inside the ballroom, people are now milling about on one side, perusing books written by the authors at the event. Zoe imagines what it would be like to have her book here, and to be teaching one of the workshops herself. But she's always been a terrible public speaker, and the idea alone causes her palms to sweat. There's a reason she's a writer and not a talk show host.

Everyone seems to know each other, and small groups have formed near a table with snacks and drinks. There are more women than men, which is usually the case at writing events, and the crowd definitely veers toward senior citizen. Not surprising when you figure the high price tag of the conference plus room and flights. No starving artists here. Zoe floats around, picking up books, looking for an in with one of the groups, but they all seem wrapped up in their conversations and don't even glance her way.

Since this is just a meet and greet, and she's not that interested in meeting or greeting, she slips out the door and waits in front of the elevator. She has nothing against people, but right now she has no time for them. She takes in the breadfruit-patterned carpet and a polished wood table with a leafy and enormous pink flower arrangement on it that smells like summertime in the jungle. It all feels so classic Hawai'i. When the doors open, she's face-to-face with a man, a little too close. They both freeze for a moment. He's tall with dark tousled hair, hazel eyes and pale freckles peppering his cheeks. His clothes are slightly disheveled, and he has a crease down one side of his face as though he's just woken up from a nap.

A look of recognition flashes, and Zoe feels it too. This guy is an author, she thinks. He nods, she nods, and one side of his mouth lifts, almost imperceptibly. She feels the urge to say something smart, but a woman steps past her and into the elevator, and the trance—or whatever it was—shatters.

"Excuse me," he says, stepping out and around her just as she tries to move out of his way but instead blocks him.

She feels clumsy. "I'm sorry."

They do this dance a few more times—awkward to say the least—and the doors begin to shut, ready to smash them both. His arm shoots out fast to stop a door from hitting her shoulder. And then she's in, and he's out, and she's riding back down to the lobby so she can grab a bite to eat and watch the sky fade from orange to pale blue to indigo.

Because if there's any place in the world that might warm her up to romance again, it's Hawai'i.

FROM THE JOURNAL OF
'ILIAHI BALDWIN, 1901

I HAVE NOT been able to write lately, because I have been flattened with grief. On the one hand, I've been fearing it my whole life. On the other, I am still in disbelief, the likes of which I've never known. Over the years, there have been people in our neighborhood there one day and gone the next, taken by the officers and held under arrest until they could be shipped off to Moloka'i. I have seen how their families suffer. I have witnessed the drawn faces and hunched backs, hearts caved in from hurt. But I have also seen how those left behind force themselves to carry on, because what else can they do? There are families to feed and children who need love, and it is brutal and ugly, and also it is the way of life here in the islands.

But now, I weep as I write this. See the water stains on the paper? Those are my tears. Ma has been wearing more clothes lately, long-sleeve blouses in the heat, and I thought nothing of it until I was braiding her long, thick hair last week. There were several spots on her shoulders, lighter than the rest of her skin. She was seated on the lauhala mat, weaving a new hat for my father. When I saw them, I felt a cold, dark drum beating against my ribs. At first I was too scared to say anything, but then she said in a very calm, almost dead voice, *'Ili, I have the disease.*

No no no no no, I screamed. But in my heart, I knew. Everyone knew what to look for. They had drilled it into us since we were little. Her left hand had not been working as well lately, and it took her twice as long to weave a hat. She even asked us kids to help her, which she never did, and that was when I began to wonder if something was wrong. I also noticed her caterpillar eyebrows looked thinner, and her nose was continually running. The thought that there was something living inside my mother that would slowly eat away at her made me faint, and I dropped to the floor, my head in her lap. She held me and said, *I am counting on you to hold everyone together, 'Ili.*

Four days later, they took her, Pa refusing to let Ma go alone, Ma ordering Pa not to leave us, while my brothers and I wept waterfalls and clutched at Ma, hoping for one last feel of her smooth, warm skin. The men took her away in a dark car, and just like that we are four, not five. I have no desire to go on, nor does anyone in our house. I will never get on with my life. I know that. Nor will Pa. He will either go to Ma one of these days, or die here without her. I can feel it. He loves us, but he loves her more. It's just the way it is.

THE NEWS

Jane

January 20

THE THEME FOR the night was Gold Rush, and Jane had spared no expense in turning the formal Nob Hill dining room a dripping, golden yellow. The help had set the massive table with her finest china, freshly polished silver, and crystal. Entertaining was something she greatly enjoyed, and even though tonight she was feeling congested, she managed to perk herself up with a special nerve elixir for the occasion.

Before the guests arrived, she dressed in one of her favorite Victorian dresses—gold satin with elaborate stitching and embroidered flowers on the lapels. Her waist was not as narrow as it once was, but she had long ceased worrying about that. She also donned an eighteen-karat gold necklace with a diamond-studded topaz pendant, a personal favorite she had kept after giving most of her jewel collection to the university. The feeling of cool, heavy gold on her skin always had a calming effect, and she was looking forward to her guests arriving. Mostly old friends from Sacramento, her brother Charles, and Jennie, his daughter.

But the minute she looked in the mirror, melancholy pinched at her heart. Almost every piece she once owned had been a gift from her husband—Tiffany diamonds and emerald sets, an Egyptian collection of beaded amulets, South Sea pearls—and this necklace was no exception. She had collected jewels the way some people collected butterflies or stamps. With passionate abandon. Leland's railroad money had provided more abundance than they'd known what to do with.

He had not always been a wealthy man. His industriousness, however, was legendary. And Jane counted herself lucky that of all the young women in New York those many years ago, Leland had set his sights on her. At the time, he remained at the periphery of her mind—once having seen him drive past, red flannel shirt catching her eye, wood piled high in the back of the wagon in Albany. She remembered thinking how piercing the cold was, and that his lips were the color of blueberries. There was something in his profile, though. Determination. Pride.

Later, Leland befriended Daniel, her eldest brother, in an attempt to finagle a meeting with her. The first things that struck her about him were his stunning light eyes, framed by dense eyebrows, and a commanding presence, as though he knew what he wanted and would get it by any means. Jane included. A man like Leland was going places, and she wanted to go along with him, wherever that would be.

"I have big plans, Jennie. Just you wait and see," he'd told her with that sly smile of his.

Not long after, he proposed. Jane was elated. When she traveled to the Stanford farm to meet his parents and his five brothers, she was greeted most warmly by a Negro family who lived and worked on the farm. They seemed exhilarated about the upcoming marriage—possibly even more so than the Stanfords—and threw a raucous celebration, singing and wailing into the night. Jane was touched. She made herself useful, and helped with the sewing of the flannel shirts Mrs.

Stanford fabricated—but in the end feared she did more harm than good. Sewing was not in her blood.

A bell downstairs startled her out of her reverie. "Ah, my Leland. I miss you more than ever," she said, heart twisting in on itself.

She touched up her lipstick, tightened the tie around her waist, and headed down. Being around people—especially Charles and Jennie, she hoped—was sure to bring up her spirits.

IN THE MORNING, Jane lay prostrate in the bed, tired and bloated from overeating pot roast and fig pudding. The slight cold she'd been nursing had turned in the night and now felt like it was strangling her. The party had been a success—at least there was that—but as often lately, she had overdone it. If only she could stay under the covers all day, but Charles and Jennie had spent the night, and she wanted to see them before they left the mansion.

She found them already in the sunroom, with steaming mugs of coffee before them. Golden light streamed through the thick glass, setting the room aglow. Once again, she'd overslept, but Ah Wing had seen to her guests, like he always did. The man was fastidious, and she was fortunate to have him on her payroll.

"Good morning, brother. Jennie," she said, moving in to join them.

Charles, nose in the newspaper, startled slightly. "Jane, dear, how was your sleep?"

Though much younger than Jane, he had grown wealthy through his connections with Leland, and he often felt more like an older brother and trusted adviser. More than anyone, she could talk to him about her mounting frustration with university matters.

Her eyes burned and were red and inflamed, as was often the case. It often made her look tired and weepy, but she was used to that. "Decent, all things considered, and you two? Were your sheets soft enough?"

Jennie smiled. "Like lying between clouds, Aunt Jane, pure bliss."

Leave it to Jennie to warm her up on the inside, a sunbeam in her life.

"Just what I want to hear. Will you two stay for brunch?"

"We wouldn't miss it."

Jane went into the kitchen, where she ordered up spinach and mushroom omelets, popovers and fruit salad, then joined her brother and Jennie again, sitting in her wide leather chair, the one her husband used to favor.

After a short coughing fit, she said, "I've made up my mind. Dr. Jordan has to go."

This time, Charles dropped his paper. "What?"

"I can no longer sit by and watch as he destroys what Leland and I so carefully built. Our views have become too disparate, and he continues to run the school as only he sees fit. Stanford is not Dr. Jordan's university. It's mine."

You could have heard a hair split. She knew that Stanford had taken on a life of its own, but it would still always feel like hers.

"I think that's a bit rash."

"He knows I'm not pleased with how he's running things. Morally, the place is falling apart, and he's only fueling that fire. And lately, he says one thing to my face but goes on and does as he likes. Ridiculously high salaries for his favored professors are only the latest in a long string of grievances I have."

Charles scooted forward on his chair. "Will you address it at the next board meeting?"

"I already have. And I think the board will support me."

Just then, Eliza showed up carrying an envelope in her hand, delicately, as though she was delivering a baby bird. "Mrs. Stanford, this just arrived in the mail."

When Jane saw who it was from, her mouth puckered. *Wakelee's Pharmacy* was the return address.

"Eliza, please fetch Thelma for me. Tell her it's an urgent matter," Jane said.

Eliza nodded and rushed out of the room.

"What is it?" Charles asked.

"The results from the chemist." Charles's eyes widened slightly. He too had been anxious for the results ever since Jane told him the tale.

She found it impossible to move, as though a strange magnetism was drawing her down into the chair.

"Well, are you going to open it?" Charles asked, wiping the coffee from his well-trimmed mustache.

Jane closed her eyes. A flush fanned out across her cheeks. "I can't bear to myself. What if the news is bad?"

Jennie chimed in, trying to sound sunny. "But what if the news is good, Aunt Jane?"

Footsteps echoed down the hallway, and Thelma appeared only moments later, breathless. Eliza trailed after her. "Mrs. Stanford, is everything okay?"

"That remains to be seen. I've just received a letter from Wakelee's. Will you read it for me, please?"

Thelma, wearing a high-necked silver dress and looking radiant, dimmed at the news. "Why, of course I will."

She took the letter in her long fingers and went to a table where the whalebone letter opener was kept, then slowly sliced the top open. Time moved like molasses as she unfolded the paper. Jane watched as her eyes scanned the page. She waited for Thelma's expression to shift. But the woman did not flinch.

Then, finally, she addressed the room while her eyes took in the carpet underfoot.

"It says it's only a preliminary report, but that the water contained three-quarters of a grain of strychnine."

Jane's throat burned. "What does that mean? Are there further details?"

"According to his notes, half a grain is usually fatal."

Jane fell back in her chair and groaned. Since the incident, she had been making light of it, as though wishing it away might somehow sway the results. But in the recesses of her mind, something had felt off-kilter.

"Dear Lord, I firmly believed no one would want to hurt me. But I was wrong, wasn't I?" she whispered.

Everyone in the room glanced at each other, afraid to speak, it seemed. People always walked on eggshells around her, something she'd grown used to. But now, it only infuriated her.

"Say something, will you?" she blurted out.

Thelma handed the letter over, her hand shaky. "I'm sorry," she said.

Jane read it, though it was hard to focus on anything other than her thundering heart. "The indignity of it."

Eliza, whose face had gone slack, backed up and said, "I will leave you in privacy. Excuse me."

"Wait. You must not speak a word of this to anyone, do you hear me?" Jane instructed.

"Of course," she said, and was gone.

Charles stood up and came to the chair closest to Jane. "We'll get to the bottom of it, I promise you. Tell me, who all was in the house last Saturday?"

She and Thelma had already run through the list, a very short list. "The servants—Ah Wing and Ah Young, Thelma and Eliza. Mr. Wilson came by. Other than that, no one that I'm aware of."

"I know this is a tough question, but would any of them wish you dead?" he asked.

Jane looked to Thelma for moral support. "I should hope not. I've been nothing but generous with all of them, and I put food on their tables and clothes on their backs. Isn't that right?"

But a small voice inside her said, *Not entirely*.

Thelma nodded enthusiastically. "Certainly, Mrs. Stanford."

"Is it possible the bottle was mixed up with an old one that perhaps stored rat poison?" he asked Thelma.

She threw up her hands. "I suppose anything is possible. But it's absolutely blasphemous. Had I perished, it might have looked like suicide," Jane said soberly.

Charles's face went white. "Don't even speak those words."

The earlier sun had been stamped out by a hazy layer of fog, and Jane could have sworn the walls were pressing in on her, making it hard to catch a breath. She thought of Mable Sommers, the wife of a university employee, who had swallowed a dose of rat poison to end her own life. Almost one year ago exactly. Jane remembered thinking what a horrible way to die. Since then, strychnine seemed to have become a poison of choice for those with murderous or suicidal urges. The newspapers loved it.

Jennie had come over to sit beside her and was rubbing her hand, soothing her some. "You feel hot. Are you okay?"

"I've been better, that is for certain," Jane said, hacking up another ball of phlegm into her handkerchief.

"I say we call in a detective agency on the double, not the police. We need to keep this quiet," Charles said.

There had already been enough scandal lately—the Ross affair, the spooning coeds, her court case with the United States government, which wanted all of Leland's railroad money. That had almost done her in, and it would have certainly put an end to the university. Yes, he had taken out a fifteen-million-dollar loan for the railroad, but not personally, and thus Jane was not liable. She had little energy for another of her affairs to be splashed across the front page of the papers.

"Agreed," she said.

If there was a person out there with murderous intentions, she and her people needed to quietly root him—or her—out.

Jane's mind flashed to Eliza, and how she had been strongly massaging her neck yesterday, hands closing in like clamps. Jane had asked her to go lighter. Could Eliza have been involved? The thought scratched across her skin. Especially in light of that business with Albert Beverly. Perhaps a talk with either of her Lelands was in order, though she would not mention that now. She was feeling feverish and needed to lie down.

THE DETECTIVES
Jane
January 21

THERE WOULD BE no séance that day or any of the days following, because Jane was flattened with a bad case of grippe. High fever, chills and a cough that made her feel in danger of cracking a rib. The attempt on her life had frayed her nerves and made her susceptible to unsavory pathogens, that much was clear. She rarely went to the doctor anymore—they had failed her son in Europe—but Charles had insisted on calling in Dr. Boericke.

He came that afternoon, and again on Sunday, gave her a cough remedy and quinine, which she was reluctant to take thanks to a new aversion to bitter substances.

"Mrs. Stanford, are you ready to end up in that mausoleum of yours?" he asked.

The mausoleum in question was the one at the country house, where Leland and Leland Jr. lay in rest. And leave it to a doctor to not be afraid of upsetting her.

"No, I'm not."

"Then take this."

She did as she was told and was glad she did, for that afternoon, she had a visit from Jules Callundan of the Morse Detective Agency. Hired by dear Charles.

Dressed in black, with a deep voice and gruff demeanor, he struck Jane as the classic detective, though he was younger than she might have guessed. Once again, she told her story, outlining who had been in the house, but was adamant that no one she could think of would want her dead. Thelma sauntered into the room to join in for the questioning, but he held a hand up to her.

"Just Mrs. Stanford and me for this, sorry, ma'am."

"I trust Thelma with my life."

"I wouldn't if I were you. I wouldn't trust anyone. Not until we flush the rat out of the hole," he said with a casual shrug.

Jane watched Thelma pale some, then slink out without a word.

He continued. "So let me get one thing clear. The three people known to have come in contact with your Poland Spring water were Eliza, Thelma and Ah Young, the boy who brings it up every evening."

"Yes."

"One by one, tell me what each of them might have to gain from your death. Start with Thelma, and give me her full name."

Thelma had been with her for almost twelve years, since Leland passed. The relationship was not without issues, but what relationship is? Thelma had a father and twin sister who her first loyalties were to, and she was constantly negotiating for time off to see them. Whenever Jane said no, which was more often than she cared to admit, Thelma would go rigid as an ironing board, her voice changing in tone, and say, "Very well, Mrs. Stanford." But it was clear that she was not *very well* with it. Of course, that didn't mean she should want Jane dead.

"Thelma Bellingham. I've written her into my will. She would inherit a small sum of money if I die. But our relationship is on solid ground and God-given."

He ignored the last part. "How much?"

"Fifteen thousand."

"Most people would not consider that small. And her salary now, is she paid handsomely?"

"Adequately, I would say."

"So, are you worth more to her living or dead?"

Anger swelled in her aching chest. "Mr. Callundan, I don't appreciate your line of thinking. I would not have spent the last twelve years with a murderer in my home and not had even an inkling."

"Guilty until proven innocent, ma'am. It's the name of the game in my business. And believe it or not, most murders are perpetrated by a close relative, friend or business associate," he said, those dark eyes burrowing into her, as though he might be able to see her thoughts and deduce the guilty party that way.

"So, you two get along well. No reason for her to be disgruntled?" he asked.

Jane thought back to the times she had told Thelma in no uncertain terms that she would not support her flirtations with men. Thelma drew looks from the opposite sex and often used that to her advantage. Over the years, she had cavorted with more men than Jane cared to admit, both married and unmarried. To keep her under her thumb, Jane demanded that she move into the mansion if she wanted to keep her job.

"We've had our differences, but nothing out of the ordinary, I assure you."

He studied her for a moment, as though unsure whether to believe her, then said, "What about Eliza? Your brother doesn't seem to trust her."

"He told you that?"

A nod. "He did."

Sometimes it felt like there was a fine line between Charles watching out for her and meddling in her affairs. He could be bullheaded at times, but then again, so could she.

"There have been whispers of misdoings by Eliza, yet I've kept her on. Now I'm not so sure I want her here."

"What kind of problems?"

"Did Charles not tell you?"

"He said that she and your old butler, Albert Beverly, had been suspected of skimming off of purchases he made for you. Is that why you gave him the boot?"

"I don't tolerate thieves, Mr. Callundan. That, and he no longer wished to travel with me, and that would never do."

A woman of her age could not be expected to travel the world on her own, could she? She had Thelma, of course, but having a man in your party tended to open more doors. Like it or not, that's how it was.

"He resented you for firing him, didn't he?"

"Most assuredly yes."

"But you didn't fire Eliza."

"I don't think she was in on it."

He scribbled madly. "Why not?"

"Eliza seemed upstanding to me, if not a little hotheaded, but looking back, I'm beginning to wonder."

Just the other day, Eliza had burst into a fit of anger when Jane made a simple demand. Jane had asked nicely, but Eliza had said she was busy. When Jane pushed, Eliza's face turned beet red, and she said coolly that she could not do two things at once.

"They're both British, that so?"

"What does that have to do with the price of eggs?"

He shrugged. "Just dotting my i's and crossing my t's."

By the end of his inquiry, she almost felt as though she were on trial, and her energy was sapped. She sagged back in her chair, struggling to maintain composure and rubbing her aching neck. Thoughts of Beverly always brought on tension. She had trusted him, and all the while he had been skimming off purchases he'd made for her. More than anything, he'd made her look like a fool, and that she did not tolerate.

Callundan closed his notebook, looked her square in the eye and said, "I'm going to tell it to you straight. People with your kind of money and power make enemies, period. My job is to locate the source of the poison, to investigate every soul who was in the house that day, and to seek out those with motive. In the meantime, Mrs. Stanford, I suggest you get out of town for a bit."

As soon as the door closed after him, she curled into a ball on the chair and felt her resolve crumbling. Something about hearing the word *motive* brought the seriousness of it all into sharp focus. She had now crossed the threshold and was a proper victim of a crime, and the thought saddened her above all else. Face buried in her hands, she began to weep.

THE WORKSHOP
Zoe

I T'S STILL DARK when Zoe wakes. She lies in bed, eyes closed, and enjoys the velvety warm air blowing into the room. She'd slept with the patio door open, quickly lulled to sleep by the ocean, and feels more rested than she has in a while. Maybe because the room is small, almost cocoon-like, and swaddles her. There's a retro vibe to everything here that makes her feel like she's stepped back in time. Arched windows, large verandas lined with rocking chairs, black-and-white photos adorning the walls.

It feels decadent for a ghostwriter from Oregon who hardly ever leaves her home state. Though she reminds herself she is a real author now, not just a ghost. Doesn't she deserve to be here just as much as anyone? Maybe even more so. She's spent the last decade blotting out her own sparkle, afraid to show her light. But whose fault is that really? It's her own, and she's sick of it. Sick of that feeling that somehow she does not deserve to have a beautiful life full of love and laughter and more animals than she can keep track of. Lasting success too. Why not have it all? The idea kicks up some dust in her heart, makes her want to change how she's gone about living.

As she's lying there, she imagines herself here a hundred years ago, standing on the pier out front, watching the surfers ride long wooden boards. But wait, there is no pier in front of the Moana, or anywhere nearby that she's seen.

That's when the haze of a dream surfaces. Actually, it hovers just beneath her consciousness, seeking to break through. Ah yes, the pier was in her dream, and she was watching a shark swim leisurely beneath her. A beautiful creature with a white tip on its dorsal fin. And then the image fades, and she remembers nothing else. Sleep pulls her under again, and she wakes to sun streaming in the window and the sound of screeching birds coming from the banyan tree out front. She checks her pocket watch on the bedside table, and it says 8:18. Her first workshop starts at 8:30.

She sits upright and flies out of bed. The yellow light comes from behind the hotel, so it's not direct sun, but the water out front now looks clear as spring water and just as calm. After a speedy shower, she towel-dries her hair, throws on the same outfit she had on yesterday, figuring no one really saw her and she wore it for all of half an hour, and hurries to the workshop, *Think Like a Detective*, taught by Dylan Winters.

When she gets there, the ballroom doors are closed, and the lobby area is silent. She slips in as unobtrusively as possible and stands along the back wall. It's a medium-size room with chairs packed together, and it looks like they are all taken. The teacher is the man from the elevator, and he stops talking for a few beats, looks at her and says, "There's a chair up here."

The chair in question is front and center, and she would much rather stand in the back so she can leave if she hates it, but obediently she slinks past the crowd and sits down on the well-padded chair.

"Sorry," she mouths to Mr. Winters, who is staring at her like he's trying to place her.

Today he looks different. Clean-cut, in jeans, a brown long-sleeve button-up and boots. You could stick a cowboy hat on him and he'd look right at home. He's perched on a stool so close she can almost reach out and touch him. There will be no escaping.

He continues speaking. "So, by the end of the morning, it is my hope that you will all walk out of here thinking like a detective, and that is what will give you the tools to set your books apart. Yeah, there are a ton of rules on how to write murder mysteries, and those are great and we'll get into that, but today we want to get into the head of the main character, and the underpinning of how *his* brain operates when he—" he's lost her at *his*, and she raises an eyebrow, silently begging him to also say *her* "—or she—is on a case."

Zoe rewards him with a tiny smile.

"And for the rest of the week, you've seen my rundown of classes. They'll build on each other, but if you skip one and go to another workshop, you can still pop back in. My feelings won't be hurt. I have thick skin. You have to in this line of work."

It is a truth she despises, because she is about as thin-skinned as they come.

Then he changes course and asks, "So, just out of curiosity, how many of you have read at least one of my books?"

She wishes she could raise her hand, but she has never heard of Dylan Winters before. Though there is a familiarity about him, same as she felt at the elevator, that makes her wonder if they've met in some literary circle sometime in the past. She's attended conferences and book talks in Portland over the years, so it's possible.

People behind her are mumbling, and the woman to her right raises her hand. "I'm a big fan. All of them. I've read them each twice. You're my favorite author." His eyes fall back on Zoe, and he seems to be waiting for her to raise her hand or say something. She almost wants to, just to be polite, but doesn't.

Someone calls, "*The Ice Train* is my favorite."

Zoe cringes. *The Ice Train* is written by DS Wilder, not Dylan Winters.

A few others chime in and agree. "Mine too," they say.

Dylan smiles, small dimples appearing in his cheeks. "Glad to hear it. That's still my favorite—if I have to pick favorites, which I hate to do."

Wait a minute, what is she missing here? And then it hits her. Dylan Winters must be his real name, and DS Wilder his pen name. Oh crap. No wonder he looks familiar, though as with her author photo, he seems like a completely different person off the page. It's been eight years, and her memory is gauzy, but she remembers thinking from his photo that he looked kind of harsh, with a buzz cut and a stern look on his face. In real life, he seems less scary, more rugged. Zoe immediately wishes she could fade away, hoping and praying he does not recognize her.

He looks her way again and she quietly says, "I love that book."

And she truly does. Full of twists and turns, it had her riveted. Not like his first novel, the one she ripped to pieces in *The New York Times*. The book bombed, probably sold less than a thousand copies. She'd landed the gig through a friend of her agent, and every now and then, the *Times* editor sends her a new crime book to review. *Be honest*, they told her. And so she had—maybe a little too much.

She swears his eyes light up at her words, and he says to the class, "I'll be using examples from *The Ice Train* today, so it helps that many of you have read it."

Zoe settles into her chair, feeling more confident that he has no idea who she is. After all, the *Times* does not publish photographs of their reviewers, and even if they had, her old author photo looks nothing like her now, in the same way that Dylan has morphed into a different person. It is her *name* he knows. Thank God she signed up for the conference as Bridget.

This workshop feels like it's going to be more useful than she expected, though she also worries it might dredge up memories. The subject matter is volatile and close to home. Teenage girls disappearing. Every now and then, she wishes she could write the story of Ginger, to turn it into a novel. But the minute she begins actually trying to plot it out, the nightmares begin to swarm, and she stops.

Now she blocks all that out as she listens to Dylan Winters discuss timelines and motives and alibis, and how to get into the mind of the victim and the perpetrator. He's no longer on his stool, but is pacing the room, almost catlike, and his words flow easily. How nice it would be to be so confident. Zoe takes notes and thinks about how she might apply this to her own work.

"When you're writing about a crime, remember that there will be someone investigating the crime, even if your main characters are not the ones doing it—"

A loud blaring of a trumpet interrupts him mid-sentence, and she's wondering what rude person forgot to silence their phone, when Dylan pins his gaze on her. Oh, God, please say it's not hers. But it is. She is that rude person. When she finally finds her iPhone in the bottom of her bag, she sees *Avery Silver* flash on the screen. Her agent. *Shit, shit, shit.* She's been waiting for this call for days now and cannot let it go to voicemail.

Bent over and head down, she is about to answer when she sees she's missed it. She immediately turns the ringer off and sits back up, phone in her lap. Dylan watches her like an annoyed high school teacher.

Again, she mouths, "Sorry."

He looks away. "You know, while we're at it, how about everyone make sure their phones are silenced." After a bit of rustling in the room, he starts up again. "So, let's talk about how you reveal your characters to the reader. You as the writer are going to need to know them inside and out . . ."

Zoe is dying to run outside and call Avery back, but she feels like she's already reached her rudeness quota for the day—for the month, actually. She chalks up leaving the ringer on to absentmindedness, since rudeness is not in her nature. Still, the desire to text Avery also causes her fingers to twitch. Avery is the most impossible person in the world to reach, and Zoe can almost guarantee that by the time she makes it outside, Avery will have moved on to something else.

Dylan gets back into his groove, and she admires his passion. Maybe that's been her problem with the next novel. *The Marriage Pact* began as more of a side project, in some ways mirroring her own life, and she was *all in* when writing it. The writing had felt like therapy and revenge and freedom. Now she's coming to believe it was a one-off. If she were standing in front of the room teaching people how to write a romance novel, would she be so magnetic? Probably not. Because the real truth is, Zoe Finch is an imposter.

The book deal, the top editor, the sales—all flukes. She just happened upon a high-concept story idea after her love life imploded, borrowing from *Bridget Jones*, and everything fell into place. A scenario often referred to as fairy dust in the industry. When Avery first called with the news, she was practically screaming into the phone. *Wait, say that again, I can't hear you*, Zoe had to say three times, blood pressure rising because they had a poor connection, and she was worried something awful had happened.

Now her phone buzzes against her thigh, and she jumps. She glances around to make sure no one else notices. It's Avery again. I spoke to Melinda, call me ASAP. Melinda is Zoe's editor at the publishing house, and though she's whip-smart and great at her job, she's all business. There have never been any warm fuzzies between them, no matter how hard Zoe has tried. It grates on her, because she and Avery clicked so well, and she'd love to have that in her editor too.

Zoe looks up again, and her foot begins to tap nervously as Dylan launches into the common types of villains in fiction. The classic villain, the noble villain, the power-hungry. Out of the blue, she catches herself noticing how good Dylan looks in those jeans. Narrow waist, thighs filling out the worn denim nicely. When her eyes make it back to his face again, he's watching her, and her cheeks instantly heat up.

As more time passes, she feels like she will spontaneously combust if she doesn't get outside and call Avery, but does not want to interrupt Dylan yet again, or draw any more attention in her direction. She tries to convince herself to wait for a break, but she's unable to concentrate on anything he's saying, and the itch is too strong. Every now and then, he checks his notes on the table, and she waits for just the right time. The minute he does it again, she grabs her bag, stands up and dashes out.

FROM THE JOURNAL OF
'ILIAHI BALDWIN, 1903

THIS AFTERNOON, THE SUN shone bright on Kalaupapa, and the grass was such a vibrant green I wanted to lie down and roll in it. Max and Liko and I were damn happy to get off that smelly boat full of cattle. We had first made land at Kaunakakai on the leeward side of Moloka'i, where we picked up thirty head of scrappy-looking longhorn, then sailed a rough passage all the way to Lana'i and Lahaina, and then finally back to Moloka'i. With all of the stops we made and the circuitous route from Honolulu, we might as well have traveled to California and back.

This remote peninsula, with its shocking cliffs and lava-laced coastline, would normally take my breath away, but we are not here for the beauty. We are here for the love of our dear mother, Haunani. And for pain, the depths of which I cannot explain. We were all desperate to see Ma. The longer we are apart from each other, the more the fever burns inside me to see her again—see, but not touch.

She's been here for almost two years now, and this is our third visit. I scraped together every cent I had to get the three of us here. I almost just sent the boys, but at the last minute, Liko managed to help Mr. Kamalani with his taro harvest and earned enough for one more ticket on the steamer *Likelike*. In the last few months, I have seen him turn that anger inside him into fuel. One minute he's boy, and the next man. It's a turning I've been waiting for since they took Ma, and since Pa died. Has it really been over a year?

Unloading at Kalaupapa is a dangerous affair if there is even a ripple of surf breaking at Kalawao. Today, breakers peeled across the mouth of the bay in neat white lines so clean, had the situation been different, I would have wished for my surfboard. Liko and Max noticed too. I could see them eyeing the surf.

A gruff man named Gilbert brought us ashore in a long, unseaworthy rowboat. On our approach, I could tell we were going to have to time the waves if we wanted to make it in without *huli*-ing. A canoe would have been a better choice, but these white people always think they know best. We took on water as a wave broke over our gunwales, but at least we were not forced to swim in our Sunday best.

In the rowboat, we were joined by John Kaʻaua and his three girls coming to visit their brother, and Mr. and Mrs. Holt, who are here for their teenage twin sons. It is a somber feeling, to come here, knowing you will not be able to take your loved one into your arms. Knowing that the only way that will ever happen is if you yourself are brought to the island, also affected. Or choose exile as well, as my father did. Leprosy is a ravaging, family-splitting disease, one for which there is no cure.

We were brought to our separate quarters and kept distant from Ma until the appointed time, just before dinner. Knowing we were so close made me want to abandon all care, climb the nearest tree and fling myself over that fence. Missing my parents is the only constant in my being. When the time came, I spotted Ma from afar, walking our way with determination, even though she's limping. In her last letter, which was carried up these cliffs by a line of old mules, she mentioned her left toes have been affected. And yet I have never seen anything or anyone more beautiful. I held my brothers' hands, and we all stood crying.

Her eyes are the same dark koa-wood brown, and her lashes curl up at the tips. She took us in for a few moments, and then all her attempts at being stoic dropped away. The sight of us three brought her to tears. Our exchange started off slowly, as though we all had fallen mute, but soon we were speaking over one another, trying to make up for lost time. My mother has made friends. She spends the days weaving and reading and watching the seabirds float on the wind. They watch movies, they write letters, they tell stories about their families on the outside. And they pray for a cure for this disease so they can return to us and resume their stolen lives.

I had this feeling that I needed to slow time. The need to be with her longer consumed me so greatly, I had trouble concentrating on what she was saying. I can be my own worst enemy this way, not enjoying what is happening before me because I am too wrapped up in what might lie ahead. This awareness struck me while Max was telling Ma about the ulua he speared, and I managed to salvage the rest of our time and keep my feet planted on this Moloka'i soil.

Her hair has turned silver, and her long fingers appear more bony. But *mahalo ke akua* she still has all ten of them. There are people here with no fingers. Missing noses. Lost legs. Fractured hearts. It also makes me worry that one of my brothers or even I will come down with the disease. But if we did, there is comfort in knowing we would be with our mother again. Prisoners of time in a lush and beautiful place. What a strange and painful contradiction.

THE LELANDS
Jane
January 27

JANE LAY ATOP the plush bed at the Hotel Vendome in San Jose with the curtains drawn, listening to the caw of crows and the muffled sounds of carriages outside. The resort was one of her favorites, and she and Thelma had been holed up here for days now. Her cough lingered, and she was feeling morose and listless. On her bedside table, she kept the locket with Leland Jr.'s photograph. She picked it up now and gazed at his beautiful face.

Her sweet, precocious and curious boy, who had graced their lives for only fifteen short years. The pregnancy had been tough, at age thirty-nine, no less. But it had been more than worth it. Those years with Leland Jr. were easily the best of her life. When he'd been born, her husband fell to his knees, overcome with unfettered love for this small, gangly and hairless creature. Something she'd never seen him heretofore do. But she understood why. A baby after all these years was a miracle. A rosy bundle of pure and all-encompassing love.

And the dinner party they'd thrown soon after young Leland's arrival and the prank the elder Leland had pulled were still talked about to this day. It hadn't been so funny back then, but now she remembered fondly. The guests had all been seated at the table, in lively discussion, Jane among them, having recovered some of her energy after a grueling childbirth. With a nervous look on his face, the servant came in and set a large covered silver platter in the middle of the table. Leland stood up and tapped his fork against a crystal glass, eyes aglow and one side of his mouth turned up in a half smile.

"Dear friends, I have an important person to introduce you all to, and I'm so glad you are here."

And with that, he lifted the tall cover and revealed baby Leland, lying atop flower blossoms, cooing like the great sport that he was. Gasps and exclamations swept around the table—some finding humor in it and others horrified. Jane leaped up to snatch her baby, but Leland beat her to it, then proceeded to walk him around and show him off. Leland Jr. smiled the whole time, a perfect little human specimen.

"My Jennie has brought us a little angel who has made me more proud and joyful than any other accomplishment in my life," he said.

It turned out, though, that angels were meant to be in heaven, not on the earthly plane. A mother should not have to bury a son, but that's exactly what she and her husband had done after he'd succumbed to typhoid fever. On the night that he died, young Leland Jr. visited his devastated father in a dream and told him he and Jane must live on for humanity, and all the children of California shall be their children.

"Mrs. Stanford," Thelma said, standing over her holding a steaming mug and startling her. "It's time you take some tea for your lungs."

Jane sat up, hacked a few times, then took the mug. "Thank you, dear. I'm lucky to have you."

"That makes two of us."

"I was missing my Lelands, and thinking I want to get back to San Francisco. The weather here is no less dreary."

"But we've been advised that it may not be safe."

"You're right as usual, but I feel so useless here, like a sick cow. Unable to get to the trustee meeting, unable to do anything, really. Not even go for a walk."

Walking was a form of religion for her. A way to get closer to God and to keep her body strong. As the mother of a university, she needed to keep her fitness and wits about her.

"Your job right now is to get healthy, so we should focus on that," Thelma said, hovering there with her mouth drawn down in that way she did when she wanted to ask something of Jane.

Jane pretended she didn't notice. "Please get me my stationery and you can be excused, if you wish. Go downstairs, get some fresh air."

Thelma went to the desk and came back with paper, pen and a small tray. She helped prop Jane with pillows so she was upright.

"There you go. Are you comfortable?"

"Fine. I've been thinking . . . I think it's time to let Eliza go. I no longer feel safe with her around, and I don't want her anywhere near me once she knows she's being investigated."

Thelma nodded. "I think it's a wise move. She thinks she's too good for her britches, in my opinion, on top of being untrustworthy and possibly even responsible for the rat poison."

"Exactly."

"Speaking of home, would you be all right if I go home for a night to check on my father tomorrow? I could get back before nightfall the following day."

Jane was taken aback by the bold request. "And leave me alone in this state? I'm afraid I can't grant you that. Not now, anyway."

"He's quite ill."

"So am I. You can go to him on your day off, but please, I need you with me."

Thelma's eyes watered, and she backed away. "Whatever you say, Mrs. Stanford," she said, drawing out *Stanford* as though it was the most vile word in the dictionary, then turned and marched out of the room.

Jane shook her head. These small tantrums were becoming more frequent of late, and she needed to put an end to them. She pulled out a sheet of paper and jotted down first the note to Ah Wing to get rid of Eliza, and next a note to trustee Judge Leib, demanding Jordan drop his ludicrous salary raises and make no more faculty appointments on his own. They *must* be approved by the board. Everything he did of late made her blood steam, and she was tired of it. Her hand shook as she wrote, though with weakness or anger, she wasn't sure.

THE CAT
Zoe

Zoe goes back to her room to call Avery, because this is a conversation that she needs to have in private. So much is on the line, and she doesn't want to be seen having a breakdown outside the ballroom. On the patio, where she can see the surfers and swimmers and sailboats out front, she makes the call.

Avery answers after one ring. "Thanks for getting back to me so quickly."

There's a plum pit in Zoe's throat. "Sure."

"Are you really in Hawai'i, Zoe? Please tell me you were kidding," Avery says.

Zoe had sent her a one-line email before leaving Oregon. I'm heading to Waikiki for a writers conference, promise to have a proposal to you by next Monday. Z. They are beyond niceties now, after working for seven years together. Avery is savvy and creative and funny, but she's also very direct. Zoe appreciates that because she knows she needs someone to bring her down to earth sometimes.

"I wasn't kidding. I'm watching the waves as we speak," she says.

"Melinda told me in no uncertain terms that if we don't deliver, you're going to have to give back your advance. So I suggest you forget about the conference and hole up in your room and figure it out. Just get me something. Anything. It's not that hard!"

Zoe groans. "I am here for that exact reason."

"Listen, how many books have you written since I've known you?"

"One."

"No, you've written six. I know you were ghostwriting, but you are brilliant and talented, and you can do this, Zoe. Do not overthink it."

But overthinking is a tendency she inherited from her mother, and once she goes down that path, it switches something on in her brain that causes a spiral of self-doubt. If only she could figure out how to permanently remove that switch. "I know I've been stringing you along, but when this conference appeared, I had a feeling this was exactly what I needed."

"What you need is time and your laptop."

Zoe feels so helpless in the face of this deadline and can't seem to force out any brilliant ideas, hard as she tries. "And I have both of those here."

"I know it's February and Februaries are hard for you, but this is a dire situation."

"I know that. But I feel stuck."

"This is business, Zoe, just like ghostwriting. You put the words on the page."

"It's not the same at all."

Avery blows out into the phone, and Zoe can tell she is smoking again. She hopes it isn't her fault. "Is there something else going on?" Avery asks. "That you aren't telling me?"

Zoe isn't even sure herself. "Ginger and I were supposed to come to Hawai'i for our eighteenth birthday, and now I'm turning thirty and she's not. Maybe it's causing some kind of disturbance in my field, I don't know?"

That she is more sensitive than your average person, Avery knows well. "Aw, hon. I'm so sorry. I didn't realize."

Zoe rarely talks about it. All Avery really knows is that Zoe had a best friend, Ginger, who had died when they were teenagers, in February. "There's no way you would have known. It's okay. But you're going to have to have faith."

Then Avery surprises her. "Do you want me to fly out there?"

"That is sweet of you, but no. The conference has some top-notch authors, and it's going to spur something, I just know it. I'm fine, really."

If only she felt so sure.

"Just say the word and I will."

"Thank you."

The minute they hang up, the tears come in big, gasping sobs. She has this feeling that there's a storm brewing in her chest, blowing her feelings around and bringing them closer to the surface. She keeps having mini-flashbacks of Gin, and she senses these will only intensify as she's here, because everything she sees and does carries a vacancy with it. Zoe minus Ginger. But crying feels good and needed and cleansing, so she sinks into it.

Her hand goes to the tiny pocket watch that hangs from a gold chain around her neck. Over the years it has worked like a pacifier, and she holds it, feeling the gentle and familiar *tick*. Ginger gave it to her on her eighteenth birthday. "And with this being so close to your heart, you will always know when it's time for love," she said with a stupid grin.

Zoe rolled her eyes. "Please."

"I swear when I'm anywhere close to someone I like— really like—the watch starts warming, like it's some kind of weird sensor."

Zoe scrunched up her face. "You're full of it, Gin."

"It's true."

The pocket watch looked expensive—gold weave, with a diamond inlay in the middle. According to the engraving on the inside, it was a gift given to a beloved in 1868. Ginger had no idea who, though, since she'd said it had come from Uncle Leo's collection of estate sale finds.

"Whatever. I can't take this, though. Your mom would kill you if she knew you gave something so precious away."

Ginger waved her off. "We both know my mom is too busy to notice. Plus it has no sentimental value."

Now, coming from out front, Zoe hears a small noise, almost like a cat. It sounds close, and she stands up to look down below, but sees no sign of any creature. Then she hears a more definitive *meow* and realizes there is a fluffy black cat sitting on a branch of the banyan tree not ten feet away.

"Hello, kitty."

Meow. The branch comes to within a few feet of her patio but looks too thin to hold the cat's weight. Nevertheless, the animal begins moving toward her. Below, there are plants and bushes and grass, but it's still a long way to fall.

"No, no, no . . . stop," Zoe says, but the cat keeps coming.

Its nose is pink and it looks young, maybe not even full-grown. There are missing patches of fur on its tail, and she can see the outline of its ribs beneath the scruffy fur. When the branch starts bobbing, the cat crouches down, still watching Zoe with intelligent yellow eyes.

"There you go. Good kitty," she says.

Another squeaky *meow*.

She loves cats disproportionately, and having one outside her window lifts her mood. It feels like a special visitor, like she is the chosen one. She watches it for a while, trying to coax it to turn around, but it's futile, really. The cat just sits there.

AFTER LUNCH, RATHER THAN go back to the workshop, Zoe holes up in the room and tries to plot out a story about a single woman who attends a writers workshop in Hawai'i and falls for the famous author heading up her class. She toys with several versions of why the woman is there, and why she's single. Maybe her husband cheated? Or maybe he died and he's left her a list of things he wants her to do, and this is one of them. Writing is a love of the heroine that she's never pursued. It's not great, but it's something.

As she writes out the first page, she draws on her experience from the morning, and pretty soon she has several decent paragraphs. This is the first time in months that she almost likes what she's written. Probably because there's no pressure—it's just an exercise—and that offers a sense of freedom and the ability to let her mind wander and jot down notes and not think too hard. Thinking gets in the way of flow, and flow is what she's chasing.

She takes breaks, eating banana bread on the deck and getting dive-bombed by mynah birds. Watching a canoe glide down the face of a wave. Admiring a trio of large black frigate birds floating on air currents overhead. The breeze has all but stopped, and the ocean is blue and inviting. As soon as she makes five hundred words, she'll go jump in.

When describing the love interest, she borrows characteristics from Dylan Winters and has no trouble remembering the structure of his face. Well-defined jaw, full lips, almond-shaped eyes that stand out among otherwise dark features. Also, how his hair is beginning to salt-and-pepper at the temples, and his forearms are veined and strong. There is no denying that the past eight years have been good to him. For a nanosecond, she imagines what he might look like with his shirt off, then catches herself and puts an immediate halt to that line of thinking. Desire has lain dormant in her for so long, she's forgotten what it feels like. The slow burn, the fast pulse, the softening behind her knees. She fans herself and chalks it up to being an observant author, because the last thing she wants is to be swooning over the teacher of her writing workshop. The man whose career she badly dented all those years ago.

THE MINGLING
Zoe

Even though it's just past four o'clock, the Hawaiian sun is melting Zoe's skin off her body. She strolls along the shoreline as far as she can, passing a couple of lifeguard towers and a trellised area where people are playing chess and cribbage, until she hits a wall and a jetty across from the Honolulu Zoo, where she hears a lion roar. Her body is screaming for the ocean, her translucent Oregon skin already pink from just ten minutes of afternoon exposure, and she turns around.

Back in front of the hotel, she jumps in, and the water feels as good as it looks. It's warm but not too warm, and she swims out a ways and floats on her back, extra buoyant in the salty water. A strange sense of timelessness comes over her, and for a moment, she is eighteen or forty or seventy. She almost feels like she's one of those frigate birds looking down on herself. It unsettles but also reassures her, as though there is a fluidity about time that she has never considered. Around her, she feels a presence, but when she looks, there is no one near.

"Is that you, Gin?" she says.

But then she remembers the shark in her dream. Hawai'i has had its fair share of shark attacks. She doesn't want to be the next victim, so she swims back closer to shore, hoping her foot doesn't get munched on the way.

A woman is wading into the water, and Zoe recognizes her from her short time at the opening of the conference yesterday. The woman is about her age—early thirties, with long black hair and silver jewelry on every appendage. Zoe smiles.

"How is it?" the woman asks.

"Amazing. I've been dying to get in ever since I arrived."

"I saw you in the workshop this morning. What did you think?"

A rush of embarrassment. "Oh gosh, I hope I didn't cause too much of a disturbance. It was my agent calling—"

The woman laughs as she eases into the ocean. "It happens to the best of us. I'm Tara."

Giving her fake name feels disingenuous, but Zoe goes with it. She has no choice. "Bridget. Nice to meet you."

"And did you just say your *agent*?" Tara asks, caramel eyes bright and inquisitive.

"Yes . . . I have an agent but am still working on getting that book deal," she says, lingering on the fact that using a fake name is really no different than authors writing under a pen name—something she has never quite understood. Until now.

"Then you're probably ahead of most of us here. Is your agent one of the agents at the conference?"

"No."

Tara is now up to her slender waist in the water. She's got a lovely hourglass figure and a sweet air about her. An innocence, kind of like Gin. Zoe decides she likes her.

"You must write mystery if you were in Dylan's workshop. What is your book about?" Tara asks.

Zoe uses her idea from earlier. "It's about a woman who goes to Hawai'i for a writers conference after losing her husband. He's written her this list of things to do after he's gone."

"I like the sound of it. Not based on a true story, I hope?"

"Thankfully no. What about you?"

Tara sinks down to her neck. "Ah, this water is delicious . . . I've written a few books. One is a thriller set at a lodge on Vancouver Island, where I'm originally from, but I also have a love story with magical realism notes and a time slip book set on an imaginary island in the Pacific. I guess you could say I'm a mood writer with no real plan."

"There's nothing wrong with that. They all sound fascinating," Zoe says, enjoying the sun on her shoulders and having someone to talk to.

"You think so?"

"I do. For real."

"I wish everyone thought so. I met with agents in Santa Barbara last year and was told I'm not quite there yet by one, and that the writing is good but I need a bigger hook by another."

"All it takes is one. You know that. And having an eye on your work can only make it better," Zoe says.

Tara dunks under. "Are you going to go back to Dylan's workshop tomorrow?" she asks when she comes up, sleek as a seal.

"Nah, I'm sure he doesn't want to see me again. I'm going to try to squeeze into *Romancing the Reader*, which is way more up my alley," Zoe says.

"Me too. I love Olivia Owens's books. They're smart and fun and have just the right amount of heat. I think I might alternate between the two each day. What about tonight? Are you going to the cocktail hour?" Tara asks.

There is nothing worse than wandering through a cocktail party where you know not a soul. You're all dressed up and you think you're going to have this grand time, and it turns out that after a few rounds of small talk, you end up at the bar sitting next to a drunk man with a comb-over who shows you pictures of his kids. Besides, she should be banging out words.

"I'm not sure. Are you?"

"I paid a lot of money to be here. I wouldn't miss it for anything. Want to meet me in the lobby at five forty-five and we can go together?"

"I would love that."

Evenings are her least productive time, or so she reasons.

ZOE WAITS IN the lobby, taking a closer look at the wall-size old photographs of the hotel. In one there is a pier out front, and it makes her think of her dream again. This must be where she got the idea from. Only she doesn't recall seeing the picture when previously walking through. Cold sweeps down her neck.

The Moana evokes a bygone era, even as the old Waikiki around her has been replaced by high-rise hotels, pavement and tourist traps. The charming building is a regal old woman amid a younger, far less polished crowd, and Zoe loves the oldness of it. She often feels as though she's been born in the wrong century, and has an intense fondness for vintage things.

Tara arrives, looking like a goddess in all white and silver. Her hair is coiled up in a bun, and her skin shines like copper in the sun, as does her smile. "Sorry I'm late. I was working on my pitch," she says.

"Priorities."

"I'm so nervous about meeting the agents, and I keep rewriting my query. To the point where I think I may be making it worse."

"Trust me, I do the same. There certainly is a tipping point, and it's hard to know with your own work."

Tara nods. "So how do you remedy that?"

"I remember looking at a ton of back covers, getting a sense of what works and using the same structure." Zoe thinks for a moment, flashing on how far she's actually come since then, when she used to model her work on that of other authors. "I guess I've also learned to trust myself as a writer. There's power in that."

"I have a ways to go before I get to that point."

"One million words, that's what they say."

Tara tilts her head. "Have you written that many?"

Close.

"No."

They step out onto the lanai and walk toward the Banyan Courtyard. Under the shade of the sprawling tree, it feels ten degrees cooler. Roots hang down like living pillars, and the birds are chattering away. "I could look at it if you want, and give you my opinion. Maybe tomorrow afternoon?" Zoe says.

"That's incredibly generous of you. Yes, that would be such a help."

They approach Susan, who is handing out stickers and a Sharpie so people can wear name tags. The entire courtyard has been cleared for the group, and there are cocktail tables already full of people. The swimming pool at the edge reflects torchlight. Zoe recognizes some faces from the workshop, and the woman in the black suit from check-in, who she assumed is an agent.

She nods toward her. "Do you know who that is?"

"Kate Allison, from Writers Group. She's at the top of my list. And over there is Andy Burns. He's good, but he's not looking for romance novels. I'm signed up to talk to him anyway."

"Agents don't like that, you know. They only want pitches that are in their wheelhouse," Zoe warns.

"For real?"

"Yes, I'd cancel."

"Okay, thanks for the tip."

Once armed with name tags and two drink tickets each, they head to the bar. Zoe is relieved to have someone to hang with, but her conversation with Avery is still front and center in her mind.

"What are you having?" Tara asks.

"Something strong?" Zoe says.

"I hear you. This writing business is not for sissies."

"Nope. It's for people with an elephant hide who enjoy torture," Zoe says with a shrug.

Tara laughs. "That may be a little extreme."

Maybe not, but Zoe does not want to shatter Tara's enthusiasm for being here. "Totally joking."

If she's honest with herself, author life might be hard, but there is nothing else she'd rather be doing. And therein lies the problem. Sometimes it feels like self-imposed torture, but she knows she will never quit.

While they wait for the bartender to make them two blended margaritas, Tara asks, "So tell me your story. How'd you get into writing, and more importantly, how did you land an agent?"

Just then, Zoe sees Dylan Winters standing with a few people, one of whom is Olivia Owens. The others look familiar, and she realizes they must be the other authors teaching workshops here. He looks casual in an aloha shirt and leather flip-flops, and there is a pretty woman by his side. Zoe watches their interaction, trying to decide if they are together. He looks taller out in the wild, and even more intimidating.

"There's something appealing about him, isn't there?" Tara says, eyes on Dylan.

Zoe startles. "I suppose, but he's not my type—not at all."

"I love a strong and intelligent man, but I'm married, so I just admire from afar." She holds up her hand. Earlier there had been no wedding ring, but now she's wearing a chunky diamond.

The bartender hands them the margaritas. Zoe takes a big gulp, dusting her lip with salt. "Back to your question about how I got my agent . . . I got my MFA at Antioch, and when I finished this latest novel five years later, I had a teacher who referred me to a few agents. Right from the beginning, I clicked with Avery." She stopped there, not wanting to get herself too far into details that she might later forget. Everything she'd said so far was true.

"Avery Silver?"

"Yes."

"Damn, girl, you're legit. Avery is an A-lister."

Zoe has never taken for granted her good fortune. "I feel lucky to have her. And your time will come if you just stay at it."

"Fingers crossed," Tara says.

"Patience and perseverance is my motto."

"And a mountain of hard work and luck."

Zoe laughs and raises her glass in cheers. "That too."

Two musicians strum guitars at the far end of the courtyard, and their mellow music, mixed with the sound of the ocean and the birds, as well as the glow of the tiki torches, has a calming effect on her nerves. She feels her whole being loosening. When the song is finished, Susan gets on the mic and welcomes everyone.

"And now, we're going to do three rounds of an activity to encourage everyone to mingle. We know that many of you are introverts, so this is just a boost to help you get to know your fellow attendees. Because it's a truth universally acknowledged that writers need other writers."

That drew a bunch of cheers.

"First up, find someone whose first name begins with the same letter as yours, say hello, and ask them what they hope to gain from this conference. You have five minutes. Go."

B is far easier than *Z*, and Zoe goes off in search, feeling like a grade-schooler again and not really minding. The margarita in hand helps. People around her are quickly pairing up, and she's about to lose hope when she comes upon a dapper old fellow with a tall straw hat on his head named *Bill*.

"Bridget, my dear! You are a sight for sore eyes." He holds out his hand and bows slightly. "I'm Bill. A pleasure to make your acquaintance."

She shakes his leathery hand. "Likewise."

"Ladies first. What brings you to this island oasis?" he asks.

His eyes sparkle with genuine curiosity, and she feels the need to give him a good answer. "I guess you could say I've been feeling rather stuck in my writing, and I'm hoping for ideas and inspiration. Also, I've always wanted to come to Hawai'i, so it felt like the perfect opportunity. What about you?"

"Ideas and inspiration, I like it. I'm here because I promised my beautiful wife Betty I would finish my memoir about my experience at Pearl Harbor and hopefully get it out into the world. I was ground zero in 1941, you see. A nineteen-year-old pilot fresh off the boat from Oklahoma. Thought I had died and gone to heaven when I arrived. And then a few months later, I almost did die . . . not sure if I would have gone to heaven at that point, though," he says with a wink.

One of her first ghostwriting jobs was for a man who'd survived Dunkirk, and it had been such an honor to work with him even though she had been a puddle of tears throughout. That was when she realized the emotional toll that inhabiting another person's life could take. Necessary to do the work, but sometimes gut-wrenching.

"That's incredible. How far along are you?"

"Not as far as I'd like to be. You see, I lost her last year, and I shelved the whole thing. But I have never broken a promise to my Betty, and I'm not going to start now. So, here I am," he said, sadness tugging at the corners of his eyes.

"I'm sorry for your loss. It sounds like she was a lucky woman."

"I was the lucky one. No doubt about that."

Zoe places a hand on his forearm because it feels like the right thing to do. "I'm glad you came, Bill. I imagine you'll have all kinds of help here—"

Susan on the mic interrupted. "Time's up. I saw a few of you in groups of three. Even better."

"We'll catch up later, dear," Bill whispered.

"Yes, let's."

"Now, for our second round, please find someone new, someone whose last name has the same first letter as yours. And please share with each other your greatest takeaways from today's sessions. Five minutes. Go."

Zoe sets off again, in search of someone whose last name starts with an *F*. She spots a puffy-haired woman with the last name Flanders and is about to go up to her, but remembers the last name on her sticker is not Finch but White. She knows one person in the crowd whose last name starts with *W* and heads in the opposite direction from Dylan, just to be safe.

"Ah, you're White. I'm Watanabe. Iris is my first name," says a pretty young woman who looks fresh out of high school.

"Hello, Iris, it's a pleasure to meet you."

Zoe likes meeting people this way. It takes the pressure off and gives everyone an immediate opening and something to talk about. She makes a mental note to thank Susan later.

"Which workshop did you attend?" Iris asks, all perky and sweet.

"I was in *Think Like a Detective*, and it was great. What about you, and what was your takeaway?"

"Valerie Johnson's class on plot. I loved it! I think the thing that stayed with me most is that a good plot always trumps good writing. Which is why she said it's so important to spend more time up front figuring out your road map. I've been so focused on producing beautiful sentences and just winging it with my plots. I'm a pantser all the way."

"How many books have you written?" Zoe asked.

"Four. Two while I was in high school and two in college so far. I'm a senior at UH now."

Iris looked so pixie-like, it was hard to picture such a young thing having four novels under her belt. But Zoe knew it happened.

"Impressive! What genre?"

"I'm interested in the supernatural, so they're all about witches and werewolves, and they're also love stories."

"Are you majoring in English in school?"

She shook her head. "I'm pre-med. Writing is just a hobby."

"Even more impressive. I hope we end up together in a workshop one of these days so I can hear you read."

"I'm scheduled for the open reading Thursday night. But how about you? What was your favorite today, and what do you write?"

It took her a moment to come up with something. "I love how Mr. Winters showed us the depth of understanding often required by an author to get into the story. Sometimes, most of what you learn and know does not make it into the book, but it is required anyway. And how layered stories make for a much better reading experience."

"I've heard he's a genius."

Zoe had been too distracted with her own stuff to pay full attention, but there had been glimpses. "It's worth popping in, even if you're not writing mystery."

"What do you write?"

"Romance, primarily."

Iris tilts her head. "What were you doing in the mystery class?"

She's perceptive, this one.

"I signed up late, and that was all there was. Tomorrow I'll see if I can squeeze into Olivia's class."

"I heard it was great, but I'll be doing the world-building session."

Susan reads the third activity backlit by a flaming orange and rose-colored sky that can only be heralding some kind of weather change. "Now for the last mixer, find someone who is wearing the same color shirt or dress, and share when you first knew that you wanted to be a writer, and what led you to that point. Take as long as you need, as you're on your own after that. Enjoy!"

Zoe doesn't have to look around to know who is wearing the same burnt ochre as she is.

FROM THE JOURNAL OF
'ILIAHI BALDWIN, 1904

WE HAD FISH and poi for supper the other night for the tenth night in a row, and when Max opened his mouth to complain, I slapped him. Immediately I regretted it and wrapped him in my arms. Max is so good-natured that it hardly bothered him, but I am unraveling thread by thread, and am not sure how much longer I can go on feeding the three of us and paying our bills and keeping up our house, the one Pa built in the shadow of Diamond Head.

I know Tutu wants to help, but she has her own troubles to worry about with Grandpa. Every time I see him, he makes less and less sense, and on our last visit to Kailua, he failed to recognize any of us as his grandchildren. He can still ride the horses, so Tutu keeps him busy with them, grooming and walking and feeding the herd. The horses are smart, and they take care of him. They know he's not all there in the head. She has suggested we move in with them, but I know we would be a burden, and none of us want to leave Waikiki, and the *mālie* ocean.

On Wednesday, when I heard through Mrs. Kahakui, whose husband works at the Moana Hotel, about an employment opportunity, I immediately began plotting how to get myself hired. I borrowed a white eyelet dress from Lilith Steiner, who has a wardrobe every girl at our school envies, braided my hair and pinned a red hibiscus behind my ear, and marched down there bright and early this morning. It was Lilith who suggested I fudge my age, because she knows how much I need this job. I pride myself on honesty, but I am not beyond telling a white lie now and then, as long as it will harm no one.

Everyone I know considers me bold, but I assure you I was not feeling bold this morning. It took everything I had to keep my whole body from breaking out in the shakes as I walked up to the entrance of the grand hotel. The First Lady of Waikiki is what people are calling it. Mr. Price was not expecting me, and so it took a precious bit of convincing the bellman to let me in. It's mostly white folk who are guests—rich white folk. Though I am half English, my complexion says otherwise, and usually I like it that way.

When I walked into the sitting room, Mr. Price sized me up with a heavy-lidded gaze, his skin the color of rhubarb. My initial impression was that he was a drinker, but also that he was intelligent. He asked me if I was lost, but I could tell he was bluffing. He knew exactly what I was there for. Because wit must be matched with wit, I told him my name, and that I had come for the position, even though I was much overqualified. That caused a loud guffaw.

I am often underestimated because of my small stature, so I did not give him a chance to ask how old I am. Instead, I explained that I am the head of a household and am skilled at all things required to run a home and family, and I excel at sewing and cleaning. When he tried to interrupt, I kept going, informing him that not only can I perform multiple tasks at once, but I read and write, I sing and play the ukulele, I have read *Twentieth Century Etiquette* cover to cover, my mother taught me how to make floral arrangements, and I have since created a tiny enterprise out of this art. (Just how tiny, Mr. Price does not need to know.)

Again, he tried to cut in, but my tongue continued unfurling talents in a steady stream. I'm an adept water woman and can swim and ride waves and paddle a canoe. There is no one I cannot carry on a conversation with, and I know when to hoʻomalimali and when to be invisible. The Hawaiian word slipped out of its own accord, but Peacock seemed not to notice. At the end of my little speech, he stared at me, twirling his mustache. I feared I had gone too far, like I have a tendency to do, but he bared his yellow teeth in a smile. He told me he wished he could hire me, but that he had a string of qualified applicants yet to interview this week. If none of them work out, there is a small chance I will hear from him, but he told me not to count on it. I could tell I won his favor, but favor is not what I need.

THE DECISION

Jane

February 6

INSTEAD OF HEADING home as they had originally planned, Jane and Thelma took the train to Palo Alto, where they parted ways—Jane to her country estate and Thelma to her family home. Family had a positive effect on her, and Jane figured it might pull her out of her funk. People could be pushed only so far, and she had made it a point to pay attention to those limits. Now she wondered if her perceptions had been skewed, because there was someone out there who she had misjudged.

A screaming cold spell arrived in Palo Alto around the same time they did, but at least the sun shone and it was dry there—more Mediterranean than the city. One of the first things she did upon arrival was layer on her woolen coat and take a walk around the grounds. Trees of all variety— eucalyptus, chestnut, live oak, orange and many a unique specimen—had been planted at her and Leland's orders, and she enjoyed the birdsong and the vigor she felt returning to her legs as she moved about.

She wandered aimlessly at first, checking on the gardens, making sure every stone and leaf was in place, then eventually found herself standing in front of the mausoleum. The granite sphynxes glinted in the sunlight, and she felt a tug of melancholy looking at the imposing guards of the afterlife. No matter how many times she came here, it could never be enough.

A gust of wind stirred the branches, and she glanced around into the trees, a hint of a smile warming her insides. Most of the trees around the mausoleum had been her doing. Olive for peace and hope, cedar for eternal life, and palms for victory over death.

"Hello, my loves," she whispered.

Around her, the place was deserted, most likely on account of the glacial air. She placed her gloved hands over her heart and walked to the statue of young Leland holding the hands of both his parents. The likeness was striking, and the words felt bold and meaningful. In her grief, it had taken her some time to figure out what saying would ever be sufficient, but in the end, she was pleased at the final product. *Dedicated to Science and the Good of Humanity.*

"Leland dear, I need your guidance on what to do. Where to go. This attempt on my life has me reeling. I don't want to live in fear, but that is exactly what I've been doing," she said, speaking aloud since she was alone.

Now more than ever, she wished to have her husband standing by her side, his warm shoulder touching hers. It had never been her plan to outlive him. No, she would have much preferred to go first. But we do not choose our endings, and she had to remind herself of that daily. It had been plain to see for some time. His legs had weakened until they barely held him, and though he put up a good front, they both knew his earthly days were numbered. Even the French spa, Aix-les-Bains, had not been able to improve his deteriorating health. In turn, he became more contemplative.

The words he spoke soon before his death made her love him even more, if that was possible. "I was lying here thinking about our boy and how sad that he was taken away from us, but how much worse it would have been if we had never had him."

Jane had looked into his watery eyes and clasped his hand. "He is ours to go to—Heaven is dearer because he dwells there."

Then on the night that he passed, his final words before he retired to his bed were, "Jennie, I want to tell you that I love you."

In the morning he was gone. At first she had refused to believe it, blowing on his cheek and in his face, tapping on his shoulder, shaking him almost violently to wake him. But his body was ice, his mouth slack and skin waxen. At a loss for what to do, she climbed into his bed and lay beside him, holding his bony hand for what might have been hours. The memory etched into her mind, alive as the trees around her.

"I want to see you and Leland, I do, and yet I still feel myself tethered to this plane. Perhaps a séance is in order?" she said, glancing around, hoping for some kind of sign that he was listening. A gust of wind, a feather floating in the air, the call of a crow.

She waited in silence, and in time, a breeze rustled in the oaks, seething through her hair and under her limbs. Over the years, she had become used to the subtleties of communication with the otherworld, and she took this as an acknowledgment. When she arrived back in San Francisco, she would set something up, behind closed doors.

Dr. Jordan continued to try to persuade her that séances and Ouija boards and mediums were nothing more than hoaxes. Real science did not support any of it, and the people who peddled in it were merely preying on grief. She knew her spiritualism was an embarrassment to him and that he worried it might be a real threat to all the grants and wills that funded the university. But there was no disputing that her husband and son visited her regularly in her dreams—consoling her, advising her, reminding her that she had work to do. And that they would be there with open arms when she took her final breath, she had no doubt.

THE FOLLOWING WEEK, she and Thelma rode the train back to San Francisco. Along the way, Jane took a catnap and dreamed of her husband. He was sitting on the steps of the mausoleum when she showed up, and he embraced her with branch-like arms. His clothes smelled of cedar and incense, and he had a wild look in his eyes. She wanted to hang on to him, but he said he had an important meeting to attend, and that she should leave the continent and go somewhere far away, alone.

She woke with a jolt as the train whistled, for a moment unsure of where she was.

Thelma patted her arm. "We're about here, Mrs. Stanford. You were having a dream."

That feeling of wanting to return to the dream was so strong, she closed her eyes again, hoping to climb back into that world where her husband dwelled. Nothing happened, and it began to fade, but his words were stamped in her mind.

"Leland said I should leave the continent."

Her husband was rarely scared, so seeing him so distraught in the dream bled into a sense of urgency. Jane felt a clawing need to do as he said.

"He did, did he?"

"Alone, of all things."

"Leave the continent. It may be a good idea. But alone?"

"My thoughts exactly."

Thelma knew enough not to question when Jane spoke of visits from her boys. Nor did she act surprised or disbelieving.

The unspoken agreement between them made Jane feel safe. It was one of the things she appreciated most about Thelma and was worth its weight in diamonds.

When disembarking, the first things she noticed were the moisture in the air and the gloom. Her lungs still squeezed when she overexerted herself, and she worried that a full recovery would be slowed in this climate. Then, looking to the far end of the depot, she swore she saw her brother Charles standing with two other men.

At the same time, Thelma pointed. "Isn't that your brother and Judge Leib?"

Just then, the third man turned. She was surprised to be looking at Mr. Wilson, her attorney. Dressed in black, they looked like they'd just come from a funeral. They hurried over to the women, puffs of breath steaming around them.

Charles spoke first. "You're looking much improved, sister. I'm pleased to see it."

Jane nodded to him and the others. "Judge Leib, Mr. Wilson. To what do I owe the honor?"

She said it lightly, but inside felt fingers of dread creeping around. Why were they here? The men grabbed their bags and Charles said, "We have a car waiting. We can talk there."

Thelma shot her a look. There was nothing to do but follow, legs weakened with dread.

Once away from the bustle, Judge Leib spoke up. "Unfortunately, your house is under lock and key, with no one allowed to come or go. The investigation is in full swing, and it's better for you to steer clear. We have a room waiting for you at the St. Francis."

Charles wore a serious expression. "The full analysis came back from Mr. Falkenau, the chemist, and it showed traces of other impure substances. According to Falkenau, the likely culprit in your water was rat poison."

"Common rat poison?" Jane repeated, as though she had to sound the words out in order to make sense of them.

The affront of it struck her, and a strange buzzing took up residence in her head. She doubted there was rat poison at the mansion, but she had just seen bottles on the shelf at her estate in Palo Alto.

"Let's get you to the hotel, and we can talk more there."

"I want to speak to the detective personally," she demanded.

Charles helped her into the vehicle. "I'll arrange it as soon as possible."

THE FOLLOWING MORNING, Mr. Callundan strode into the hotel room with an extra measure of swagger. In the name of being discreet, they were meeting in private. He'd given a false name to the front desk, asserting he was a university trustee. A young trustee. From what she had learned about him since their last meeting, he'd been with the Morse agency since his teen years and had steadily climbed the ranks to captain. She felt like she deserved Harry Morse himself, ex-sheriff of Alameda County with a long line of notches in his belt, but Callundan would have to do.

He removed his hat and bowed to her. "Ma'am, welcome back to the city."

"Have a seat, Detective."

Callundan pulled out a cigarette. "Mind if I smoke?"

Jane was about to object when he lit up anyway. The man had some nerve, but she was too anxious to bother arguing over it.

"Thelma, please open the window," she requested.

Mr. Callundan's eyes followed Thelma to the window, and he lazily watched her while Jane watched him.

"Thank you, kindly," he said. "Now, once again, this is a private matter between Mrs. Stanford and myself. Would you mind vamoosing?"

Jane nodded to Thelma. "I'll fetch you when he's gone."

Thelma had an adjoining room. That way she could keep an eye on Jane, and Jane could keep an eye on her. Sometimes Thelma felt like a secretary, others a daughter, and yet others an overbearing mother.

"So, here's a quick rundown for you. Eliza Sutton was dismissed at your request, and right away, I put a tail on her. So far it's not yielded anything, but she did tell me that she gave you notice before the poisoning. That true?"

"Miss Sutton had a tendency to fly off the handle. We quarreled some a few weeks back. In a rage, she told Thelma she wanted to leave my service. But things smoothed over, and she stayed on."

"She says you had unreasonable expectations," Callundan said, cigarette hanging from his lips.

It wouldn't be the first time. "High standards would be more correct."

"She did go speak with Albert Beverly. Why do you think that might be?"

"Oh, who knows. The two were friends—maybe more— and she's probably seeking his help finding employment."

Beverly had fallen out of her graces, but he was out of her life. He would have nothing to gain from knocking her off.

"What about Ah Wing? He told me he was polishing silver all day the day your water was tampered with, because you'd had a dinner party the night before. But Miss Sutton said there was no dinner party. In fact, you and Thelma had been planning to go to Palo Alto that evening but changed plans at the last minute."

Why would Ah Wing lie about something so easy to check? "Miss Sutton is right."

"He had access to the whole mansion, didn't he?" Callundan asked.

"He did."

"You ask me, the man was sweating while we questioned him. Does he have any reason to want you dead?"

"I have pledged that if he stays on with me as long as I live, he and his family back in China will be taken care of. Plus, I've already given him a thousand dollars," she said.

Callundan slowly nodded. "So theoretically, he did stand to gain."

"And your point?"

"You think he doesn't want to get back to his family sooner than later?"

Jane thought about her attentive servant, recalling how he did return to China years ago without her permission. But that did not make him a killer, and she felt sure he was not to blame. "Ah Wing is a good man. I would focus my energies elsewhere if I were you," she said.

"We'll tail him nonetheless. How about Wong Toy Wong, then, the guy who claims to have been defrauded by you and your bank of thirty grand—"

"Mr. Callundan, surely you know there is no Stanford University Trust Bank. That letter he sent was pure cockama-mie." She thought back to the mangy fellow lurking on the street out in front of the house in the weeks before the poisoning, trying to get an interview with her. She had dismissed his accusations that someone had impersonated him and with-drawn the funds, because how could one remove funds from a nonexistent bank? "The man was a lunatic. Do you think he could be responsible?"

"If he is, we'll get it out of him. He's been admitted to the Mendocino nut house. Obviously he's delusional, and the doctors who examined him think he could be homicidal. But my gut tells me he's a loose cannon, not a potential killer. I think this was an inside job, if a job at all."

"What does that mean?" she asked, flummoxed.

Callundan jotted a few notes, then said, "I gotta be honest, Mrs. Stanford, we're struggling to find anyone close to you who believes someone wanted you dead. Nor have we found a source of the strychnine."

She told him about the poison in Palo Alto, then added, "What are you saying?"

"I'm saying it's possible this whole thing could be a big misunderstanding. There has been talk of squabbling and jealousy between your employees, and we're beginning to wonder if one of them may have put the poison there to frame another. After you drank it."

Jane shook her head. "That's a ludicrous theory. You seem to forget that the water was vile and bitter, and I vomited profusely."

"Or they could have put it in before."

"There was a dose big enough to knock me dead and then some."

"But not if they were standing by to rescue you, as two were," he said.

That meant Thelma or Eliza. "Mr. Callundan, I would like for you to keep looking for the real killer here."

"There is no killer, Mrs. Stanford, as I'm sitting here across from you, and you are very alive."

Her dander was up. "You know what I mean."

The fact that they were sitting here conversing about people who might despise her enough to poison her made

Jane want to retch. And now this. She wasn't sure which was worse, and it pained her to no end.

SHE SPENT THE coming days ruminating, sinking deeper into a panic, and remembering Leland's words in her dream. *Leave the continent and go somewhere far away.* Dr. Boericke had visited yesterday afternoon, strongly suggesting a trip to warmer and sunnier Southern California, but word was the weather down there was cold and damp too. Would she have the gumption to leave now, with so much happening and her desire to clean things up at the Farm?

Her mind went back to the bitter water and the wretched amount of vomiting, and the sheer weight of the terror she had felt. How she had been minutes away from death— possibly at the hands of someone who knew her. Maybe even someone in the household. Suddenly, she knew what she had to do. She went to Thelma's door and knocked until she was pounding.

The door flew open. Thelma stood there, wrapped in a plush white robe, hair wet. "Is everything okay?"

"We're going to Hawai'i, and on to Japan from there. Get dressed so we can plan the trip."

Thelma went still as a cactus, and just as prickly. "Well . . . I . . . what about—"

"I've made up my mind. And I need you to come with me."

"You know I can't leave my father for that long."

"Your sister is perfectly capable. This is life or death, Thelma. And you said yourself I shouldn't go alone."

"There are others who would be happy to travel with you. You could even ask Mr. Beverly."

"I don't want others, especially not Beverly. I want you. You are the only one I can trust."

A cold wind blew through the hall, or so it felt. Thelma nodded. "I'll be in in a moment."

While Jane waited, the plans for their travels began to bloom in her mind.

JANE WAS ALLOWED into the mansion during the day, with an escort from the Morse Detective Agency, to pack her trunks for the trip. She also rehired Dot Hale, a maid who had previously worked for her. Dot was young and pliable and eager to please, a slight and pale girl with dull and wispy hair. Tropical air might do her good. She had a sweet and lively demeanor, which was, frankly, refreshing.

It took days to figure out her wardrobe; Dot went through each item of clothing, of which there were multitudes, for Jane to review. *Ah, Mrs. Stanford, it brings out the gold in your eyes* or *Why, what a stunning dress on you. You look like a queen!* Almost as though they were two young girls playing dress-up, and for a slip of time, Jane was free from the constant worry that had been sinking its teeth deep into her bones and leaving her cold. Because even after tea, even after a scalding bath, it was impossible to warm up. More and more, she found herself drowning in chill.

Jane also set out the medicines she would take, including a bottle of bicarbonate of soda, serums, cascara tablets, quinine and a whole array of other remedies in case of illness. You never knew what might befall you when traveling to foreign places. She had learned that lesson the hard way. And even when you thought you were prepared, tragedy could still strike.

Feeling as though she were going through the motions, and without the excitement she usually felt before a big ocean crossing, she decided she must bring some jewelry—if only for keeping up appearances. Jane pulled out some of her favorite pieces, and Dot helped her carefully pack them. Diamonds, diamonds and more diamonds.

Dot's eyes went wide as her hands ran over each one. "They're as beautiful as the night sky, and just as bright."

She was staring at the tiara and her most brilliant Tiffany necklace. "We won't be bringing those. No need for such extravagance in the tropics, but how about these?"

Jane chose a single strand of pearls, a sapphire pin in the shape of a cross, and several pairs of dangling earrings.

"What else?" she asked.

Dot exhaled and stepped closer. "This ruby bracelet is lovely. Oh, and this. And this!"

Jane acquiesced. "Very well. They may as well see some sunlight too."

In the end, she was aware that they had chosen a hefty collection of jewels, more valuable than what most people would earn in several lifetimes. But they were her weakness, and each and every one brought back memories of Leland. As fine a reason as any to bring them along. That, and maybe by the time they reached Hawai'i, the salt air would have worked its magic on her ominous temperament.

FROM THE JOURNAL OF
'ILIAHI BALDWIN, 1904

After a dreary and melancholy week of waiting, I still have not heard from Mr. Price. I've been mending uniforms for the Royal Hawaiian band, and that has kept my hands busy, but my mind has been galivanting from one bad scenario to the next, the worst of which would be giving the house back to the bank or pulling my brothers from school to work full-time. I had arrived at the conclusion that it may be time to sell the house and move in with Tutu in Kailua. Ripping the boys away from their home and school would pain them, but what other choice did I have?

My mind was made up, and I planned on telling them this weekend. And then, a series of events unfolded that I interpret as divine intervention. I can't help feel but my father had a hand in it. I will tell it here as succinctly as possible.

Yesterday afternoon I went to pick up eggs from Mrs. Lee in Kapahulu, and I took the long way back, around Kapiolani Park. The weather had taken a strange turn, with gray clouds stacking up along the Waianae Mountains and the humidity rising. I stopped under a dense milo tree to check the ocean, and ended up talking story with Willy Akau, who was there for the same reason as me. Willy told me he'd heard the waves would soon be rising.

As we stood there, in one short hour, the ocean went from flat to filled with long, head-high peelers. Iwa birds hovered like black kites overhead, and I could see a sudden change in currents. The conditions were perfect. When I arrived home, I told the boys, and we all slept with one ear open, listening for the thrilling roar of large surf. In the morning, the air was thick with 'ehukai, and salt coated every surface in our house. Liko went around licking things like a cow, and did so until I pinched his ear. We must be civilized if we want to survive in this town.

Liko and Max are what keep me going every day. My two guiding stars. It's been that way ever since we've been on our own. Before that, they fished and farmed with Pa when they weren't in school, and I did my womanly things with Ma. Strange how it took a tragedy to bring us close. I used to think of them as muddy, foul-smelling and dumb as old man Liu's water buffalo. When we were younger, neither showed much interest in me until I came home and announced I needed help fashioning a wooden plank into a surfboard to ride the waves.

Pa knew he wouldn't be able to talk me out of it, so instead, he helped me. Ma loved the idea. Anything that went against the grain of the missionaries, she was all for. And missionaries do not approve of wave riding. Do you think I cared? When all was said and done, it took four of us to carry the polished redwood board to the beach. From then on, it was always a fight for who got to ride it, so Pa, bless his heart, helped us build two more boards, both longer and heavier for the boys.

Though I am older, Max and Liko have both outweighed me for years. At thirteen, Max is six feet tall with wild curls and lime-green eyes. Softhearted and with a fondness for animals, he reminds me of a large puppy. Liko, on the other hand, is more like a wiry stray. On the cusp of sixteen, he has yet to master the fire in his bones, and has had a few brushes with the law, mainly for taking what is not his. It's hard to blame him, since he thinks he's doing us all a favor. They are good-hearted boys, strong and sturdy, and I love them with the fierceness of a mama cat.

So, back to this morning. We have been fortunate enough to keep our surfboards in a wooden frame near the shore, built by an intrepid friend. When your surfboard weighs one hundred pounds, it makes sense. Even before we arrived at the beach, we were giddy with anticipation. The gauzy veil of salt in the air and the constant thrum of breaking waves drew us at almost a full gallop. When we arrived, the entire horizon had turned white, and waves lined up on the reefs beyond where we usually ride.

A posse of surfers was already there, including young Duke Kahanamoku, the most naturally gifted surfer on the island, lined up and watching the waves with what can only be described as awe and wonder, if not a hint of trepidation. Max and Liko immediately began debating whether or not to go out. Liko of course wanted to, and Max was afraid. Duke and his friend Tom, who had been watching it for upward of an hour, said they had picked out a channel to paddle out through and if any of us wanted to follow them, we could keep an eye on each other. What happened after that would be a matter of chance and fate.

I am one of the only females who regularly surfs in Waikiki. My mother said that before the haole came, women surfers were abundant in the islands, and just as skilled as the men, only more graceful. I dream to see that again, but for now, I am just glad to be out there. I wear a modest swimsuit so as not to call attention to myself. Regardless, people have taken notice, and sometimes when I come in to shore, I find a small audience awaiting. If only surfing paid the bills.

This morning, we waited for a lull and then scrambled out to sea, helped along by a swift current. Liko and two others remained on the beach, which, in hindsight, was the prudent thing to do. No one was sure exactly where to position ourselves, so we floated around each other a half mile out to sea. I stayed close to Duke. It was some time before a set came, but when it did, I instantly regretted my choice in paddling out.

The entire ocean reared up in a mountain of blue, heading straight for Duke and me. We were the farthest out. He looked at me, I looked at him, and we both lay down and started scratching for the horizon. We made it over that one, but the wave behind it was double the size. I glanced over at Duke, who was paddling hard toward the right. I could tell he was going to turn and ride it, so I followed suit since I did not want to be left out there on my own. The wave lifted up my twelve-foot board and I was staring down a cliff, unsure whether to remain prone or try to stand.

Through the spray, I could see Duke was up, and so I hopped to my feet and cut my board at an angle so the nose didn't dip underwater. For a few moments, I felt my board falling through air, but it reconnected, sticking back onto the face of the wave and slingshotting me along at high speed. I imagined myself an 'a'ama crab, crouching low to the board and keeping my feet rooted in place. Ahead, Duke moved freely on his board, carving generous turns and making it look like a cakewalk. I assure you it was not, as I was just hoping to survive and get myself back to shore in one piece.

When we hit the inner reef outside the Moana, the wave exploded into white water, knocking me down onto the board. Somehow I managed to hang on, careening toward the hotel on my belly, hands in a vise grip. When I popped out of the froth, I noticed a person in toward the shore feebly waving. I watched in horror as he or she then went under. I could still see the top of their head bobbing, and steered my board in their direction.

When I reached the person, I slid into the water while still holding on to my board with one arm. I grabbed for them, trying to get a solid hold. My hand found short, cropped hair, and I pulled at it with all my strength, lifting the man's face out of the water. Immediately, he started clawing at me and gagging and spitting. I yelled at him to calm down, that I had him, he was going to be okay. That's the thing with a drowning person. They will take you down with them if you aren't careful.

He was a big man, nearly twice my size, and it took some wrangling to get him on my board. Since he was useless and could not use his arms, I had to lie on top of him tandem-style and paddle us both in, where I swear to you, every occupant of the hotel awaited us on the sand. I let the white water carry us up the beach, and several men rushed forward and grabbed hold of my board, securing us. A wailing woman dropped to her knees next to the rescued man, screaming, "Henry, oh my Henry!"

I was spent, I tell you, and I collapsed into the sand myself. Max appeared out of the crowd, pushing his way through like a bull. He kneeled by my side and asked me if I was okay, since everyone else was focused on Henry. I told him I was fine, just out of breath and still a little shaky from my ride. Later, Max said that from shore, Duke and I were mere specks, dwarfed by the monstrous wave.

As I sat there, trying to regain my composure and fill my lungs with air, Mr. Price came to stand before me. I thought that was you, he said, pulling up his pants at the ankle and sitting down next to me. Do you know who that was, he asked.

I told him I did not, other than that his name was Henry. Well, it turns out he is a wealthy automobile manufacturer who Peacock says is going to change the world. I glanced over at Henry, who was now sitting up, and he gave me a curt nod and a salute. The crowd began to cheer, and wouldn't you know it, Mr. Price offered me a job on the spot.

THE TRUST

Jane

February 15

A s the trip grew near, Jane was haunted by the notion
that she might never return. She'd had these thoughts
on previous travels. It was perfectly natural. But now the idea
consumed her. So much so that on the afternoon of her departure, she asked George Crothers to pay her a call and bring
with him a copy of the trust. On top of being a board member,
he advised her on the side about university legal matters.

When Crothers walked through the door, her heart
jumped a little, as it always did. She had never told him why
she had such a soft spot for him, and it wasn't just because he'd
been one of her Stanford boys—a member of the first graduat-
ing class.

"Mrs. Stanford, a pleasure to see you, as always," he said
once seated on the brushed velvet couch.

"George dear, I have so much to tell you before I leave for
this trip of mine, and there is work to be done," she said, unable to look away from his oh so familiar eyes.

George glanced down, fumbling through his briefcase and
producing a legal tablet and fountain pen. "I'm all ears."

"I would like you to draw up a statement for me to sign
that says I approve of the trust. If anything should happen to

me, I want it clear as an alpine morning that the money I've left to the university shall remain with the university, under all circumstances. I suspect there may be those who challenge the trust, so we must act in haste. It needs to be ironclad."

She and George spent the next hour or so drafting the document, and after that, she had Thelma fetch tea and crumpets.

He took off his glasses and rubbed his eyes, then smiled. "You can rest assured, the future of the university is on solid ground. And I'm sure you will return, but . . ."

"It feels very surreal to leave under such peculiar circumstances, but leave I must. And grim as it sounds, I don't want to leave without saying my goodbyes to people I care about. Which is why I want you to know how much I value you, George. All that you've done for me—being a sympathetic ear, working so hard on the California amendment. That was a huge deal for me personally, and for the university."

It was because of him that Stanford had an exemption from taxes. Hallelujah. Without that, she would never have donated her stock holdings, which were a huge boon to the school.

Red flushed in his cheeks. "It's because of the Farm, and you, that I am where I am. I owe so much to you, Mrs. Stanford."

"I also want you to know how grateful I am for your support these last years in all other matters. You've been there in dark days, and your positive outlook has buoyed my spirits more than you know. You're a kind soul and a good friend," she said.

"As are you," he said.

She felt such a fondness for him, and wished her own son could be sitting here on the couch beside him. "I've never told you this, but with your likeness to Leland Jr., I used to seek you out on campus just to get a glimpse of your shining young face. To a grieving mother, it was a balm for my shattered soul. I wouldn't expect you to understand, but in some small way, I was able to put my son in your place, and it soothed me."

People often mentioned the likeness, so there was no surprise there, but he went solemn and quiet for a moment, mouth opening and closing as though he wished to speak but was unable.

Jane wanted to put him at ease. "I consider all the students, past and present, my children, but you are at the top of the lot. Remember when you used to drop in to see me in the early days?"

"I do."

"Ah, you were so young and so full of hope, always cheering me on and telling me what great things were in store for the school," she said.

"One of the benefits of being young and naive, I suppose," he said.

"But you were right. Look at how far we've come."

He stayed another hour as she unloaded old memories on him. Reminiscing about the early days of the school, builders and craftsmen and endless construction as the massive Quadrangle went up, and the first students arriving in long lines of carriages leading up to the Arch. All those young souls coming to begin their future lives of enlightenment and cultivation. Bless his heart, he was a patient and focused listener. After Crothers left, she took out her stationery and wrote several goodbye letters, just in case.

Thelma brought her a ham sandwich with deviled eggs as sustenance. "We have a big day tomorrow. Don't you think it's time you get some rest?" she asked.

"Not yet."

It was as though she was possessed, her mind a whirl with odds and ends and unfinished business to wrap up. Funny how in life, we humans forget how death can sneak up so quietly, so suddenly, so unapologetically. She thought of the new and immense library under construction, and decided then and there that she would—no, she *must*—write out a dedication for it. The students deserved to hear from her directly, and God only knew when she would return.

She filled her pen with ink and began, words pouring forth.

> *My health being somewhat impaired, I am advised by my physician to take a sea voyage to Honolulu. I regret this absence as it was my desire to be with you when laying the cornerstone of this library . . . these noble buildings are not for the present, but for ages to come . . .*

She then went on to tell the story of her donated jewels, which had been meant to fund the chapel but were not needed in the end. And so going forward, after her departure from this life, the jewels were to be sold. The proceeds would go into the endowment, solely used for the purchase of books and publications. Her hand began to cramp from all the writing, but she kept going.

> *I desire that this fund be known and designated as The Jewel Fund . . . God bless you all is ever my prayer, for I well know prayer is the key that unlocks the doors of heaven to us all.*
> *Jane L. Stanford*

THE MAN
Zoe

ZOE'S BURNT OCHRE, strapless dress feels like it's just caught fire. She's wearing the dress because it illuminates her coffee-colored eyes, or so she's been told. As soon as they are given the third assignment and she hears Susan's words about finding someone wearing the same color garb, her eyes cannot help but swing toward Dylan Winters. His aloha shirt is distinctively rust-orange with splashes of yellow. He catches her look, and his eyes drop down to her dress for a fraction of a second. It would be rude to turn away because they are so obviously matched, so she offers up a half smile.

He walks slowly toward her, scanning the crowd as if hoping he might find someone else. "I guess it's us. I'm Dylan, but you already know that," he says, straight-faced.

"My name is . . ." She draws out the *s*, about to say *Zoe*, but catches herself. "Bridget. Look, I am so, so sorry about my reprehensible behavior this morning in your workshop. I'm usually prompt and conscientious. It must be the time difference. It's really messed me up."

"Where are you from?" he asks.

She lifts her eyebrows. "Oregon?"

Two hours' difference is nothing, really, and he looks like he knows it. But there's also something else on his face. Surprise, maybe?

"Is that a question?" he asks.

Her mind is acting strange, and she's not sure why. She laughs. "No, it's not a question. I know where I live, Mr. Winters."

"Please, call me Dylan. So, what's your story, Bridget? When did you know you wanted to become a writer?" He asks as though he really isn't that interested in knowing the answer, and then looks at his watch.

"Why don't we start with you, since you're the real writer here," she says.

He shoves his hands in his jeans pockets. "My story isn't that interesting, and I'm tired from talking all day, so entertain me."

Zoe teeters on her heels for a moment, then notices that her glass is empty. "Okay. I . . ." She tries to come up with something, but again realizes that the truth is the best way through this. "My best friend Ginger died just before we turned eighteen, and I always suspected it wasn't an accident. I became somewhat obsessed with true crime stories. I read them constantly."

"What made you think it wasn't an accident?"

"She had started seeing someone but wouldn't tell me who—I believe it was a married neighbor—about a month before she was found at the bottom of a cliff in the woods. When I mentioned my suspicion, only one cop took me seriously and looked into the guy, but lucky for him, there was no evidence of the two of them ever being together. It would have just been my word against his."

"There's always evidence."

"You said that in your workshop, didn't you? But in this case, if no one is looking for evidence, chances are they won't find it. And I thought about writing the story as a novel, with an alternate ending where the bad guy meets his own fate, but could not get myself to put the words down. It gave me nightmares. So instead, I wrote a romance novel. Because, well . . ." she says, "I love a good love story."

The words make her feel vulnerable, and she immediately regrets saying them.

He cocks his head, autumn-green eyes searching hers. "Did she die from the fall?" His voice is softer now.

"It was presumed so. She fell from a cliff in the hills behind our houses. There's a huge network of mountainous and rocky trails, and we both knew them like the backs of our hands. We found her at the bottom of a ravine, and the official story is that she slipped and fell. Rocks were loose as she went down, she hit her head on a rock, and it shattered her skull. But that particular trail was one we never went on."

"Did they do an autopsy?"

"No. Her parents wouldn't hear of it. Her mother, mainly. Nor did she want to hear my concerns when I tried to broach the subject. Said her daughter would never have done anything like have an affair. Completely shut me out."

"Damn."

"I know."

"I'm sorry you've had to live with that. Not only losing your friend, but knowing there's a guy out there who could have gotten away with murder."

"It hasn't been easy."

In her heels, she is still a couple inches shorter than him, and her eyes keep going to his mouth and the small cleft in his chin. There is something appealing about the way his lips move when he speaks, and his teeth are toothpaste ad perfect.

"So, what about the love story? Is that what you're here for? Trying to get it published?" he asked.

She fingers her gold pocket watch, which hangs around her neck and is weirdly warm to the touch, but doesn't feel like getting into it. "I think you've run out of your allotted questions."

One side of his mouth lifts. "Is that so?"

"It is. Just tell me when you knew you wanted to be a writer—since that was the assignment and I always complete my assignments—and then you can be on your way," she says.

Actually, it's a lie. She has failed miserably at completing her latest assignment, and instead of working on it, is standing here. Procrastination has many forms, and for her it usually means going out of her way to do anything but the task at hand.

"Who says I want to be on my way?" he asks.

His tone sends a bolt of lightning up her spine.

"You did, earlier."

"You misunderstood me, then. I just meant that I'd rather you talk and I listen. And . . ." He shrugs. "I don't know, I guess I'm a curious person, and I like to hear about other people's journeys."

"Which is why you're a good mystery writer."

He shrugs. "So, back to that love story of yours . . ."

There is less than a one percent chance Dylan Winters has ever heard of her or her book, so she gives him a little. "It's about two best friends who make a pact on their twenty-ninth birthday that they will both find husbands before they turn thirty, and they embark on a hilarious and heartbreaking journey."

"You've got your pitch nailed," he says.

"Yeah, practice makes perfect, isn't that what they say?"

A gust of wind blows through, stirring the leaves overhead and filling her nose with kerosene from the torches. It feels very exotic, and for a moment, she wishes it was just the two of them, and they had all night to talk. She wants to know more about him, and he's given her nothing so far.

"Do they both find husbands?" he asks.

She crosses her arms. "I never give away my endings. You'd have to read to find out."

He looks terrified.

The last thing she wants is for Dylan to figure out who she is, but she continues anyway. "Or do you not read romance novels?" she asks.

"It's not that I don't like romance novels. I just tend to lean toward mysteries and thrillers. Or nonfiction," Dylan says almost apologetically.

"Have you ever read a romance novel?"

His long pause tells her everything, and he seems to be searching for the right thing to say. "I've read books with love stories in them."

"But not a straight-up romance or love story."

"Not off the top of my head, no. Is that a crime?" he asks, a smile creeping onto his face.

"Not at all. But it does mean you'll never get to know how my story ends."

Something has caught his eye behind her, and the air shifts between them. He moves away slightly. Zoe turns and sees the beautiful woman at the bar, watching them. When she looks back at Dylan, his face is stone.

"I've enjoyed talking with you, Bridget, but I have to go. Maybe I'll see you in my workshop tomorrow?" he says.

"Tomorrow I'll be in Olivia Owens's class," she says.

Then he catches her completely off guard. "I noticed you never came back today. Did I put you to sleep?"

She can't help but laugh. "To be honest, I was too embarrassed to walk back in after the interruptions I caused, and then after lunch . . . something came up."

They stand there for a few breaths, and she swears that a crackling current passes in the space between them, but then he nods and heads off. She watches, expecting him to go to the bar, but he kicks off his shoes and steps into the sand, disappearing onto the beach. Zoe expects the woman to follow him, but she doesn't. And now she's curious. What *is* Dylan Winters's story?

THE FIRST PAGE
Zoe

Z OE WAKES TO a monochromatic gray sky, and for a moment, wonders where she is. The stillness has intensified from last night, and a dead calm settles in the room, making her want to roll over and go back to sleep. She doesn't feel rested, and her mouth is dry and cottony. Hopefully she's not getting sick. She grabs the glass of water on her bedside table and takes a few sips, swishing it around. The weight of her predicament slams her, and she feels bad for picking the mixer instead of working on her proposal. She looks at her computer sitting on the table, and rubs her eyes.

Then a recollection of a dream rears up, vivid in her mind, and strikes hard. A crowd of people are all looking down on her, and she's lying on the floor of her room, unable to get enough air. Almost as though she's underwater. Strange things are happening to her body, and she feels rigid and immovable, made of lead. She is unable to ask for help, and no one does anything. They all just stand there gaping down at her. The ocean roars out front, and a bird comes in and lands on someone's head. It stares down at her too, black feathers iridescent. The bird drops a live fish on her chest, and then flies off as the fish begins to flop around. She tries to scream, but nothing comes out.

Unleashed from the dream, she sits up panting, drinks more water, throws on a robe and goes out onto the patio. The sky and ocean are one big canvas of gray, with streaks of bloodred here and there, and it's hard to tell where one stops and the other begins. Her hands are shaking as she tries to make sense of the vague unease that slinks around her insides. It reminds her of the dreams she used to have of Ginger, and how gutted she always felt afterward. But those were always weird and disjointed, and this one has a clarity to it that makes her shiver.

As she gets ready for the workshop, she does her best to shake it off, remembering Dylan and their conversation and the shimmer of flirtation going on between the lines. It isn't purely her imagination, she's sure of it. And as someone who has studied flirtation for a living, she should know.

She'd looked him up on the internet as soon as she'd returned to the room, under the guise of knowing more about her teacher, but not really fooling herself. He is handsome and sexy in a bad boy kind of way, and according to his website, married. Is the woman from the bar his wife? Maybe they'd had a fight. He wore no ring on his finger, but not all married people do.

Zoe learned that the hard way with Gus when she was twenty-two. He had claimed he was single, and split his time between Bend and Dallas, but she'd come to find out he was married to a model who spent much of her time in NYC. It took her a while before she was willing to trust again, but when she met Luke, she fell hard. He ticked off so many boxes—loved books, had a wildly creative mind, made her laugh, touched her in all the right places, hiked with her to her heart's content.

But that was when he was home, which over time grew to be less and less. A photographer by trade, he took jobs all over the world, and that's where things fell apart. She was blindsided. The *woman in every port* turned out to be a real thing, and it broke something inside Zoe. She couldn't eat or sleep for months and felt the betrayal in every cell of her body.

Since then, she's had a long dry spell—three years of nothing. It's been her choice, and in that time she wrote *The Marriage Pact*, but she battles conflicted feelings on the regular. Wanting a life partner, not wanting to fall for someone ever again. There is also this sense that she's running out of time. She tries to practice acceptance, because in acceptance, there is freedom. At least according to all the self-help books she's been reading lately. But so far she's not convinced. She doesn't feel free. She feels like there's something inherently wrong with her.

OLIVIA OWENS LOOKS like one of the cover models on her books. She's got long red curls, fire-engine lips and a body designed for tight jeans. Zoe is on time today and slips into a middle row. They are in a smaller ballroom with far fewer chairs than Dylan's class, and there's not a man in sight. She puts her purse on the chair next to her, to save for Tara, who shows up one minute before the class is supposed to start, with wet hair and sandy feet.

"Did you go swimming?" Zoe asks.

"I couldn't resist. Even though the sky has that ominous look, the water was like warm satin."

"I'm jealous."

"Go on your lunch break, then, because from what I hear, there's a big storm brewing out at sea."

Zoe can feel it in her bones. The lowering of the barometric pressure causes an ache in her left fibula and humerus, both of which she broke when she was riding her mountain bike looking for Ginger on the trails outside of town. Her body will always remember.

Olivia introduces herself and asks the group, which is only about twenty people, to go around and share their names, where they are from, and the title of the manuscript they plan on workshopping, if they have one.

"This is a workshopping class?" Zoe asks Tara, surprised that she'd missed that.

"Yeah, first pages."

She groans.

"What?"

"My book isn't ready for that."

"What do you mean? I thought you have an agent already?"

She catches herself. "I mean my new book, the one I've recently started."

This lying is getting harder, and she thinks that maybe tonight she'll explain herself to Tara. In the rush that she'd been in to get here, she obviously hadn't thought everything through. That she might make friends. Or meet a man.

"Even better. You'll get good feedback."

Olivia starts with the first row, and Zoe doesn't hear anything anyone is saying, because she's trying to come up with a title for the book she started yesterday. Titles never come easy for her, and now that she's on the spot, her muse goes dark. *A Wish for Zoe* is all she can come up with. Anyone who knows about titles knows that they usually change. Publishers like to come up with their own titles, so it will be enough for now.

Today's workshop is all about first sentences and first pages, and how important they are in hooking the reader. Olivia reads a few first lines aloud and asks the group to critique them. *You ask me, men are nothing more than shoulders and abs and asses, and well-defined ones if you're lucky.*

"What sense do you get from this line? About the narrator? About the story?" Olivia asks.

Zoe raises her hand, and Olivia nods at her. "I get a sense she's kind of a badass. At least on the outside. But I also wonder what has caused her to have this attitude, and if there isn't some wounded child hiding behind this tough-girl act."

Olivia clasps her hands, smiling. "Wonderful! Yes."

Others chime in, and Zoe enjoys the discourse and hearing what they have to say. The next line is *The last time I saw Joe Sumner, he was naked in a kiddie pool trying to drown me.* People get a kick out of that one. They go through a few more, with Olivia giving them a list of ways to craft a knockout first line. A shocking statement. Something curious. Drop the reader into the setting. Make them feel. It's lovely to be surrounded by others passionate about writing, and the unease from the morning begins to dissolve.

Then Olivia reads another. "Here's one from a book I love. *I'm in an ambulance the first time I see him. The second time too.* I know that's two sentences, but they complement each other well. So, what do you think?" she asks.

These are the first lines in Zoe's novel, and she feels every surface of her skin turning red. She looks down at her notebook and pulls her curls alongside her face. Maybe it might be a good time to split to the bathroom, but she doesn't want to call attention to herself.

Tara says, "I want to know more!"

"Right?" the woman next to her says.

Olivia picks up a book from a stack on the table and shows everyone the cover. "After this short prologue, the author jumps back and forth in time, but I love how she piques our interest immediately," Olivia says. "Have any of you read the book—*The Marriage Pact*?"

Tara raises her hand, and as Zoe looks around as casually as she can, she sees that about a third of the people in the room also have. "Loved it." "It was so fun!" "I hope she writes another one." That last comment gives her heart palpitations, so she tries to focus on the other two. She is extremely honored, even though she feels like a spy.

They move on from first lines to first pages, and they dissect several great first pages from *The Duke and I* to *The Secret Life of Bees* to *The Time Traveler's Wife*. She's relieved that Olivia has chosen other books, and enjoys the process of studying line by line how other authors craft their setup. Most readers have no idea how much work can go into a single page, or even a single line. And honing in like they are now reveals how expertly these authors manipulate their readers to get sucked into their stories.

During the break, Zoe meanders around the lobby, stretching her legs while Tara calls her husband. None of the other classes are out, and the space is quiet. She stands by the window looking out at a peekaboo view of the ocean through tropical plants. It's a peculiar feeling to have people know your work and yet not recognize you as you are sitting among them.

Something about it reminds her of being twelve and transferring to another school, not knowing a single person at the new one. Of sitting in class, horribly self-conscious and yet discovering that if she kept her nose in a book, and dressed in jeans and sweatshirts, she could be invisible. Her mother always said she was "quietly pretty," with her big brown eyes, dainty nose and high cheekbones, but all anyone noticed were her wild curls. No matter what she did, she could never tame them.

And now, with this storm brewing and the dense, thick air, those curls have taken on a life of their own. She goes with it—what else can she do? Behind her she hears voices and sees the door to Dylan's class is now open. People trickle out, and she's tempted to peek in for no reason other than to see him. The pull is strong, a centrifugal force that she has to work to resist, and she finds it curious. But knowing he's married has somehow taken the pressure off. Now he will take up less of her head space.

As she leans against the window frame, the woman from last night walks out of his ballroom with Dylan trailing behind. She's tall and lanky and all business in a pencil skirt and a powder-blue silk blouse. They make an attractive couple, and yet for some reason, Zoe doesn't think it's his wife. It's more a hunch than anything, but she's learned to trust her hunches.

Dylan says something, and the woman turns and laughs. Then he spots Zoe, and his expression brightens. She's about to wave, but someone from the class is waiting for him outside and stops him. Then the woman in the pencil skirt sees Zoe, and her expression flattens. She waits with Dylan as he talks to this student, and Zoe realizes it's time to go back into her workshop. She gives them a wide berth.

AT LUNCHTIME, ZOE GRABS a pesto and veggie sandwich on sourdough bread and a bag of taro chips from the buffet and goes back to her room to frantically work on her first page, applying principles she's learned in Olivia's workshop. She wants to have something to send to Avery soon, and this idea is growing on her. Pages, not just a synopsis, even though there's a chance Avery will shut the whole thing down if she doesn't think the idea is strong enough. Which, when she's honest with herself, it probably isn't. But it feels good to dust off her creative cobwebs.

In the workshop, she and Tara partner up first to read each other's work and offer critiques before they share to the larger group, which has grown smaller by four or five people. Tara's book is titled *Daughter of the Winter Moon*.

"First, I'll give you my elevator pitch, okay?" Tara says. Her skin is a shade darker than it was yesterday, and Zoe envies her ability to tan so beautifully.

"Of course, I'm dying to hear it."

"This novel tells the story of a medicine woman who lives alone deep in the rainforest, and of the injured man who shows up on her doorstep in the middle of winter with no memory of who he is and how he got there."

Zoe is genuinely intrigued. "I love it! Already it has this wonderfully atmospheric feel to it. And the title is evocative."

Tara's face lights up. "Really—truly? Because I'm here for honest feedback, not someone to just tell me they like it."

"Really. Truly. Now read me the first page."

"'*December.* Freya stood at the edge of her broad porch, admiring the quiet falling of snow. White swallowed everything and had already filled in the boot prints from her recent foray out to the barn to feed the animals. She heard King kicking in his stall, unhappy about something. There was an unusual scent in the air. Metallic. Pungent. Almost human. Over the years, she had come to trust her senses . . .'"

Zoe listened until she finished, impressed. "This is good, Tara. How many agents have you queried with this story?"

"None. This is my latest. I'm still revising it. But what would you change to make it better?"

She took the paper from Tara and read through it again. "Honestly, nothing. But I do wonder how it would sound in first person, so we feel even more of an immediacy, like we are standing in Freya's shoes. It doesn't always work, and sometimes it's hard to pull off, but when it does, it's magic."

"Hmm. I hadn't thought of that. Is yours in first person?"

"No. Mine felt better in third."

Tara makes a few tweaks, then rereads it in first person. The setting springs to life, and Zoe may as well be standing in that snowy landscape, hair up on the back of her neck. "Definitely first person. I can't wait for the agents to read this."

Tara squeals. "You're serious, aren't you?"

"One hundred percent."

"Let's do yours. I don't want to be a time hog."

Tara closes her eyes as Zoe reads, and when she finishes, Tara lets out a whistle. "This is you, yesterday, isn't it? Either that or you conjured up Dylan Winters in a séance or something."

Zoe laughs. "I wrote it last night. Something about that interaction in his class sparked an idea—though of course it has nothing to do with Dylan himself. I've been in a writing drought, so any inspiration that I get, I grab on to."

"I love the premise, and the idea of finding love after loss," Tara says.

Love after loss. The words choke Zoe up, and she's not exactly sure why. Then Olivia rings a little bell, announcing they will start reading to the group. It's not a requirement, but she strongly encourages everyone to learn to receive constructive criticism. A required skill for anyone wanting to get better at writing—or life. For time's sake, she will offer two to three suggestions per person, but the class can write down their own feedback and hand it in at the end. "And please, be kind."

Zoe loves her all the more for this last statement.

The pages are all over the place. Some brilliant and polished, others in need of rewriting altogether. Finding a good starting point to a story is an art in and of itself, one that Zoe has pursued relentlessly. But it's fascinating to hear how other minds work and what they come up with. Zoe is last, and baby butterflies are beginning to flap their wings.

Tara goes two before her, and Olivia raves about her work. "I want to read this story. Can you send me a copy?"

"Um. Well. Of course!"

Zoe is happy for her, but also feels envious, and is thankful that in the writing world, the two feelings can coexist. The clock on the wall says four, but Olivia asks that they stay for just one more—Zoe's. Reading aloud is high on her list of most dreaded things in this line of work, but she takes a few deep breaths and begins, because that's why she's here.

Time has never been on her side. Not a day in her life. Now, Fiona stands outside the mystery workshop ten minutes late, wondering if she should sneak in and stand in the back shadows or wait for a break. But she's paid a high price to be here, so she slinks in and hovers near a fake plant almost as tall as she is. From there, she surveys the room for empty seats, but there are none that she can see.

She sets her bag on the floor, and her entrance appears to have gone unnoticed until the teacher says, "Hey, you by the plant, there's a seat up here."

He points to a chair in the front middle of the room, mere feet away from the stool where he sits. She has no choice but to make her way up there, and situates herself as quickly and quietly as possible. When she finally looks up at him, her heart catches. She hadn't paid much mind to his photograph, only that he was a best-selling author, and that his workshop *Emotions in Story* is the best-attended workshop every year. He's a dead ringer for Tommy, her late husband. Same dark hair, same arctic ice eyes, and a five o'clock shadow framing his striking face.

There are differences, of course. Nose a little longer, jaw more square. But the similarity is close enough that she finds it hard to breathe. He seems to notice her struggling, and he watches her.

"Are you okay?" he asks.

"I'm not sure."

Zoe finishes there. A first page is short, since it's really only half a page. Relief and anxiety fill her in equal measure. In the reading circle, she sits with her side to the door. Out of the corner of her eye, she sees movement, and reflexively turns to look. It's Dylan Winters. He slides out the door without a backward glance. Tara has noticed him too, and gives Zoe a dramatic shrug. Zoe is dead.

Olivia has nice things to say about her opening, but Zoe can tell her socks have not been knocked off, as they were with Tara. It's impossible to concentrate, but she does her best, hoping no one notices that her face has caught fire.

"Do you think he heard me read?" she asks Tara once they're dismissed.

"I know he did. I saw him come in just as you were reading your title."

"You should have kicked me or something." Zoe wants to dig a hole in the sand and crawl into it for the foreseeable future. "I'll never be able to look him in the eye again."

Tara rolls her eyes. "Just own it. You can always tell him that you wrote this before coming to the conference. He's not the only tall, dark and handsome man in the world."

"And an author at a writers conference?"

"It's not like you have a thing for him." Then she cocks her head. "Do you?"

Zoe hangs her leather bag on her shoulder and turns to head out. "Not at all."

FROM THE JOURNAL OF
'ILIAHI BALDWIN, 1904

I BEGAN AT the Moana last week, and I have been too spent to write much, so I will catch you up now. On my first day, I woke with the roosters, as I often do, then went outside and counted stars for a time, drawing my own lines and bringing to life an aquarium in the sky. A high-finned shark, an octopus, a spotted moray eel swimming through the inky morning hours. It's something I loved to do with Pa, except Pa knew all the real constellations. Though to this day I still wonder why we don't use our Hawaiian star charts. They make so much more sense than those concocted by people in far-flung lands. Real, I suppose, is highly relative.

I spent some extra time fixing my hair, twisting two halves and coiling it atop my head, then plucking three pink plumeria and pinning them in place. My uniform is a slim-fitting white dress and a kukui nut lei, and I have never felt more elated about putting on items of clothing in my life. The white sets off my skin, and the polished lei brings out the gold in my eyes. I have to admit that I've had a few daydreams of being swept off my feet by a wealthy prince, but that would only mean leaving my brothers, and the daydream abruptly ends.

Just after dawn, I walked the mile to work, and with each step closer to the hotel, I grew more and more apprehensive until I was a living, breathing earthquake. I was fretting that I might blurt out the wrong thing, or somehow embarrass myself among such a refined crowd. Ridiculous, because I am well-versed in etiquette. Ma would have grabbed my shoulders and said, "Be strong, let your mind not be weak. *E ho'oikaika nō 'oe, e ku'?u kaikamahine.*" They said it would get easier as time went on, but I miss her more each day.

When I arrived at the Moana, a woman named Mrs. Akina was waiting for me at the front desk and eyed me with a look of concern when I told her who I was. I held my head high, grateful that the way I'd done my hair added few inches to my height, and promised her I would not disappoint. We toured the palatial property, though my brothers and I have already traipsed through the hotel on several occasions after the grand opening, and I worried the whole time that Mrs. Akina might suddenly remember me as the girl who walked through the lobby dripping salt water and leaving a trail of ocean in my wake.

On top of all my nerves today, I also felt a sense of pride. Introductions were made to other staff members, some haole, some Hawaiian, some Japanese, some Filipino, and Mr. Lee has already made himself a permanent fixture sweeping sand from the veranda and banyan court. A waste of time, if you ask me. A hotel on the beach is bound to have sand everywhere, so why bother?

Mrs. Akina showed me how to "turn down" a room, and then let me loose with my own little cart of cleaning supplies and towels and mints and linens. They call sheets *linens* here, even though they are made of cotton. The hotel is nowhere close to occupancy—I've learned a bunch of new terms, as you can see—but there are seventy-five rooms, and I cleaned half of them. After the first three, Mrs. Akina came in and inspected my work, and seemed pleasantly surprised. Taking care of two young brothers has required me to become strict as a nun in a convent, and I know my way around a scrub brush. She reminds me a little bit of Ma: tough, but fair and kind.

Over the next few days, Mrs. Akina began to trust me more, and when Lina Chong fell ill, I took up the slack and helped show people to their rooms and ran around like a head-less chicken meeting the needs of all the guests, on top of turndowns and turnovers. I hate to admit it, but twice I was so hungry I ate the mints meant for their pillows. I hope no one counts them.

Most of the guests are polite and delighted to be here, but a few have tested my ability to keep a smile on my face. As of this writing, we have a banker and his wife from New York, a duke and duchess from England, a governor, a family of aristocrats from Paris, and several businessmen who are in Hawai'i to see if they can extend their fortunes in our islands. If they rub me the wrong way, I imagine them lying naked in the sun, burnt to a crisp, and that does the trick every time. Because the way I see it, stripped bare, we are all the same.

THE JOURNEY

Jane

February 15

I F SALT WATER HEALS, salt air must have a similar effect, or so Jane believed. They boarded the *SS Korea* to much fanfare and a military band playing for war hero General MacArthur, who would also be aboard. She hoped that things would soon turn around, and putting distance between herself and a killer was bound to ease her melancholy.

There was also the matter of Hawai'i, which had captured her heart two years ago, when she had come to recuperate from surgery—the painful removal of cysts on her scalp. What a ghastly operation that had been. But the warm breezes and the slumber song of the ocean had revived her and given her a new lease on life. Now Waikiki was home to a new hotel, and perhaps it would be the exact thing she needed a second time.

Thelma and Dot accompanied her, and they were all dressed in their finest. Feathered hats, parasols, gloves. Although truth be told, the *Korea* was not a luxury liner. Jane was somewhat disappointed, after crossing the Atlantic in such grandeur, but beggars could not be choosers, and this was the soonest option to get them across the ocean.

For the first several days aboard the steamer, a biting wind blew, roughing up the surface of the water and turning half of the passengers green. Jane counted herself among the lucky to rarely succumb to seasickness, but poor Dot had her head in the toilet and one foot in the grave. Thelma spent much of her time consoling the poor woman and nursing her with ginger ale and soda crackers, which left Jane to roam on her own and socialize with the few others feeling well enough.

The ship was well-appointed, with a smoking room, a wood-paneled bar, an enviable library and top-notch cuisine. The crew was another matter, a good portion of them looking like half-starved dogs. The captain was Japanese with a fabulous sense of humor. Jane enjoyed chatting with him, and he told her of his travels in seas far rougher than this. His English was impeccable, and she found herself seeking him out during the voyage.

Three days out from the islands, the sea lay down, and Thelma and Dot were able to join her on the deck, relaxing on lounge chairs and absorbing the warm rays of the sun. Several humpback whales were spotted, spouting and breaching, and the entire load of passengers rushed to the port side of the ship, causing it to list frightfully. Jane hardly minded, feeling ebullient and lighter than she had in weeks. Something about those whales, the sheer bulk and joy with which they flung themselves out of the water, brought tears to her eyes.

It was that night at dinner, when Jane was feeling more like herself again, that she joined General MacArthur and his wife, Pinky, at the captain's table. The general was a fascinating man, full of stories of his travels all throughout Asia. His deep voice carried through the room, making his presence known. But it was Pinky who Jane was drawn to. Though slight of frame, she held her head high with uncommon poise, and brimmed with the vitality of a much younger woman.

"Tell me more about your travel plans, Mrs. Stanford," she said, while her husband conversed with a businessman from Chicago.

"Our itinerary is for three weeks in Honolulu, and then on to Japan. But things could change, as this was a last-minute trip, and I'm not opposed to spontaneity."

Pinky's eyes lit up. "Would you consider visiting me in Tokyo? My husband will most likely be off to Manchuria, and I'll be alone. It would be lovely to have a friend from the States."

"What a generous offer. I would enjoy that very much."

Staying with the highest-ranking army general's wife would certainly have its perks, with safety being a welcome byproduct.

"Forgive me for being nosy. I'm intrigued that you have the courage to hop on a ship and travel halfway around the world with only two young women by your side. Is this a pleasure trip, or are you conducting some kind of university business?" Pinky asked.

The general had now tuned in, and both of them awaited her response. She hesitated. In San Francisco, gossip would certainly be circulating about what caused her to depart under the cloak of secrecy. But here upon the open seas, why not tell the truth?

"Neither. I left town for two reasons. One, because of my health, seeking warmer weather for my lungs, and two, someone tried to poison me last month, and it was thought best if I skip town while the investigation is underway."

Pinky's hands covered her mouth. "Dear God, what a calamity! You poor dear."

Her husband frowned. "Are they closing in on suspects?"

"Nothing certain yet."

"Powerful people make enemies. A most unfortunate

truth," the general said, mustache so wide it almost flopped when he spoke.

"I can see that in your line of business, but I'm just an old woman who happened to start a school," she said.

Pinky laughed, good and hard and from the belly. "Oh, you don't fool me for a second. You're the ruler of that university. You're like the queen of California." Then her face grew serious, and she rested a delicate hand on Jane's. "But also, more importantly, you are the mother of Leland Jr., your dear departed boy. There is nothing more noble—or crushing—than being a mother."

Their eyes met, and Jane saw a deep well of sadness residing there. A look she recognized from staring at her own face in the mirror over the years. A wound that would never heal, not if she were on earth for another thousand years.

"You lost a child too?"

A nod. "Our little Malcolm. He was only with us for five years, but more love poured out of that little being than from any other human I've encountered. He was my angel. Measles took him from us far too soon."

"I'm sorry," Jane said, knowing that familiar fracturing of the soul.

Pinky squeezed her hand. "It's because of your son that you are who you are and you've done what you've done. A loss that enormous will either break a person or turn them into an agent of change. You know that, don't you?"

"Without a doubt."

"For those unfortunate enough to be in this society of women, there is also a strange kind of peace in knowing that you can survive anything. Isn't that so?" Pinky said.

"It's a conundrum that I have felt ever since he left me, and yet now, with this attempt on my life, I've been feeling bereft and not like myself at all."

"Being overseas will help. I can already see a new light in your eyes that was not there when we set sail."

Jane smiled, looking forward to meeting up with this woman in Tokyo.

IT WAS MID-MORNING several days forth when the passengers were alerted to keep an eye out for a tall, green form rising from a bed of clouds. Land had been spotted, and Jane, who had kept her telescope with her on deck ever since the seas had calmed, pulled it out, feeling as giddy as the whales they had continued to encounter. Sweeping her glass across the horizon, she came upon a hazy point of green, tall and craggy and dusting the sky.

"I see it!" she cried.

A most welcome sight after a week of nothing but open water. As they neared the coastline, a white ribbon of beach came into focus, a few houses and buildings visible, with Diamond Head asserting her presence. Coconut trees flanked the mountain's base.

Jane exhaled, that tight coil of fear loosening its grip. Instead a flutter of wingbeats appeared in its place. A few loud blasts of steam, and she glanced over at Thelma and Dot, leaning over the rail like excited schoolgirls; they seemed to get on well, even if Thelma had a tendency toward bossiness. A crowd had gathered, and everyone cheered. She smiled—a real smile that spread from her core.

Yes, coming here had definitely been the right thing to do.

February 21

IF THERE HAD been one thing lacking in Honolulu, it had been a luxury hotel on the ocean in Waikiki. That had been remedied four years ago with the construction of Honolulu's finest and most extravagant hotel, the Moana. On the deserted end of Waikiki, fronting a sandy, dusty road, the structure stood out among marshland and coconut trees like a crown jewel. Four stories high, with arches and columns framing a grand porte cochere.

As they entered the lobby, open French doors ushered in a salty breeze blended with the smell of plumeria lei, which they all wore around their necks, reminding her how far she was from home. There was a sweetness to Hawai'i, and a strange frequency in the air that made her wish she was a far younger woman, with a whole life still to be lived and Leland by her side.

The woman at the front desk had a bun on her head the size of a grapefruit and a smile as bright as the tropical sun. "Welcome, Mrs. Stanford, I presume?"

"Correct."

"Your three rooms are ready for you, if you would just sign here."

Jane noticed her hand was shaking as she handed her the pen. She couldn't have been more than eighteen, with large brown eyes and bronzed skin.

"How was your crossing?" she asked as Jane read over what she was signing.

"Lovely," Jane said.

At the same time, Dot said, "Awful."

The young woman glanced between them, then said, "Well, I'm glad to hear it and sad to hear it. At least you're on solid ground now, and the ocean out front is warm as a bathtub and just as calm." She spoke with a Hawaiian inflection that so many of the natives had.

"What's your name?" Jane asked.

The poor girl looked stricken. "Oh, my apologies. I'm 'Iliahi. I'm filling in for our regular gal, Mrs. Akina, who fell ill yesterday. I'm still learning the ropes, but you can call me 'Ili."

"'Iliahi. What an interesting name. What does it mean?"

"'*Iliahi* is the Hawaiian word for sandalwood, a once common tree here."

She was a waif of a thing, her hair looking to weigh more than she did. Just then, the porter appeared with their trunks, and 'Ili escorted them to their rooms, first to Jane's, which to her delight was spacious, with a large glass door that opened onto a porch fronting the shiny white beach. Maybe, just maybe, she would dare to take a dip this trip. An urge to try things in case there might not be another chance had begun to spring up.

"Room 120 is my favorite room. We have everything you could wish for at your disposal, a private bathroom, and your very own telephone!" The way her eyes sparkled when she said the word *telephone* made her seem like a child describing a favorite new toy. Then to the bellman, as she jumped toward him, "Here, Charlie, let me help you."

Charlie, a diminutive Chinese man who reminded her some of Ah Wing, was pushing a cart with a freight train's worth of trunks and bags. It looked on the verge of collapse. 'Ili pulled off the top trunk, bigger than she was, and hoisted it across the room as though it weighed nothing. Everyone gaped.

"Dot, Thelma, don't just stand there, help the poor woman," Jane said.

'Ili laughed. "Don't worry, I'm stronger than I look. I have two younger brothers," she said, as though that explained it all.

She helped Charlie unload the rest of Jane's luggage, and before they headed off with Dot and Thelma, said, "Once you all are unpacked, if you meet me in the lobby, I can show you around. You are going to think you've died and gone to heaven."

Her choice of words caused an uncomfortable sensation inside Jane, like a bat taking flight in her chest.

THE DREAM
Zoe

THAT EVENING, ZOE MANAGES to avoid Dylan Winters on the way to the talk, which is being given by literary master Barbara Small, winner of the Pulitzer Prize for her novel *Cloud Cover*, a postapocalyptic story where constant storms ravage the earth and sunshine is a thing of the past. Zoe's in full procrastination mode, but rationalizes that she needs to eat. She gathers a few pieces of sun-dried tomato and feta flatbread onto a paper plate, a can of pamplemousse sparkling water, and slides into the back row next to Bill, her friend from last night.

His bushy white eyebrows rise when he sees her. "How did your day go, lass?"

"Great, how about you?"

"Oh, I learned a thing or two, and figured out a way I might structure my memoir in a more creative way. Met a few nice folks too."

"That's wonderful!"

As much as she wants to talk to Bill, she is famished and exhausted and begins to wonder if maybe she should have stayed in her room and worked on her proposal, then cozied up in bed with a good book. She still has DS Wilder aka

Dylan Winters's book *The Ice Train* on her Kindle, and has entertained the idea of reading it again. Not that she plans on writing a mystery, but good writing is good writing. And the more good writing you read, the more it filters into your subconscious. The hope is, you can learn by osmosis.

If only it were that easy.

The ballroom fills up fast, and it's standing room only. Barbara gets a warm Hawaiian welcome with a lei and thunderous applause, but within minutes, Zoe finds her attention drifting. Barbara's voice flatlines about clouds in minute detail to the point where she has lost Zoe completely. For an easily distractible person, being here feels like torture. After twenty minutes or so of this, Barbara pulls out her novel and proceeds to read a scene from her book in which a woman is sewing, and it's about as interesting as watching paint dry.

Zoe begins to look for an escape route when she spots Dylan and the mystery woman sitting next to each other in the front row on the far right, closest to the door. She tries to read their body language for any giveaways as to their relationship. They are close enough that every so often the woman leans in, bare shoulder grazing his arm. Dylan has a nice profile, and his neck is the kind of neck you'd find on an athlete—a cowboy or a mountain climber or a surfer. He obviously hasn't shaved today. The truth is, it makes him look sexy as hell.

Bill, bless his heart, begins to snore softly, and she nudges his leg. He does it again louder and she shakes his shoulder, looking around to see if people have noticed. Really, it would be hard not to, but thankfully this group is cultured and polite. Bill jerks awake and gives her a little nod. Most everyone keeps their eyes on Barbara, but Dylan casually glances back. Not at Bill, at Zoe.

There is something questioning in his look, and the essence of a smile, though he does not wear one on his face. As though, somehow, seeing her pleases him. She cannot explain how she comes to this conclusion, but feels it viscerally. It's been a long time since she's been with a man, and her body responds to his gaze by sending heat waves spiraling through her. No matter that he's married, she's just looking, not touching. And there is nothing illegal about having a reaction to a handsome man.

As soon as he looks away, the woman glances back. Her blond hair falls in loose layers just below her neck, and she looks elegant in a cream-colored shift. She pretends to sweep the crowd, as though she's looking for someone in the back, but her heavily lined eyes stop on Zoe and do a once-over before continuing on. After that, she whispers something to Dylan, and her shoulders bump as though she's laughing. His do not.

Not only is Zoe exhausted and bored, now she has to pee, but she tries to wait until Barbara finishes her reading. With no end in sight, Zoe finally slides out of her seat and tiptoes for the exit. It feels like it's becoming a habit, but at this point she doesn't care. People should be more socially aware when they are putting an entire ballroom to sleep.

BACK IN HER ROOM, she stands on the lanai and watches lightning flash out at the edge of the horizon, far enough away so the thunder goes unheard. The sky feels electric and eerie in that calm before the storm kind of way. And not a star in sight. Below, the tiki torches flicker, and muted voices of lingering dinner guests float up to her room. The banyan looks alive in the shadowy light, and she swears she sees movement among its branches. The cat, perhaps?

Inside, she sits down and readies herself to pick up where she left off on her new book idea. She rereads what she's written, reworks it some and then goes back to the synopsis. What happens after the initial meetup? And what are the other things on the list? How will she create a whole novel out of this? Maybe the workshop leader was somehow her late husband's cousin. Or brother. Maybe after digging, she finds out he was adopted. Some kind of family secret. She types and deletes. Types and deletes. This goes on for a while, until she gives up. There needs to be more, and nothing is coming.

Instead, she pulls up the weather report to see what's in store. Just her luck—a Kona storm is slowly approaching the islands and should hit sometime tomorrow night. Something similar to a hurricane, but instead of having a warm center, it has a cold one. These kinds of storms can be equally destructive. Forecasters are calling for strong winds from the south and battering rain, thunderstorms, and even a chance of hail. *Hail?* In Hawai'i? Dangerous surf and coastal flooding too. It's hard to imagine any of that here based on the tranquil weather she's experienced so far.

Feeling shortchanged, she moves on from weather to Dylan Winters, hoping to find something other than the one-paragraph bio on his website. Maybe a photo of his wife. She knows it's silly and pointless, but she can't help herself. She scrolls past a handful of book reviews and comes across an interview in *The New York Times* from earlier this year. Most of the questions are writing-based, but she learns that he recently moved from Wyoming to Sisters, Oregon, literally a half hour drive from her house. Reason: divorce. No kids, but there were horses involved.

She closes the computer and feels ashamed at how happy this news makes her feel. Divorce is not something she wishes on anyone. Her parents split when she was ten because her father fell in love with his big-haired secretary, Phyllis. For some time, Zoe hated her father and the way he had literally crushed the life out of her mom. But the years crept on, and in time, her mother found a better match—another English teacher at her school—and Zoe found it in her heart to forgive him. Because while he might have been a shitty husband, he had always been a solid father.

AT SOME POINT in the night, Zoe screams herself awake and fumbles around in the darkness, uncertain where she is. Her heart bangs against her rib cage, and her chest is soaked in sweat. Lightning flashes in the distance, and she remembers she's in the Moana. The dream lingers in bits and pieces. Her sitting in the middle of the room, unable to control her limbs. Not in the way of dreams where you are moving through liquid or running in quicksand, but in a rigid, tormented manner. She also remembers a woman standing in the doorway, eyes watching, wide with fear.

She's unable to pull up any more of the dream, but the distinct feelings of terror and helplessness remain, pulsing through her body in waves. She runs her hands along her throat, down her damp chest and over the flat of her abdomen, making sure everything is still in one piece. She feels her legs, and wonders if maybe her calves had been cramping, as they sometimes do after an extra-long trail run. But no, they feel supple and warm. The clock says 11:22, and she's surprised because it feels much later.

Then there's a thud on the lanai and a moment later, a scratching on the screen. It startles her back to the dark room, and she pulls the covers up over her head, brain immediately going to what she might use to defend herself against an intruder. The lamp. No, maybe the chair with its metal legs. Another long, slow scrape against the screen, and bile rises in her throat. This is not how she pictured her Hawaiian vacation going.

And then, a small *meow*. The relief is instantaneous. "You!" she hisses, pulling the covers back down. "You scared me half to death. What are you doing all the way up here?"

In the distance, lightning flashes. The cat meows again, and Zoe switches on the light to its dimmest setting. The tiny animal circles back to the outer edge of the lanai, then sits, yellow eyes blinking in the light. On the lanai, it looks smaller than when she'd seen it in the tree. Maybe the lightning has scared the poor thing.

"You looking for shelter, kitty?"

It tentatively comes back to the screen, letting out a high, squeaky meow.

"Is this your MO? Wake the guests in the middle of the night and swindle them with your cuteness? Well, it's not going to work with me."

A gust of wind shakes the leaves on the branch and blows into her room, and now she can taste the rain too. It's near. She fetches a towel and opens the door to fold it up in the corner of the lanai, and the cat shoots through the open crack in the door.

"Oh, come on, cat, I cannot deal with you right now."

But the cat has gone under her bed, and Zoe is tired and disturbed and just wants to fall back asleep and wake in the morning free from whatever nightmare she'd been having. So she puts down a cup of water for the animal and climbs back under her fluffy covers. Far away, thunder rumbles. Sleep comes quickly, but she tosses and turns with a horrible sharp taste in her mouth and a feeling of gaping loneliness.

In the morning, she wakes to a new sound in the room. One eye opens and there's the cat, curled up against the pillow on the other side of the bed, not three feet from her head and purring loud as a motorboat. Very dim light surrounds them, and she watches the rise and fall of its tiny chest. There is nothing more peaceful than watching a cat sleep, and this one is in such a tight ball that its face is hidden by its back legs. A softness flows through Zoe like warm honey.

She slips out of bed, feeling the need for a beach run. On the way to the bathroom, she sees a piece of paper on the floor and leans down to pick it up, figuring maybe the wind blew it from her table. But there are words scrawled across it in large, scratchy block letters.

HELP ME, I'M DYING.

She drops the paper as though it's on fire, and stands in a shocked daze trying to make sense of it. The paper lands face up, and the words scream up at her. Did someone slide this under her door in the night? It's the only explanation and a creepy one at that. Probably a kid playing a prank, because if someone were in fact dying, they would not have the where-withal to write a note and slip it into some random person's room.

She picks up the paper again. It's Moana stationery, message written on the back side. She has a pad next to the archaic telephone on the bedside table. All the rooms would have them. Coupled with her fitful night of sleep, she feels even worse than the previous morning. Hair askew, mouth dry, eyes slightly scratchy, no doubt from the cat. She's surprised they aren't worse. The need to get out of this room and onto the beach presses in on her from all sides. So as fast as she can, she gets ready, leaves the screen open for the still sleeping cat, and heads out.

THE GIRL

Jane

February 21

WHILE UNPACKING, JANE PERIODICALLY had to steady herself against the wall. Her equilibrium had been worsening with age, and after so much time at sea, her legs needed to adjust to firm ground. Each time she wobbled, her eyes sought the horizon—a habit from being aboard so often. The first floor was really a floor above the main lobby, so she had a bird's-eye view of the water. Dot and Thelma had returned and were hanging dresses and folding undergarments, busy as bees, but she could tell both women were antsy to get outside and see the place. As was she.

After freshening up, Jane decided she was in the mood to make a splash, and donned a pale blue dress with a lower neckline to showcase one of her favorite diamond necklaces, a single strand of round-cut diamonds with a teardrop star sapphire pendant. Leland used to say it was his favorite, but he said that about every piece she wore. Always a charmer. She sighed at the memory. Heavens, she missed those blue eyes and larger-than-life presence.

They took the elevator downstairs, a real treat, and 'Ili was right where she said she would be. When she saw Jane, she locked on the necklace for a few moments before looking up and making eye contact. It was a common reaction to her jewelry, and Jane felt pleased.

"Well, if it isn't the most lovely woman—women, I should say—on the entire island of Oʻahu," ʻIli said, clasping her hands.

She liked this girl. "You flatter us."

"I never tell a lie, Mrs. Stanford."

ʻIli led them through the main parlor, with its high and airy ceilings, polished wood trim, and colorful furniture, on to a billiards room, a saloon lined with crystal bottles, and a library of books neatly filling in all four walls.

"This is my favorite room. You will find all the classics, as well as modern fiction by the likes of J. M. Barrie, Mark Twain and Jack London. Mr. London even came to Waikiki last year and caught a few waves out front. That was before I started work here, but I was surfing next to him. A highlight to be sure." She went straight to the shelf and produced *The Call of the Wild*. "Have you read it?"

Jane wasn't a big reader—reading hurt her eyes—but she had a fondness for books because they reminded her of her son. Leland never met a book he didn't love. Often, she asked Thelma to read to her.

"I regret to say that I haven't."

Dot nodded. "I have. Mr. London knows his way around a story."

"When we came in from the water, I worked up the nerve to talk to him, and he encouraged me to begin a journal, which I have—"

Thelma interrupted. "Miss ʻIli, we would love to get out to the beach and kick up our heels. As you can imagine, it's been a long day."

"Forgive me! My Ma always said I had a tendency to ramble, and she was right, I'm afraid." She held out her hand toward the veranda. "Follow me."

Past tense, Jane noticed. "No need to apologize. I would want to talk about Jack London too, had I ridden waves with the man. Which begs the question: You surf?"

"Oh yes, I learned when I was a young girl. A bunch of us kids from the Waikiki Grammar School would paddle out every chance we got. Old man Makua let us use his old wooden boards, and even though I got splinters, I—" she said, then clamped a hand over her mouth. "Oops, there I go again. I have to remember to only answer what I'm asked. Come on, let's go!"

She was so animated, it was hard to be cross with her. 'Ili took them outside. There was something feline about her, the way she slinked cautiously around, eyes not missing a leaf out of place. Jane was intrigued for no other reason than it had been a while since she'd met someone so endearing and so unusual at the same time.

A banyan tree stood at the center of the patio, and guests sat at tables, playing cards, conversing and nursing cocktails. To the right was a structure whose concrete posts came right to the water's edge. "This is our waterfront dining room, where you can gorge on mahi-mahi to your heart's content."

Directly in front of the hotel, a long pier jutted out, and now with the sun dropping closer to the horizon, the water took on a golden hue.

"Tell me, 'Ili, where is the best vantage point to watch the sunset?" Jane asked.

"That would be at the end of the pier, in the gazebo. That way you can watch the fish swim to the surface. I bet you didn't know that fish also enjoy a pretty sunset."

Thelma laughed. "Nonsense."

"Oh, just you wait and see. And if you're lucky, you may glimpse a very friendly white tip shark cruising in between the posts."

"No thank you!" Dot exclaimed.

"White tips don't bother anyone, and they're about as sleek a thing as you've ever set eyes upon. All grace and beauty."

"Do you write about these things in your journal?" Jane asked her.

"Sometimes."

They stopped and took in the sights on the beach, Jane feeling a bit out of breath. People in bathing suits sat on the beach and frolicked in the water, and just out front, an outrigger sailing canoe that looked dangerously full of passengers was setting sail, only the wind was so light, they weren't likely to get very far. Dot watched them intently with a look of longing. If Jane was feeling generous, perhaps she'd let her take a ride one of these days.

"You seem to know a lot about this place, 'Ili. I would like for you to plan an itinerary for us this week. You see, I want to pass the time here pleasantly, and need diversions from a difficult matter at home."

'Ili frowned, and for a moment Jane thought she might ask about the difficult situation, but she refrained. "I would love to, but Mrs. Akina usually does that."

"Well, I'm sure that Mrs. Akina won't mind, especially if I'm personally requesting it."

She curtsied. "As you wish."

And then they followed her down the pier and hoped to not see any sharks.

IN THE MORNING, Jane took her time in the shower, letting the steam loosen her lungs. Even after one night's sleep in the salty Hawaiian air, she felt like a new woman. Dot came in first to check on her and help her dress for breakfast. Then the two of them walked arm in arm to the elevator and on to the lanai below. The day's first sunrays cut through the coconut trees, creating a crisscross pattern in the sand that was lovely to behold. Thelma had already secured them a table, even though hardly anyone was up yet.

Jane felt ravenous and ordered a mushroom and spinach omelet, and the two girls both chose eggs Benedict. The waiter also delivered a basket of steaming sweet, sugary buns called malasadas, which gave everyone at the table a sugar mustache. Usually, she avoided sweets for the sake of her digestion, but these smelled too good to pass up.

While waiting on their food, Jane observed the other diners. A younger couple, head to toe in white. Two women, probably a mother and daughter because they both had curly locks of spun gold, and a lone, bespectacled man reading the newspaper. Everyone had a languid quality about them, which she hoped to acquire as the days unfolded.

Suddenly, 'Ili appeared at their table, holding a piece of paper. "Mrs. Stanford! I have what you asked for. Each activity on here should entertain and delight you and Miss Bellingham and Miss Hale. Would you like me to read you the highlights?"

"Why not?"

'Ili turned out to be quite a planner, and arranged for a sightseeing ride in the carriage, card games, watching a polo match in Kapiolani Park, a ride in an outrigger canoe, a visit to the Bishop Museum and a picnic in the mountains. Jane wasn't sure she would have the energy for it all, but she could pick and choose. It would be nice to have options.

"I've also pulled some books for you in the library that I thought might be of interest," 'Ili said.

"Thank you, dear. I don't suppose you have anything by William James?" Jane asked.

A smile broke on her face. "Wouldn't you know it, we do. *The Varieties of Religious Experience.*"

Jane felt a jolt of surprise that the hotel would have this book available. She had a particular proclivity for Mr. James. His layered theories on religion and reservoirs of consciousness had become almost an obsession to her. She'd been trying to snag him from Harvard as a professor but had yet been unable.

'Ili eyed Thelma, who was surveying her with an equally surprised face. "A little bird told me about Mrs. Stanford's interests."

"Are you interested in spiritualism, 'Ili?"

"I believe in spirits, if that's what you mean. This island is full of them. Ancestors, warriors, lost souls."

"Not exactly what I meant, no. Spiritualism involves contacting the deceased and communicating with them."

A flash of fear in her eyes. "Oh, I don't mess with that kind of thing, I leave it to the kahuna. My father comes to visit me now and then, but I let him decide when and where. And anyway, I'm too busy with the living."

"My condolences on your father. What happened?"

Now 'Ili's entire being wilted. "My mother was ordered to Kalaupapa when she contracted leprosy. She was turned in by her boss who noticed spots on her arms, and my father went with her and died within the year. His heart gave out on him."

Jane felt her heart lurch. "My word, this is devastating. And your mother, is she still alive?"

"She is. I took my two younger brothers there last month to visit, but they make us stay on the other side of a chicken wire fence, and there is no way to hug or kiss or hold her in my arms. She's alone there now that my father is gone, and it gnaws away at me day and night," 'Ili said.

Jane almost keeled over from the sheer force of 'Ili's grief. "Dear God, child, what your family has endured!"

"It has tested me and gutted me, but I have my brothers to take care of. So I can't dillydally, and I work as much as I can, which is why this job is everything to me."

Jane took her hand. "A most admirable young woman you are."

Tears shone in the girl's eyes, but she stood up tall, smiled and said, "Enough about me. What would you like to do today?"

Jane knew that door was closed, but she felt a deep tenderness for her and wanted to extend some kind of help or support.

"I think today we will stay here and gain our bearings, but tomorrow we will be ready to branch out. Say, how long does it take for the mail to arrive from San Francisco?"

"About a week, why?"

"I'm looking forward to some news from back home."

"The moment I see anything, I'll find you."

"Thank you."

Again, she looked on the verge of inquiring more, so Jane decided to tell her. She summed it up as quickly as she could, and found that with each telling, it eased her burden ever so slightly.

"*Auwe*—" 'Ili covered her mouth again and glanced around. "Pardon me, I meant outrageous, horrible, terrifying! I'm so glad you left, and I assure you, you will be safe in this hotel."

"I'm sure I'll be fine here too, thank you," Jane said, though a small but insistent voice nagged at her that even on this far blue shore, she was anything but.

THE RAIN
Zoe

THE BEACH IS EMPTY, the sand damp and cool on her feet. Thankfully, it's not raining yet, but Zoe can see pillars of rain squalls out to sea. The water gives off a scent of melancholy, which she feels between her bones. She doesn't bother stretching and sets off toward Diamond Head at a fast walk. Her head feels foggy from the poor sleep, and she's not sure if the scratchy throat is from cat allergies or maybe she's coming down with something. In front of the lifeguard tower, she begins to run.

Running has always been her solace. Cross-country soon transformed into a love of trail running in her junior year of high school. After sitting in the classroom all day, bored and fidgety, taking to the hills felt like letting out a giant exhale. Trees and rock and rivers, meadows and open sky. These were the things that she craved. Her creative writing teacher, Mrs. Foster, encouraged her to write about them, and soon the class became her favorite. It was like a crack in her mind opened, allowing her to travel to other realms.

There are ripples on the water, small islands of breeze, but other than that, it's silky smooth and slate gray. She runs hard and fast, toes squishing into the sand. Her heart rate picks up, and she breaks a sweat almost immediately. It feels like she's running from something, and she tries to bring back the dreams from last night but cannot. A heavy raindrop lands on her shoulder and a few seconds later, another on her head. The clouds are low, dusting the top of Diamond Head. Moisture clings to every inch of her body, and to say it's muggy is an understatement.

When the beach ends, she continues along on the grass, the sole person around, save for a bony old man with a terry cloth headband running past on the street and the occasional car rolling down Kalakaua Avenue. It's just past seven and there is no sign of the sun, other than a slight brightening behind the clouds. She makes it almost to a building she believes to be the Waikiki Aquarium when the sky opens up and unleashes the heaviest raindrops she has ever felt.

There's an arbor up ahead, and she beelines to that, already half soaked. This Hawaiian rain is warm and feels delicious and cleansing. She stands looking out to sea, waiting for the squall to pass. The beauty of the moment takes her breath away, and for a fleeting moment, she feels very much like she belongs here.

And then, from behind, a voice. "It was bound to happen sooner or later."

She leaps into the air, annoyed at this interloper into her peace. "Oh my God, you scared the—" it's Dylan Winters, drenched "—shit out of me," she says, voice trailing off at the end.

"Sorry."

"What are you doing here?" she asks, as if she owns the arbor, and realizes it's a dumb question, but she's feeling jumpy after finding the note this morning.

"Same as you, I think. Avoiding this deluge. Though I'm a little late for that. Looks like you are too," he says, eyes drawing down over her slick body.

"I meant, are you out for a walk or a run?"

His smile unties the knot that has been in her stomach all morning. "Run. It's my jam."

She smiles back. "Mine too."

He nods at her bare feet. "Are you one of those barefoot runners?"

"Ha! Not usually. I rarely get to go barefoot in Oregon, so I figured I better take advantage while I'm here."

"Speaking of Oregon. Where in Oregon do you live?"

"Bend."

"I'm just outside of Sisters."

I know. "Ah, you didn't mention that the other night. How long have you lived there?"

He shrugged. "Not long. I moved there in September."

She waits for him to say *after my divorce,* but he doesn't.

"It's a good place for writing," she offers.

"And horses. You ride?"

"I *have* ridden. But I am not a horse person, if that's what you mean. I love them, though. Their bigness and beautiful lines and soft noses."

"Yeah, I'm addicted to their soft noses," he says with a grin that opens up a boyish side to him.

It's raining even harder, trickling down between the tangled bush growing atop the arbor. A drop hangs from the tip of Dylan's nose. He wipes it away and turns to look out at the ocean. She turns too, and they are standing side by side. She feels small next to him without her shoes, and at five-foot-nine, she rarely feels small. Up until this very second, she's been so in the moment that the reading yesterday slipped her mind. But now she remembers and feels a tingle of embarrassment.

But he doesn't seem fazed. "They're saying it's going to get wild. I love a good storm, how about you?"

"Absolutely. Though I was hoping for blue sky and sunshine this trip, and that I might learn to surf. My friend and I were supposed to come here on our eighteenth birthday and do that, but we never got the chance."

As if she'd have any time to learn to surf with a looming deadline to address.

"The one who died? Ginger?"

It touched her that he remembered her name. "Yes."

"Whoever said you can't surf in a storm? It would definitely add an element of excitement."

"Are you kidding me? Have you heard the weather report? They're making it sound like the storm of the decade, though newspeople seem to like to do that these days."

"We'll see," he says.

The pause between them grows awkward, and she contemplates broaching the subject of her reading. Then decides against it. Better not to break the spell of the moment. The dull rush of the rain. Heat coming off his left shoulder. And then, out of nowhere, an atomic bomb of thunder explodes overhead at the same time the sky flashes electric.

Dylan yells. "Whoa!"

She screams, and her natural inclination is to grab on to his arm. "Oh my God!"

His bicep is hard and ropey, and he flexes it, or at least it seems like he does. For a few seconds, she hangs on, soaking up his warmth and his male energy. He doesn't seem to mind, and it feels more intimate than it should. Reluctantly, she lets go.

"Are you coming to my class today?" he finally asks.

"Your class is full, so I signed up for Kristin Baker Wells's class on plot."

"You can't go wrong there. We're going more in depth on plot today too."

It almost sounds like an invitation, like he wants her there.

"You know, you never really told me your story, and how you got into writing. And how you honed your craft. Will you be sharing this in class today too?" she asks.

"People don't want to hear my story. They want to know how to write their own."

"Oh, I don't think that's true at all. Readers love to know about the person behind their favorite books. People always ask me—I mean, when I'm at conferences, people always ask the author, especially well-known ones like you."

He gives her a funny look. "My bio is online. That should be enough."

"I guess. But still, I would want to know. Theoretically . . . say, if I happened to be one of your fans," she says.

"Didn't you say you loved my book?"

She feels bad now for deceiving him. If he ever finds out, he's going to hate her. But if he hasn't figured it out yet, he probably won't. So long as she's Bridget, not Zoe. She can pretend for the week, and then she'll never see him again, and he'll forget all about her. It'll be fine.

"Right. I did, didn't I? So I guess that makes me a fan. Which is why I'm asking to hear your story. Not like a stalker or anything like that. 'I guess I'm a curious person, and I like to hear about other people's journeys.' And this *is* a writers conference, isn't it?" she says.

She risks a look up at him. He's grinning, and she feels remarkably pleased with herself for quoting him word for word.

"How about we meet up for a drink in the bar before the luau, if they even hold it in this weather, and I'll tell you anything you want to know," he says.

His offer catches her off guard. "Sure, why not?"

The rain has let up slightly, now coming down in a hazy drizzle. "Great. I'm going to run back now so I'm not late. See you at five in the bar, if not before that."

And with that, he's off. Loping away, splashing through puddles. He runs like a football player, light and springy. Fast. As though he could outrun lightning if he had to.

WHEN SHE GETS back to the room, the cat is gone, and she's relieved but also slightly disappointed. She takes a hot shower and before her workshop goes to the front desk to let them know about the note. It's early enough that the front lobby area is empty, and she walks right up to the counter. No one is there, so she rings the bell. A few moments later, a silver-haired woman pops her head out from the office door.

"Aloha, how can I help you?"

Zoe suddenly feels weird about showing anyone the note, but pulls it out from her purse and sets it on the counter. "I just wanted to give you a heads-up that someone either slid this under my door last night or actually came into my room. I'm a light sleeper, so I doubt that happened, but it's still troubling."

The woman steps out and looks down at the paper, face turning sea-foam white. "What room are you staying in?" she asks.

"120."

A cold wind slips in through the ocean-side door. Zoe pulls her sweater tight around her. The woman does not look up. Does not say a thing.

"Excuse me, but is everything okay? I'm a bit freaked out by this, as you can imagine," Zoe says, trying to prompt some kind of response.

Finally, Manu—as Zoe can see on her name tag—raises her head and makes eye contact. She smiles, but the smile does not reach her eyes. "I can assure you that no one would have entered your room last night."

Zoe doesn't like her coolness. "Well, have you had issues like this before?"

Seconds pass, as though Manu has to think about her answer. "Not like this, no. None that I'm aware of, at least. And I've been here a long time."

The woman is probably in her early sixties. Skin smooth as polished wood, hair pulled into a tight bun, and pointed eyebrows. Her arms are covered in gold bangles with black engravings, *Manulani* and other Hawaiian words, Zoe sees.

"I guess there's always a first. I'm hoping it was just some kid, a prank of some kind. But please let the manager know."

"Was there anything else?" Manu asks.

"What do you mean?"

"Like, did you hear anything, see anything . . . smell anything?"

It's a weird question, Zoe thinks. "Did I smell anything?"

"Yes."

"Not that I recall. But there was a cat. He jumped onto my lanai from the banyan tree in the middle of the night."

She leaves out the part about him sleeping on her bed. Not that it's her fault, but she doesn't want to be the cause of the cat being taken away to the pound. And any guilt she feels about harboring a cat in her room is overshadowed by the note.

"Oh? Did it cause you any trouble?"

"No. I was already awake from a bad dream."

Manu gives her a hard stare. Her eyes are so dark, it's hard to tell if they're brown or black, and Zoe gets the feeling she knows something more but isn't letting on. "I will notify the staff to keep an eye out for anything strange, or any other papers like this. Can I keep this?" she asks.

Zoe pulls it back. "No, if you don't mind, I'd like to. But if you need it as any kind of . . . evidence, just let me know."

Manu nods. "As you wish. Have a nice day, Mrs. Finch."

Everyone always assumes she's married. She's not sure why. She smiles to herself at this thought, doesn't correct her, then heads off to find her workshop.

THE PLOT
Zoe

PLOT IS EVERYTHING. We as humans are designed to constantly seek out plots in the world around us. Since the earliest of time, story is how we have made sense of our lives. We crave story almost as much as we crave food and water, and whether we know it or not, all of us are storytellers in one way or another. Zoe believes this with her whole being.

She's read about plot, listened to experts talk about plot, spent countless hours plotting other people's books, and most recently her own, but she still feels like plot is as elusive as a snow leopard or a giant squid. One of her favorite quotes on plot is "There is only one plot—things are not what they seem." An author and screenwriter named Jim Thompson, a man she has never read, said this, and it rings so true.

There are countless writing programs that guarantee to help you easily plot your novel. Yet if it were easy, everyone would be doing it well, and everyone would be a bestseller. And so, eager to hear yet another perspective, she sits in the back of Kristin's class, hoping to learn something new, and perhaps stumble onto a cache of magic that will help her figure out how to brilliantly plot this pathetic new novel idea of hers for Avery.

Kristin Baker Wells is sunshine in human form. Blonde and tan and emanating warmth, she seems to be in a perpetual state of smiling. She's best known for her American Psychic series about a psychic who helps solve mysteries and crimes. Zoe hasn't read any of her books, but she's a multi–*New York Times* bestseller, and her books have been translated into dozens of languages.

Zoe feels secretly proud that up until now, *The Marriage Pact* has sold in six countries. Not bad for a first novel, and a romance no less. No one here would know that, though, and she wishes a little that she hadn't lied about her name. Quite honestly, she doubts anyone would even care. There are so many authors in this world, and most of them are just regular people who happen to also write books. Often in bed. Wearing pajamas. Messy hair. Very unglamorously.

Tara has popped in next to Zoe, smelling fresh and flowery, and a minute later, another woman slides into the seat on the other side of her, at the edge of the row. Zoe looks up, ready to smile, until she sees it's the one who's been with Dylan. Now she has to force the smile, and the woman's mouth barely moves, just a quick widening of lips, no other facial parts involved.

That's all forgotten when Kristin launches into her method, which involves first filling out a beat sheet that lays out your three acts, much like a screenwriter would. But a screenplay is only ninety to a hundred twenty pages, where a novel is generally three hundred plus—ninety thousand words, give or take. She has everyone pull out a piece of paper and begin by listing—one or two lines, max—their opening scene and their inciting incident, which may or may not be the same thing.

As Zoe puts her pen to paper, she feels mildly self-conscious with this woman sitting next to her, spiking the air with her rose-scented perfume. She is mid-sentence when she remembers something from last night. A smell. When she'd woken from the dream the first time, there had been a light scent of honeysuckle or maybe jasmine in the room. Something delicate and floral aside from the salty air. Manu's question now gives her the chills.

As they work through the beat sheet, she struggles to focus. This workshop is exactly what she needs, and now she's fumbling along, twitchy and unable to concentrate. Both Tara and the lady next to her are scribbling away and seem confident in their stories. In fact, everything about the woman she'd seen with Dylan oozes confidence. Her perfectly applied makeup, her cuffed gray pants and white blouse, fitted perfectly, her loopy and neat handwriting. Even the way she crosses her legs and holds herself.

Zoe fidgets, wishing she could take flight, and bumps the lady in the arm. "So sorry," she says.

"It's fine."

When they are finished, Zoe decides hers could have been done by a kindergartener. She sometimes hates the fact that she's so sensitive, and things don't roll off her back like they do with most people. Last night's dream, for example. She feels things so deeply and so intensely that it worries her. Right now, though, this sadness she feels is out of proportion to anything that is happening. She breathes deeply while tapping her left chest with two fingers as inconspicuously as possible, and soon feels her nerves settle. A trick from her therapist friend that has saved her hundreds of times.

"Now, I'd like you to turn to the person next to you, preferably someone you don't know, and share what you have. This can be brief, but it should be fruitful. I want you to really dig in. So when it's your turn to give feedback, be nice but honest. It's what editors do, and you need to learn how to accept and use feedback—and give it. It's the secret to improving your writing."

The lady turns to her. "I guess that's us," she says with a little flip of her hair.

Zoe tries to sound upbeat. "Yes. I'm Bridget."

"Hello, Bridget, I'm Sam. So, what do you think? Would you like to go first, or shall I?"

She speaks with a slightly hoarse voice, and possibly even an accent.

"You should," Zoe says.

"Sure. So, just to give you some quick background, mine is a historical novel about the eleven-year-old daughter of a missionary in South Africa who comes home one day to find her entire family has vanished. Then we follow her twenty years later, when she returns to find answers. And possibly vengeance."

The words flow eloquently off her tongue, and she sounds sophisticated and a tad full of herself. But as much as Zoe hates to admit it, she's intrigued by the story. "I like the sound of it."

"The opening scene, we have Solana sneaking back from the river, where she's been told not to go alone, and she comes upon an empty house—mum, dad and older sis—strange because the old Land Rover is still there. The place is eerily quiet and she waits and waits, searches the entire area, braving wild critters and poachers. We see her lying down in her bed at night, alone and terrified, and the chapter ends there. So, for the sake of the beat sheet, this is both the opening and the inciting incident. What do you think?" Sam says.

Zoe wants to read this book. "I think it's a perfect place to start. Without knowing anything else, it gives me *Poisonwood Bible* vibes."

"Ah, yes, many readers have compared it to Kingsolver."

Isn't that nice. "It should be a breeze getting it published, then. Straight to bestseller-dom for you."

She's being snarky, but she can't help it. The Kingsolver comment was over-the-top. In her experience, people who make a point to tell you what great writers they are, are usually not.

Sam flashes a white smile with a little too much gum. "I expect I'll have an offer by the end of this conference, so yeah, that would be lovely. Now, how about we hear yours?"

"Mine is a love story. The opening scene involves a woman walking into a writers conference workshop late, and she realizes the teacher is hot, and he looks exactly like her dead husband. I haven't quite figured out my inciting incident," she says, finger twirling a curl all the way around it. "It's a new project."

"Is this based on a true story?"

"I'm not sure."

Sam laughs. "I was in the workshop on Monday. It reminds me an awful lot of that."

Zoe can't quite grasp if Sam is laughing at her or with her, so she assumes the latter because she likes to give people the benefit of the doubt. "It does, huh? Well, nothing to do with Dylan Winters himself, but the experience sparked an idea."

"Dylan is handsome, though, isn't he?"

Zoe shrugs. "I guess. I hadn't thought too much about it. It looks like you two know each other."

"Ah, yes. We go way back. My family moved from South Africa to Texas when I was fifteen. Dylan was a year ahead of me, and we had the same friend group. We've always been tight," she says, stopping there.

And there it is. Mystery solved. "Back then, were either of you writing?" Zoe asks.

"Dylan carried around a small leather journal and liked to record things. I remember he took a shine to Jack Kerouac in our senior English seminar—something about the Beatniks and their antimaterialism appealed to him. Being nerdy clashed with his bad boy image, but he couldn't have cared less. That's the thing about bad boys, no? They do whatever the hell they want."

Zoe nodded. "Oh yes."

"But other than that, no. And I was too busy with all my AP classes and dance and art to pursue writing. I took it up a few years ago when I attended the Sun Valley Writers' Conference. Dylan used to run it, and—"

A bell rings, and their conversation is cut short. Zoe has forgotten all about her story and wanted to keep mining Sam for information about Dylan. He seems to be taking up an awful lot of mental space and is proving to be a big inconvenience. Yet she is having a difficult time squashing her curiosity.

Kristin tells them to save the rest of the beat sheet for later, and they move on to conflict. The critical ingredient to all compelling stories. The lighthouse through your whole journey. The driving force. Conflict exists when your character wants something, but there is an obstacle in the way. Zoe thinks about the conflict in her own story. Maybe Fiona desperately wants to write a novel, but instead all she can think about is the workshop leader and what it would feel like to have his hands all over her body.

THE TOUR

Jane

February 24

IT WAS EASY to fall into the island rhythm of cloudy mornings with light squalls of rain, followed by trade winds gaining speed midday and ushering in clear skies and sunshine. 'Ili had been right about the pier, and Jane and Dot and Thelma would sit out in the gazebo and watch the sun go down. 'Ili's shark had made an appearance, and she had actually been right—it was lovely to watch. Four feet long, and mostly tail, it looked docile as a pet dog.

Off to both sides, men and women rode long wooden boards, sometimes in tandem. The waves were barely there, but 'Ili had explained that the great length of the board caused it to pick up the smallest of swells. Dot hung over the railing, clapping and jumping up and down when they rode past, sometimes all the way to the beach. Her pleasant demeanor was catching, and Jane felt herself buoyed up in her presence, almost forgetting what she was running from. Thelma, on the other hand, seemed listless, as interesting as a wet rag.

"Is everything all right with you, dear?" Jane asked after dinner one night, as Thelma helped her prepare for bed.

Her face remained unreadable. "I think it's the heat. It's never agreed with me, and I haven't been sleeping well."

As far as Jane was concerned, the temperatures had been perfect. Chilly enough at night for a blanket, and in the daytime, warm in the sun and cool in the shade.

"Perhaps tomorrow you should take the morning off and rest. Dot and I will be fine, and maybe I can persuade 'Ili to join us on our tour."

"I'll be fine, but I appreciate the offer. Not only that, but 'Ili works here. She can't just take off as she pleases to ride around the island," Thelma said, coming behind Jane and unclasping her necklace.

Their eyes met in the mirror. Jane smiled. Thelma didn't.

"Now that I think about it, it's not a request. I would like for you to stay here and get some rest so that you are fit to see to your duties as a travel companion. Nor do I appreciate this ungrateful behavior."

"Mrs. Stanford, I've left my ailing father to travel halfway around the world, so please know that I am not ungrateful, but rather, I'm drained and scraped bare."

It was hard not to feel for the woman, and Jane softened. "Even more reason to take a day for yourself. Consider it a gift."

AS USUAL, JANE GOT her wish, and she and Dot and 'Ili set out the following morning with a carriage driver named Israel, a portly Hawaiian fellow, with bushy mutton chops and a good nature about him. The two horses, a chestnut mare and a spirited black stallion, pranced them down Waikiki Road toward Diamond Head, the clip-clop of hooves muted by the sand-swept road. Jane had asked Mr. Price himself—the owner of the hotel—if 'Ili could accompany them for the day.

"Anything you desire, Mrs. Stanford. I'll arrange the best driver in town."

They didn't have to go far to reach their first stop—Kapiolani Park, with lakes and an island with a large bandstand in the middle. Peacocks roamed, and bird calls echoed through the trees. The sheer amount of green around them was staggering, and it felt more like summer than winter. They were here for a horse race, though Jane wasn't a better.

"King Kalakaua had this park built to honor his wife, the queen," Israel said, then chuckled. "But as you can see, he had a fondness for horse racing—and betting."

The racetrack and its accompanying building were well maintained, and manicured green lawns spread out in all directions. It had a San Francisco feel to it, minus the biting cold.

"He and my husband would have gotten on well, then," Jane said.

'Ili, perched next to him, turned and said, "This whole area used to be a swampy wetland. It's hard to picture it now. And up there—" she pointed to the crook of Diamond Head "—was a surfing *heiau*, a place where people came to pay their tributes and ask for guidance and help in the waves. The location had been chosen carefully, with a birds'-eye view, and the kahuna there had some method to alert everyone when the waves were big."

Israel slowed and turned down Makee Road, heading inland.

"This is the second time you've mentioned a kahuna," Jane said, her interest piqued. "Tell me, what exactly is a kahuna?"

"You know, we really aren't supposed to talk about Hawaiian ways nowadays, but I say, why not?"

Jane swore she saw Israel's cheeks flush, but he kept his eye on the horses and his mouth shut.

"Who says?" Jane asked.

"The United States government, that's who. I was ten when they locked up our queen, and before that, we spoke Hawaiian—obviously, since this is Hawai'i. But the missionaries thought we were heathens and set out to tame us and—"

Israel cleared his throat, loudly.

"Ah, I digress again. To answer your question, I suppose you could say a kahuna is an expert in their field—a teacher, a priest, a caretaker. The word doesn't translate well into English, and means so much more. Mastery can be a long and arduous undertaking, so kahunas are often elders. But not always."

As young as 'Ili was, there was a timelessness to her, and she was illuminating a side to Hawai'i that Jane found fascinating.

"So, there were kahuna for all fields?"

"There *are*, not *were*. We may be a territory of the United States now, but they can't erase us so easily."

"Nor should they want to. Tell me, do you know of any of these kahuna who might be willing to visit me at the hotel? Say, one who communicates with those in the afterworld. I believe it would be an enlightening experience, and would give me a chance to learn more about your ways," Jane asked.

Israel and 'Ili exchanged a look. "We would have to be discreet," she said.

"I'm good at discreet, and so is Dot," Jane said, patting the young woman's knee.

"I can't promise you anything, but I can ask around."

From the park, Israel took them on a coastal tour around Diamond Head, with a vista overlooking the wind-chopped blue ocean below.

"This side picks up the trade winds, far more than Waikiki, which has about the best weather on the whole island," 'Ili told them.

From there, they rode through Kahala, a flat area with vast pig farms, chicken farms and a dairy that stunk up the air. Jane could not wait to get back to the hotel and enjoy lunch under the shade of the banyan tree, and perhaps play a game of cribbage with some of the other guests. It was rumored that her friends the Hightons would be arriving, so she also had that to look forward to.

FROM THE JOURNAL OF
ʻILIAHI BALDWIN, 1905

TIME HAS FLOWN like a swift-moving seabird, and it has been over a month since I began my employment at the Moana Hotel. The work is all-consuming, and Max and Liko have both implied that they actually miss me, imagine that! But they do not miss eating the same meal for days on end, and they welcome the new sets of slacks and button-ups and shoes they have for school, and the leftover food from the kitchen I bring home when I can. Max asks for the potatoes au gratin, and Liko loves the glazed York ham. As for myself, I would never tire of the spring chicken with Virginia bacon or the pineapple and cottage cheese.

The sheer amount of food wasted daily astounds me. The kitchen is a busy place, and the chef, a stern and high-strung man named Oswald, brought in from New York, spends much of his day red-faced and yelling. Being anywhere near him makes me nervous, but when night comes, and I've done a late shift, he is generous with leftovers and allows me to fill a small pail to take home. The boys and I have gained at least several pounds because of it.

I consider myself successful in my role for the most part, and have shown that I can keep cool under pressure. I've decided that the rudeness of guests falls into two categories: those who order me around like an indentured servant, and those who act as though I don't exist. More often than not, it's the women. The folly of men is that they openly leer, causing jealousy in their wives. Mrs. Akina had some wonderful advice, and told me to keep a smile on my face and kill them with kindness, that these people thrive on causing a reaction. It makes them feel important because deep inside, they are not secure in themselves. By the end of the day, I tell you, my cheeks ache from smiling.

Last week, we got wind that a very important new guest would be arriving soon. A Mrs. Jane Stanford, same as the university, which I had never heard of but pretended to. Apparently, she is the richest woman in San Francisco, and she's known to be difficult and a bit eccentric. Well, she and her two travel mates arrived yesterday morning with more trunks than a band of elephants. As fate would have it, Mrs. Akina came down with a cough and asked me to fill in for her.

Something about the way everyone talked about Mrs. Stanford caused a buildup in my chest, and by the time the woman actually arrived, I was near full of hysteria. Jane was older and taller than I expected, and commanded a presence like no one I have ever met. As though the world belongs to her, which it probably does. I was tongue-tied to start, a rare thing, but she soon put me at ease and allowed me to show them around the property. To my surprise, when that was done, she said I'd made an impression and asked if I would help plan her itinerary while here. Mrs. Akina won't be pleased, but what can she say?

During our tour, Jane—as I will call her for the sake of ease—wore a diamond necklace so brilliant I was blinded. No one but our Queen could get away with such opulence. I found it all to be a strange contradiction, though, because this morning as I presented her with my itinerary, the conversation turned toward me and my life. No one here has ever asked me one word about myself. And here Jane asked after my family and showed real emotion when I told her our story. I don't want anyone's pity, but I admit it is nice to feel understood. Isn't that what every human being longs for?

THE VERANDA
Zoe

BETWEEN THE WORKSHOP and going to the bar, Zoe lies on the bed and shoots off an email to Avery, telling her she's made splendid progress. She knows how much Avery worries, and better to have only one of them stressing. She is still on the fence about actually running with this idea, but as of now, it is the only thing she has. A kind of *if you can't be with the one you love, love the one you're with* in book form. Later, or in the morning, she will spend more time on the beat sheet, and maybe that will spur something.

In the past half hour, the wind has gained speed and now blows in angry off the ocean, a choppy gray-and-white frenzy. The temperature has plummeted, and she climbs under the covers to stay warm. No one has warned her of the possibility for foul weather, and she hasn't packed for the cold. No fuzzy Patagonia jacket or wool socks. Then from outside, a small thud.

She sets her computer aside and sits up on the edge of the bed. "You again?"

Meow.

Wind blows the tufts of fur on the side of its face forward, and the cat is so small and narrow, she worries it might blow away. "If I let you in, will you promise not to sleep on my bed?"

At that, it stands up and rubs its cheek against the glass. Zoe opens the door, and it shoots in.

"And if we are going to continue seeing each other like this, I'm going to have to name you. But first, are you a boy or a girl?" she says.

The cat darts from chair leg to table leg to Zoe's leg, rubbing its face against her shin. She lifts her leg quickly because while it is adorable, it also looks a little bit wet and sandy. She wants nothing more than to scoop up the cat and give it a warm, soapy bath, but knows it's a far-fetched wish. Cats and baths do not go well together. Instead, she leans down to scratch behind its ear with one finger. The cat leans in and begins to purr. It's so dainty, and with those big eyes and sweet little meow, she is almost positive it's a girl.

"How about I call you Storm? That way, if you turn out to be a boy, no biggie."

She then recalls the half tuna sandwich in her mini-fridge, scoops out a clump onto a napkin and sets it on the floor. Storm inhales it, making smacking and little grunting sounds as she eats, and her tail twitches.

Zoe reaches down and lightly pets her back. "You like that, huh?"

She knows if she so much as touches her face, she will puff up, so she pets Storm for as long as the cat eats, then goes to scrub her hands in scalding hot water. When she comes back, Storm is back on the bed in the same place she slept last night, making biscuits on the pillow. Zoe doesn't have the heart to kick her off.

"That is your side, and this is my side. Are we clear?"

Something about the way the cat looks at her gives her the impression Storm understands. And just to be safe, she goes into the bathroom for a towel, folds it neatly and sets it next to where Storm is kneading, as far from Zoe's side as possible.

"There, your own little spot."

Having another being in the room with her makes her feel safer, even just this little stray cat. Because the truth is, she is dreading going to sleep tonight.

IT IS DEFINITELY not luau weather, but Zoe puts on her turquoise flowered dress and sandals because she wants to be festive, hoping the event will still be held. Now that she knows a few people, she feels much more at ease. Her pocket watch rests in the middle of her chest and draws attention to her nonexistent cleavage, but she likes how it looks on her ever so slightly more tanned skin. Over that, she wears her jeans jacket, but it hardly keeps her warm, even indoors with the air conditioning off.

Down on the veranda, they've rolled down a thick plastic wind block, much as you'd find on a boat, and it keeps the place dry, but there are still bursts of wind sneaking in. Dylan is already there, sitting at a table off in the corner with a beer in front of him, staring out to sea. There are only two other couples out here. Everyone else is packed inside at Vintage 1901, the lobby bar where it is far warmer.

"I'm surprised they're open out here," she says on her approach.

This time, he jumps. "Geez. You're soft-footed."

Pussy-footed. "My dad used to say that."

She's still standing, and he suddenly hops up and pulls out the other chair for her. "Have a seat."

The chair is cool and she feels it through the thin cotton fabric, causing goose bumps to run up her arms. "Mahalo."

He raises an eyebrow. "Embracing the language, I see."

"I've learned a few words. *Aloha, mahalo, lanai.*"

"You could accomplish a lot with just those three."

A woman comes by and asks what she'd like to drink, and Zoe orders the same kind of beer he's having. A Big Swell.

"How about you?" she asks, aware that being in his presence causes an uptick in her heart rate.

"Believe it or not, I went to college here."

She scrunches her eyebrows, surprised. "You did?"

He nods. "My dad's best friend was a swimmer, and he went to UH and loved it. So I applied and got in on a football scholarship."

"You seem so . . . cowboyish. I would not peg you at all as having anything to do with Hawai'i."

Tonight he's in jeans and a long-sleeved brown checkered shirt, almost like a tablecloth, and boots. He also smells of citrusy aftershave, and his five o'clock shadow is gone. Zoe realizes her hands are trembling and wonders why she's so nervous.

"Anything to get me out of Texas. Long story, but things were rough—my real dad died, and my mom ended up marrying an asshole."

"I'm sorry."

"It's life, you know?" he says softly, and for a moment, his soul seems so wide-open.

"I do know, only too well. For the longest time, I thought I hated my dad because he fell in love with his secretary and left my mom. I took it so personally, when really he and my mom had been unhappy long before the secretary."

It's a lot to divulge right off the bat, but she feels the need to let him know she shares in the pain.

"Are you on good terms now?" he asks.

"We are. It turned out he could love the secretary and still love me. What about you and your mom?"

"Yeah, eventually the asshole husband got replaced with a decent guy. He makes my mom happy, so that's all I care about."

His eyes are aglow, almost from the inside out, and she realizes if she's not careful, she could easily fall into them.

Thankfully, he changes course. "As for those Hawaiian words, hmm. *Mauka* and *makai* mean toward the mountains or toward the ocean. *Pau* means finished. *Pau hana* means end of the work day. Like right now, you and I are having *pau hana* drinks."

On cue, her beer arrives, and he taps the glass with his. She takes a long, cold sip and wishes she had ordered a hot chocolate instead.

"It's freezing."

"It's only going to get worse before it gets better," he says.

She teases. "What are you, a weatherman?"

"No, but I pay attention. It's my job."

"So, yeah, about your job, you said you would tell me how you ended up with your illustrious career as an author," she says, wanting him to know she views this meeting as writing-related and nothing more.

"My interest in law enforcement started when I was a kid. In our town, we had this gang of horse rustlers, and no one could ever catch them. We finally had this detective come from out of town. A real cool cat, and he arranged some kind of sting that finally nailed the guys. For a young boy who loved horses, he was God as far as I was concerned. So at UH, I studied criminal justice, but it also so happened that I needed an elective, and the only one that fit my schedule was this creative writing class."

A gust of wind pounds against the plastic shield, startling them both as a new round of rain thrashes down. It feels as though they are on the brink of something, though she's not exactly sure what.

Dylan swigs his beer, then goes on. "Ursule Molina. A real quirky lady with black nails and dark glasses that she never took off. She was goth way before her time, but she was also genius. We had this assignment, and I wrote a short story about the horse rustlers, and she loved it. Raved about it and told me that I had talent. That was the first time anyone, besides my dad, really praised me."

She's both touched and surprised by his openness. "Sometimes all you need is that one nudge," she says, thinking about Mrs. Foster.

"Writing felt good. I liked that I could create my own form of justice for the bad people, and I liked creating my own worlds, you know?"

His left leg is bouncing up and down, and she wonders if maybe he's nervous too.

"Yes, I do."

"When I graduated, I went to Wyoming, because, well, horses. I joined the sheriff department's investigative division and was living my dream. But after five years or so, I realized I enjoyed writing about crime more than actually living it. I'd been writing all along, just short stories, not really finishing much, and when I attended the Sun Valley Writers' Conference to see if I could give it a go, a light bulb went off.

"My first novel was crap. Shitty reviews, dismal sales. But that only made me more determined to figure it out, master the craft. It made me hungry."

Zoe grips her glass hard enough to break it, but it holds. All this time she'd thought she had ruined his life. And now this. It would be as good a time as any to come clean, but her throat constricts at the thought of actually speaking the words. *I'm Zoe Finch, and I wrote that review.* His eyes follow something behind her, and she senses someone coming, but it's only the waitress, bundled in a thick sweater as though they are in the arctic circle.

"Can I get you two something to eat?" she asks.

"No thanks, we're going to the luau," Zoe says.

The woman points up at the sky. "No luau tonight."

"You didn't get the message?" Dylan asks.

Zoe is heartbroken. "Oh no! I was so looking forward to it. I was actually a drop-in, so maybe I'm not on the texting list?"

Dylan orders a burger and fries and one more beer.

"Nothing for me, thank you. I can get room service. I have a lot of work to get done, and I'm dragging," she says.

"Am I boring you?"

It feels like he's testing her.

She laughs. "Hardly."

"Then join me for some grub."

She sits up a little straighter. "Fine. I'll have what he's having."

When the waitress leaves, he says, "To be honest, I'm kind of glad the luau got canceled. Last year's was pretty hokey. I'd much rather sit here and unwind and not have to make small talk with anyone."

"You too, huh?"

"Put me in a herd of horses any day."

"So, why do you do it? Come to these conferences, I mean," she asks.

"Because I love writing, and I love sharing my process with other writers and helping them find a way through. Even those writing romance novels," he says with the lift of an eyebrow.

She sets down her beer, hard enough so that some splashes out. "Waaaaait a minute. *Even?*" This is a hill she will die on.

"Romance novels keep the publishing industry afloat. More than crime and thriller, more than self-help. So, please don't *even* me."

He holds both hands up. "Whoa, there. It was a simple statement. All I meant was that I love sharing with anybody who will listen, really. I don't care what they are writing. All walks of life. And since you happen to be writing a romance novel, well?"

"I've written more than one novel," she says, feeling the need to add in, "and not just romance."

"I thought you said you had tried writing crime before and you couldn't?"

She backpedals. "Yes, but I've written other stuff."

In front of them, the banyan's long branches flail around, and she thinks about Storm, hopes the cat is still in the room. With the note, and the residue of dreams, all waiting for her.

"So, what's your day job, then?" Dylan says. He seems a little buzzed, and looser than he's been so far. Almost playful.

"Again, you've reached your question quota," she says, attempting a smile as a feeling of dread scales up her back.

He seems to sense her unease. "Hey, is everything okay?"

She wants to say yes, everything is perfectly fine, but instead, she says, "I'm not sure."

He leans in. "I'm a pretty good listener, if you want to get it out."

The male variety of good listeners is hard to come by these days, and the way he's looking into her feels so honest and tender. She believes him.

"I've been having bad dreams the last couple nights—waking up kind of terrified to be honest, and this morning there was also a note on my floor. On Moana stationery. Someone must have slid it under the door as a prank, but I can't stop thinking about it."

"What did it say?"

"*Help me, I'm dying.* In block letters."

His eyebrows pinch together. "Weird. Did you hear anything?"

"Not a thing. Except there was something on my lanai scratching on my door that turned out to be a cat."

"How the hell did a cat get onto your lanai?"

"The banyan branch. It's a waif of a cat, and she must have made the leap. I figured she got freaked out by the lightning and thunder."

"What did you do with it?"

"She's sleeping in my room as we speak, even though I'm allergic. I'm calling her Storm."

A slow smile spreads across his face. "So, you're a sucker for animals in need."

"Who isn't?"

"Plenty of people, unfortunately. Did you tell the front desk about the note?"

She thought of Manu and her odd questions. "Yes, no one else reported anything, and the woman seemed like maybe she knew something she wasn't telling me."

"And they don't have security cams set up in the hallways, or you would know your answer."

"I never even thought of that. How do you know?"

He taps his temple. "It's hardwired into my brain."

"Of course it is."

"Probably just kids, and you're safe with the chain lock, but let me know if you get any more. We can set up a sting."

Even though she's cold, perspiration breaks out on her palms. The creepiness of the whole thing has stuck with her. She tells herself he's right, though. It probably was just some kids. But then, why the odd reaction from Manu?

He then asks, "Which room are you in?"

"120."

"I'm in 127, so feel free to come bang on my door if anything else happens, no matter what time it is."

She's surprised she hasn't run into him on the stairs or in the elevator, but knowing he's so close makes her feel better. Men, for all their faults, can be handy to have around.

"Thank you. Now, back to your story. You never finished, and I'm curious how you made the leap from lawman to author," Zoe says, always intrigued at people's path to publication.

"After my epiphany, I started writing whenever I had downtime. A stolen hour here and there adds up, and I somehow managed to finish a novel—an expanded version of my horse rustler story—and I thought it was the best thing ever. But no one wanted it. So I dug deep, went to a few more conferences and then wrote another. That one landed me an agent and a publishing deal, and the rest is history."

"Living the dream," she says, happy for him. "It doesn't always happen so smoothly."

"I wouldn't call it smooth. Remember, my first book tanked? That was rough. I pour my heart and soul into these books—maybe even too much," he says.

Hearing him say this makes her heart sting. It hadn't been until she published her own book that she realized how painful a bad review can be. How even one sentence can flog you and threaten to burn you to the ground. Had she known what she knows now, she would have never been so hard on him. A reviewer can dislike the book without flogging the author.

"Do you ever have trouble coming up with new story ideas?" she asks.

"Nah. I have the opposite problem. Too many ideas knocking around in my head. My agent has rationed me to sending him only two new ideas a month," he says with a chuckle.

Lord, if only she had that problem. When their food comes, they eat and continue to talk and laugh. It feels so natural to be with Dylan, like she's hanging out with an old friend at a campfire, plaid blanket around her, roasting marshmallows. She doesn't want to be enjoying herself so much, and feels a dangerous and familiar tug toward him. Then reminds herself that what they are doing is perfectly acceptable. Two writers, talking craft and sharing war stories.

Though she has to hold back a lot. Damn, she wants to tell him her real name is Zoe and how she might have had a hand in that first book tanking, but huddled here with him as the storm whips around them, she's more relaxed and cozy than she's been in a long time, and she just wants to savor it.

Tomorrow. She'll do it tomorrow.

Now they are done eating. They've both finished their second beer, and Zoe has no idea how long they have actually been sitting here. It feels like a lifetime. They have completely blown off the rest of the conference goers and stayed out in their little cocoon. Realizing it's late, they both rise to leave, use a side door and bypass the lobby, taking the stairs to the first floor. Neither says anything as they approach the junction where they'll part ways.

When they get there, he turns to her and cocks his head. "So, Miss Bridget White, it was a pleasure weathering the storm with you."

She feels lightheaded. "Same."

"And I meant what I said. Any funny business, just come get me. Or call." He gives her his number, and she punches it into her phone.

A better idea might involve him staying in her room, but she doesn't say that. "Thank you."

He looks as though he wants to say something more, standing there with his hands in his pockets. His eyes drop down to her pocket watch, setting it aflame on her skin. Suddenly, he doesn't seem like a cocksure author and ex-detective. More like a man trying to decide what to do with this woman before him. She can see the muscles in his jaw tighten, but then he says, "Everything's going to be fine. Good night."

FROM THE JOURNAL OF 'ILIAHI BALDWIN, 1905

MA BELIEVES IN SPIRITS. When I was a child, she told me that all things on earth have their own form of energy, even rocks and trees and waves. When I was five, I came upon a dying seabird on the beach. Holding it as the life waned out of it, I rushed the bird home, with its drooping wet feathers and limp neck, in the hopes that Ma could help it back to life. When she told me that the soul of the bird had returned to the earth, I cried so hard my eyes nearly bled. Until that point, I believed my mother could do anything, and wielded the powers of the sun and moon and the sky.

The bird was a type I had never seen before, with wings as wide as a carriage. Mōlī, Ma called it. An albatross. We took the bird back to the beach and buried it in the sand, and Ma quietly chanted for its spirit to be returned to the *aina*. That day changed me, and I started watching for signs of spirits everywhere.

Soon, I began to sense that many of the animals around me were there for a reason, and I discovered an ancient intelligence in their eyes that I had never before noticed. Since we spent so much time near the ocean, collecting 'opihi and limu, I developed an affinity for swimming. Hawaiian children are amphibious. We are taught to swim as infants, not like the malihini that come here and sink like lead weights. The area where we frequented was home to a small family of *manō*, white tip sharks, and I befriended them. Or perhaps they befriended me.

Ma told me that the shark is our 'aumakua, our family's protector, and I have nothing to fear from them. So when I spied the small white fin cut through the water as Jane Stanford and Thelma sat at the edge of the pier, I felt like maybe it was trying to tell me something. Though what, I am not sure.

THE MEETING
Jane
February 26

A QUIET KNOCK came at the door the following afternoon. Jane was resting on the bed after a long and hot morning in a canoe, being paddled back and forth by two young men and Dot, who was about as poor with a paddle as humanly possible. The woman most certainly had two left arms.

"Who is it?" she called.

"It's 'Ili."

"You can let yourself in, dear, it's unlocked."

'Ili slipped in, then shut the door silently behind her. She glanced around, as would a ferret coming out of its hole to check for predators, then spoke. "I have someone who will come tomorrow evening. But she doesn't want anyone to know the reason for her visit, so if anyone asks, just say she was fitting you for a mu'umu'u, since she is a well-known seamstress. She normally does not do this for strangers, but she is a friend of my mother's and will do anything for me."

Jane sat up and smoothed down her unruly hair. "Your kindness will not go unappreciated."

She noticed 'Ili was not looking at her but eyeing the jewelry laid out on the table. Jane had been planning her dinner outfit and arranged all of her necklaces and bracelets in a row so she could determine which to wear.

'Ili took a step toward the table. "*Auwe*, they look like they belong to a queen."

The jewels always garnered people's admiration, though since the loss of her husband, showing them off had lost its shimmer somewhat. The way he looked at her when she wore them always set her heart aglow. No one would ever look at her like that again, and the realization pained her.

"I am a fan of Queen Victoria, so it's only fitting," Jane said.

'Ili leaned down to inspect the collection for a moment, then backed away hurriedly. "I'm not a jewelry person myself, aside from the shell necklace my mother gave me, which I keep in a box under my pillow. Anyhow, I need to get back to work, but wanted to tell you that I'll bring Mary up here tomorrow at 7:00 p.m., after dinner."

And then she was gone, the faint smell of flowers and salt water in her wake.

GRAY SKIES AND rain filled in the following morning and lasted throughout the day. Truth be told, it was a nice excuse to lounge about and enjoy cribbage and reading, and gorging on malasadas, club sandwiches, and fresh tangerines that were so bright and juicy, Jane began plotting how to get her own orchard back home.

At seven o'clock sharp, Thelma greeted 'Ili and the older woman, Mary, at the door, peering out to make sure no one else was around to notice. Dot had been given the night off because Jane felt it would be better not to frighten the poor woman. Mary stood a good several inches taller than Jane, with one braid down her back, thick as a horse tail.

In greeting, she stepped close and pressed her nose against Jane's, inhaling deeply. "Tonight is a waning crescent moon, a time when the divide is gossamer-thin. It is a good night to be open to what spirits are with us. Come, let us sit."

The four of them sat around a table that Thelma had cleared earlier, and Mary pulled out a small bottle full of a brown liquid, four cut-out gourds of some kind, a bunch of bananas and a candle. Gold bangles adorned her arm. There was little talk, and the sound of raindrops on the window made the room feel cozy as a cocoon. Jane's whole body was tingling with anticipation.

Mary lit the candle, poured everyone a small amount of the liquid, closed her eyes, and reached out to Jane and 'Ili, who both latched on to her fleshy palms with their hands.

"We pray," she said, mumbling words so softly Jane could not make out what they were. After the prayer, she dipped her fingers in her cup and flung a few drops into the air. "The essence is yours, the substance ours."

Then, to Jane, "Drink."

Jane did as instructed. Normally, she would have demanded to know what this foul and pungent-smelling brown liquid was, but she trusted 'Ili, and by default, she trusted Mary. Over time, one developed a sixth sense about people. Some gave off a particular vibration so powerful you could feel it the minute they stepped into the room. Mary carried this force field, and it blanketed Jane in a kind of calm she had not felt in years.

Mary then nodded to 'Ili, and 'Ili drank. Then Thelma. And finally, Mary downed hers. After that, she peeled open the bananas and broke them apart, handing pieces to each woman. A strange numbing sensation began to creep onto Jane's tongue and lips, but her mind felt sharp and alert. She took the banana, and the sweetness counteracted the earthy taste of root on her tongue.

"We four are here to witness, as we invite Jane's loved ones to join us, should they be in the mood. Our intentions and hearts are pure. Now, let us close our eyes," Mary said in a full-throated voice.

She squeezed Jane's hand and Jane squeezed 'Ili's hand as the light danced beyond her eyelids. Rain spattered, and the ocean crashed—the door had been left cracked slightly, and humid air poured into the room. Jane swore she could hear her own heartbeat slowing down.

Nothing happened for a while, and Jane went off into a dreamlike state, remembering vividly the moment she first held baby Leland in her arms, and the weight of love she'd been struck with. The fresh smell of his skin, and his first cry announcing his arrival into this world. His life played out like a silent film, and then she saw herself at his deathbed, weeping. She had thrown herself over his body while inhuman sounds spewed forth from the recesses of her body.

A gust of wind blew through the crack in the door, howling and drawing her back to the hotel room. The curtains whipped around, and suddenly the room went dark. Mary's hand heated up, and Jane felt something warm brush against the back of her neck. She opened her eyes and turned, but it was almost impossible to see anything but the black forms of the other women, and shadows from the flailing trees outside.

Mary spoke in a much lower tone. "There is someone with us."

"Can you tell who it is?" Jane asked, feeling slightly feverish.

Strangely, the smell of wine and horse manure wafted up around them. Scents of the stock farm. Scents of her husband.

"Your work in this life has been transformative for many, and there is much to be proud of, but I am getting the sense that you are not safe, even here, in the islands."

"Shall I light—" Thelma said.

Mary cut her off. "Hush, let me continue. You are trusting to a fault, and this must change. But if you remain vigilant, all will be well."

A knock came on the door then, loud and insistent, and whatever charged energy had caused the hair on Jane's arm to rise suddenly whooshed away. Thelma switched on the light at the same time 'Ili slid into the bathroom. Then Thelma opened the door just a crack.

It was Mrs. Akina. "Please, forgive the interruption, but I have confirmation that your coachman, Israel, will be waiting for you in the morning at ten o'clock, and the gingerbread that Mrs. Stanford requested will be baked fresh and ready to go. Is there anything else we can get for you?"

"That's perfect. No, thank you," Thelma said, shutting the door in her face.

Talk about bad timing. The spell was broken, and Jane sat on the chair next to Mary, thinking perhaps this had not been the brightest of ideas. The trip had been a most enjoyable one, and now these words would stubbornly lodge in her mind.

"Is there anything else you can tell me? I felt a presence in the room, and it smelled like my husband, but I need assurance," Jane said, trying to keep the pleading from her voice.

The wind whistling in had all but stopped, and an eerie calm befell the room.

"There is never any assurance when dealing in this realm, but there was a masculine energy, and I felt that you were most loved. Did you feel it?" Mary said.

"Leland."

'Ili poked her head back out, then joined them. "I told her I was going around the hotel, making sure the windows were closed with this weather. If she saw me in here, it would have drawn suspicion."

"You don't have to worry, 'Ili. I am more than happy to cover for you," Jane said, turning her attention back to Mary. "I'm not a young woman, and I've known love and heartbreak in equal measure, but I will tell you this: I am not ready to be murdered."

There, she said it. She felt like a caged animal, or a man waiting for his execution. A rush of hot tears came on suddenly, cascading down her cheeks.

'Ili came and sat beside her, wrapping an arm around her and resting her head on Jane's shoulder unabashedly, as though she had known her her whole life. "It's a heavy weight to bear. But you are not alone, Mrs. Stanford."

It was strange how the touch of this peculiar young woman brought her so much comfort. It almost seemed as though God had set them up together, a motherless girl and a childless woman.

"I believe there are several moments in time set aside for all of us, crossover points that are open to us, when we leap off into the next world. Only if we pay attention to signs are we able to bypass one of these openings. Many factors are out of our control, but you have been warned, and that is a gift," Mary said.

Was it, though?

Mary began packing the bottle and gourds back into her bag, but left the leaves on the table. Jane felt cheated. "Can we try again?"

"In my experience, the corporeal visits do not last more than a few minutes. You will only be disappointed. But have faith, he is always with you. Relax and enjoy the effects of the awa, and maybe you will get another visit in your dreams."

Jane's tongue felt thick and heavy—come to think of it, her whole body did—and thankfully, sleep came swiftly once they were gone. It was a deep and restful slumber. But there were no dreams.

FROM THE JOURNAL OF
'ILIAHI BALDWIN, 1905

I TOOK A risk by bringing Mary to the hotel, but if anyone knows the desperation one feels after losing a loved one, it is I. There was no way I was not going to help Mrs. Stanford in any way I could. And what I have observed in my short time here is that wealthy folk are not immune from the tribulations of life. I might even go as far as saying that they are even more prone to it, with all their galivanting around the globe exposing themselves to exotic diseases, as young Leland was, and their lavish lifestyles and overconsumption. You ask me, the simple life is the best kind of life. Earth, ocean, sky, family. That is all I need.

But I must confess, there is something magnetic about those jewels that Jane wears each day, and how they catch the light in such captivating ways. I have drifted off in several daydreams, imagining what just one necklace could purchase. To walk around in broad daylight with such expensive adornments seems like asking for trouble, but she seems not to care. Around Mrs. Stanford and these rich folk, I often feel like I'm studying a foreign species, and the thought causes a lightness in my being.

As much as Jane can be difficult and bossy, I like the woman. Though I cannot say the same for her secretary Thelma, an overbearing nag who treats Mrs. Stanford like a child. Thelma has made it a point to show me that she holds a special relationship to Mrs. Stanford, and that no one else could possibly know or care for her like she does. Not only that, but she pouts and sulks and seems otherwise preoccupied all the time.

Mary's words to Mrs. Stanford echo in my mind: *You are trusting to a fault.* It is obvious to me that Jane trusts Thelma, but less obvious that Thelma trusts Jane. I sense that Thelma feels wronged in some way, and there's a dark energy seething beneath her skin. Again, so much can be told by watching the language of the human body. A tight mouth, shifty glances, fidgeting hands. Jane would do well to leave the woman behind.

All this talk of the dead has me longing for Pa with a keen tightness in my chest. Even when Ma was exasperated with me, and my curious ways and eager tongue, Pa seemed amused by me. Much older than Ma, he arrived in the islands from Boston as a merchant marine, already having lost a wife, Mary Jane. He was highly sought-after as a builder, but still made time for us. And it crushes my heart every day to think of what he went through at the end of his life. Heart broken in two. Half on Oʻahu, half on Molokaʻi.

Not many people can understand the kind of grief our family has experienced, but Jane does. Just being in her presence, I can feel an outpouring of empathy. Though different as can be, we share the language of grief.

THE NOTE
Zoe

JUST TO BE SAFE, Zoe puts a chair in front of the door that opens to the hallway. She feeds Storm part of her burger, which she saved in a napkin. The cat happily gobbles it up, then curls up on her towel. She's looking cleaner and shiny, having had a whole day to do nothing but sleep and bathe herself. It's nice to know Dylan is close, and Zoe is too tired to even attempt writing, so she drifts off to the sound of wind and rain and purring.

She sleeps through the night—a dark and dreamless slumber, thanks to exhaustion and two strong beers. When she wakes, there is something warm breathing against her stomach, and she sees that her body is wrapped around Storm, spooning the little animal. Surprisingly, her eyes are not swollen and scratchy. Going against her best judgment, she reaches down and pets Storm's head with one finger running down between her shoulder blades. The purring kicks up a notch.

"Morning, friend."

Storm shifts, pressing her head into Zoe's finger.

"Are you my little guardian angel?"

A mewling sound.

Carefully, Zoe slides out of bed without disturbing the cat. Silver light filters into the room, and the sky still looks brooding. Not that she's expecting it to change—the storm is supposed to last for days, but one can hope. On the floor, something catches her eye, and her stomach drops when she sees it's another piece of Moana stationery. A chill spreads from her fingertips to her toes as she reads, and her body turns to ice.

I'VE BEEN POISONED!

She lets the paper flutter to the floor and climbs back in bed. *Poisoned.* Again, if anyone in the hotel has been poisoned, why would they slide a note under her door? It makes no sense. But the word reminds her of the dream in which she is dying, and the tightness in her chest when she wakes. A prickling of unease moves through her.

Zoe picks up the phone, ready to call and demand a new room, but then looks at Storm and sets the receiver back down. There is no way she can leave the cat now. Not in this weather. But staying here is turning her blood cold. It's almost as though she's the heroine in a horror novel, when you're reading and wondering why the character doesn't just get the hell out. Then her rational mind takes over and reminds her she's in a packed hotel in Waikiki, people everywhere, Dylan just down the hall. There has to be an explanation.

The cat stands up and arches her back, stretching, and looks at Zoe, then tries to climb onto her stomach, delicate white whiskers tickling her arm. Zoe nudges her away with one leg under the covers.

"Do you know anything about this?" she asks. "Because if you do, now would be a good time to speak up."

She feels weird talking to a cat, but having Storm here lessens her anxiety. And Storm somehow feels like an old soul, like she's been around the block for at least a few centuries.

With her head back on the pillow, Zoe debates texting Dylan. He seemed so sincere with his offer to help, but now, in the light of day and not under the influence, she's not so sure. Part of her wishes she was going to his workshop, but then what? Watch him and his sexy mouth all day, and not learn a thing? Nope, not today. Not with her deadline. Her future depends on it.

She decides to run down to the lobby before getting ready, and throws on yoga pants and a T-shirt. Her whole body is tense, and that bitter taste is back in her mouth. This time, Manu is standing at the front desk, and when she sees Zoe, her mouth pulls down.

Zoe slides the paper over the cool wood. "I got another love note this morning, and I have to tell you, it makes me very uncomfortable. Especially with the dreams."

"Dreams?"

"I've been having weird dreams ever since I got here, where I feel like I'm dying. Or maybe I really am dying?"

Manu stares at the note and does not make eye contact. "How are you dying in your dreams?"

"Like I can't move, and I'm calling for help but no one will help me. I know that sounds like a typical nightmare, but these feel real, and I can't shake the feeling even after I wake. Look, if there is something I should know, please tell me," she says breathlessly.

Zoe is pretty good at reading people, and she can tell that Manu is uncomfortable—the way she shifts on her feet and fusses with the giant red flower in her hair. Voices grow louder behind her, and she turns and sees a couple approaching.

"Please," Zoe whispers.

Manu nods. "I get off at four. I'll come to your room."

ZOE MAKES IT to the workshop with ten minutes to spare and opens her manuscript file. Aside from the premise and the opening, she is still struggling to make it a big story, something mind-blowing or earth-shattering. Then reminds herself that her last book wasn't either of those. It was a sweet and funny story about two best friends trying to find love in a world where love doesn't always want to be found.

Because despite Zoe's professional success, and outward appearance that she has her shit together, her heart still desperately longs for a deep and unwavering love. Other people of all shapes and sizes and personalities have managed to find it. So why can't she? The hope is still in there somewhere, but it's been slowly eroded, and now she's almost thirty and still unattached.

A few minutes later, Tara sits down next to her. "Hey, pretty woman."

Zoe looks up. "Good morning."

"I noticed you had a date last night. I thought about coming over and saying hi but didn't want to interrupt anything."

"Not at all. We just had some unfinished business from the mixer that first night to wrap up."

Tara gives her a look like she doesn't quite believe her. "Are you sure? Because it really didn't look that way. Tucked away in the corner of the veranda like that, beers, eyes only for each other. Neither of you even noticed the gala affair that was going on in the lobby. I miss that—the early excitement, the falling part."

"No, no, no. It wasn't like that at all. It was all writerly talk."

"Whatever you need to tell yourself." She seems to assess Zoe, then asks, "You sure nothing happened afterward? You look like you had a long night."

She doesn't have the energy to draw Tara into her strange room drama. "I think it's probably the two beers and a restless sleep. Nothing happened."

Tara leans close and whispers, "I bet he's a good kisser."

"I won't tell your husband you said that."

"Thank you. It'll be our secret. But you have to promise to tell me if it lives up to expectations when you do kiss him."

Zoe can't help but smile. "I can see why you write romance, among other things. And speaking of secrets, I have something I want to tell you. Please remind me after the workshop, okay?"

Telling Tara who she really was felt like the right thing to do.

"Sure." Tara looks at her watch. "We should probably go in."

Throughout the morning, they work on perfecting their beat sheets to make sure their plots are as tight as can be. Sam is not there, and Zoe is happy about it, and she and Tara partner up. Tara is workshopping her thriller set on Vancouver Island, and this one sounds utterly intriguing. It strikes her how fascinating the evolution of a story is.

Looking at Tara, this sweet and beautiful woman, you would never know that in her mind, she's carrying around entire worlds. Several of them. And if—actually *when*, because Zoe knows it will happen for her—she gets published, her stories will then enter the minds and hearts of countless others and take on a life of their own. The words will always be the same, but no two people will experience them in remotely the same way. Some will love the story. Some will hate it. Some will think about their own lives and how they might need to change something. Some will laugh. Others will cry.

During the lunch break, Tara is talking to Olivia, so Zoe sneaks out and takes a handful of her turkey from her sandwich up to Storm, who is now in a ball on the chair. Zoe's happy the cat is not outside in this, as the sky has turned black again, like it's nine o'clock at night. When Storm sees Zoe, she hops off and starts rubbing against her legs. Zoe reaches down and pets her, puts the turkey down, washes her hands, then hurries back downstairs, hoping to catch Dylan before the afternoon session and tell him about the disturbing new note.

She goes straight to his ballroom, not really expecting him to be there yet. But he is. And so is Sam. Zoe stands suspended in the doorway, poised to back up silently and leave unnoticed. But they both turn, so she has no choice but to interact.

"Sorry to interrupt. I can come back later," she says as casually as possible. "I just had a writing question, no big deal."

She searches her mind for something to ask.

Dylan waves her in. "No worries. That's what I'm here for."

Sam does not look pleased, nor does she move. So Zoe walks in, smoothing down her wild hair, and says, "I was just wondering more about surveillance equipment in hotels, say, if your novel takes place in one and there has been a crime."

"Aren't you writing a romance novel?" Sam says, a tone of skepticism in her voice.

Dylan doesn't look away from Zoe as he says, "Would you mind, Sammy? I promised a short consult with her earlier."

Sammy?

Sam grabs her purse from the chair and slings it over her shoulder. "No problem. I'll see you later," she says and heads for the door.

"Really, this could have waited," Zoe says.

"You came at a good time, actually. Tell me everything."

So she does, speaking fast. As the words tumble out, it becomes harder to catch a breath, and she feels lightheaded.

He places a hand on her shoulder. "Bridget, slow down, take it easy. Everything's going to be fine."

His touch sends a wave of warmth down her arm, and she leans into it. Human touch is something she's been lacking lately, and she soaks it in like a dry old sponge. But she also feels awful that he is so kind and helpful, and she's so dishonest. It's actually the first big lie she's ever told, and she does not understand how some people do it so effortlessly. It would be one thing if she and Dylan were not developing some kind of friendship. Or attraction. Or . . . *thing*.

Several deep breaths later, she says, "I'm so curious what Manu is going to tell me. And I want to move rooms, but the cat and—"

His hand drops. "Whoa there. There has to be a reasonable explanation. Why don't you see what she says and go from there."

She looks up at him, arm still tingling from where he touched her. "Will you be at the open mic readings this afternoon?"

"Supposed to be, yeah. Either find me there or text me after?"

"I'm sorry to be a bother. I just don't know who else to turn to."

Dylan inches toward her. "Don't be sorry. We'll figure this out, I promise."

In such close proximity, she notices gold flecks in his irises. The look he gives her unnerves her. *He* unnerves her.

THE PICNIC
Jane
February 28

ROCKING CHAIRS WERE one of life's greatest pleasures. That gentle back and forth had always had a lulling effect, and Jane felt tranquil as she watched the ocean from their perch on the arched veranda. Between yesterday and today, the water appeared an entirely different entity. No longer a turquoise blue, it now boiled white and soupy with surf. The beach was strewn with sticks, and sand crabs scurried around, trying to make sense of this foreign debris on their turf.

They had eaten a light breakfast and now were waiting on the coachman. The sun was just starting to break through the clouds, but there was no sign of rain, and for that she was thankful. She checked her pocket watch. Almost ten.

"Say, shouldn't we be leaving soon?" she asked the girls.

"I'll go check on things," Dot said, hurrying off toward the lobby.

A few minutes later, she returned. "There has been a problem with the gingerbread. It's not rising."

"Oh, for heaven's sake. Let's just go, then," Thelma said.

Jane remained planted in her chair. "We can't leave without the gingerbread. I've had my heart set on it for days now." Gingerbread was one of her favorite guilty pleasures.

"Well, I don't know what else to say," Dot told her with a shrug.

"Why don't we go have a peek in the kitchen, perhaps that will speed things up," Jane said.

In the lobby, 'Ili intercepted them. "Ah, there you are. Everything is packed up for the picnic, and Israel is here, but a calamity has befallen your gingerbread, I'm afraid."

"What sort of calamity?" Jane asked.

"All I know is it has not cooked as planned."

Jane marched on toward the kitchen, irritated, with her entourage falling in behind her. Once there, a man in white garb stood bolt upright when he saw them, having been peering into one of the ovens.

"Mrs. Stanford, this is our cook, Oswald," 'Ili said.

Rivulets of perspiration ran down the man's bony face. "Lord, it's been a morning! Our oven went kaput and I've lit this one up, but it's taking its sweet time. The bread should be ready in about a half hour or so."

This kind of foul-up would never happen in her own kitchen. "I was assured of our meal last night, and that we were to leave no later than ten. Whose responsibility is it to keep the ovens working?"

"Um, mine, ma'am. But—"

"Then I will be having a talk with Mr. Price," she said.

A heavy feeling came over the room. Jane felt bad for about half a second, then thought about how much she was spending to stay here, and turned to leave. "We will expect the gingerbread in thirty minutes, no more."

TWENTY-NINE MINUTES LATER, 'Ili came to fetch them, carrying a picnic basket under her arm. "Calamity averted. Are you ready to be awed by one of the most beautiful views on the island?" she said with a wide smile, though her eyes looked tired. Had Jane been expecting too much of the girl?

They rode down Waikiki Road and turned up toward the mountains before they reached the overcrowded streets of Honolulu and Chinatown, crossing bridges over wide streams that ran out of each valley. Large swaths of land with paddies of heart-shaped leaves covered much of the area, and ducks and cats seemed more populous than humans on their route. Lazy clouds draped themselves low on the ridges.

"Do they have names?" Jane asked, then added, "The mountains, I mean."

"Yes," 'Ili said, while at the same time Israel said, "No."

Jane laughed, her mood much improved by the excitement of being off on an adventure. "Well, which is it?"

"They have long Hawaiian names that you would never be able to pronounce, but not English names," 'Ili said.

"Try me."

'Ili pointed to a closer one, and then in the direction they were headed. "Kalaepohaku is that one, and that is Pu'u 'Ōhi'a."

The words slid fast off her tongue.

"You're right, I suppose. But what do they mean?"

"*Kalaepohaku* means point of rocks, and *Pu'u 'Ōhi'a* is hill of 'ōhi'a tree, our beautiful red-blossomed trees."

"The language is lovely," Jane said.

"Yes," was all 'Ili said.

When they arrived at the mouth of Nu'uanu Valley, on a street lined with royal palms, they veered up toward a high wall of cliffs that cut along the whole east end of O'ahu. Along the way, they came upon the summer house of the late Queen Emma and her husband, Alexander Liholiho. It looked straight out of New England with its high columns and neat white paint, and it reminded Jane that while she often thought of herself as royalty, these people actually were.

The air cooled as they neared the mountain pass at a place 'Ili called the Pali, and Israel started singing. He had a warm, melodious voice that caused the horses to lift their heads and prance, and birds swooped down from the trees. Vegetation thickened along the base of the cliffs, and Jane had the feeling they were about to enter another dimension.

"Now, hang on to your hats. When we round the bend ahead, it's going to get windy enough to blow your stockings off," Israel said.

The mountains appeared impassable, but the carriage wound its way up a road that had been carved out of the near-vertical rock. Just as a gust of wind assaulted them, a panorama came into view below that rendered Jane speechless. Green plains a thousand feet down met up with an endless blue ocean dotted with small islands.

'Ili turned and smiled at the three women, loose strands of her hair whipping wildly. "It is a good day to be alive, is it not?" she yelled.

A good day indeed.

THEY SURVIVED THE perilous traverse down the cliffs and rode to a flat place flush with palms and an open grassy field not far from the ocean, sun-splashed and salt-scented. By now, the whole group was singing along with Israel, everything from "In the Sweet By-and-By" to "Amazing Grace" to "In the Good Old Summer Time."

"In the good old summer time, strolling thro' the shady lanes," they all belted out together as they rolled to a stop.

Jane didn't know all the words, but filled in where she

could, and honestly could not remember a more pleasurable ride in recent years. 'Ili's voice was pitch-perfect and throaty, which was a delight. They set up under a wide canopied tree with tufts of coral flowers that looked ready to take flight. Israel let the horses loose to drink and graze in a brook nearby, then laid out the carriage pillows for the women to sit upon.

'Ili stood with her arms wide open, breathing in sky. "My mother loved this spot for its ideal positioning, close enough to the Pali but far from civilization," she said.

A trio of long-legged birds landed across the clearing, sparking Jane's interest. Whenever she saw things in threes, it felt like a sign from God that she was in the right place, a representation of her own little family, the holy trinity, and the rule of three. She took it as a good omen.

"I've always believed that places hold the residue of past experiences and people, in a kind of spatial memory that enhances our own. It's why we're drawn to certain places," Jane told them.

"Oh, I believe that wholeheartedly," 'Ili said.

Israel nodded. "And I agree."

The pair of them—'Ili and Israel—felt so . . . connected. So in tune with their surroundings. Far more so than many of the intellectuals back home, or even the noble folk in Europe. The idea boosted her feeling that coming to Hawai'i had been the right thing to do, though the undercurrent of worry about the university had not left her completely. Who knew what Jordan and the board were up to without her. And she was eager to hear of any updates on the investigation. Surely they must have found something by now—a fortnight had passed since her departure. She tried to put it out of her mind for the time being.

Everyone helped carry the baskets of food, and Thelma produced the book Jane had picked out from the hotel newsstand that morning and set it on the picnic blanket. *The Mighty Atom.*

"How about a reading? While we work up more of an appetite," Thelma said, more chipper and like herself today. Perhaps the stress of the past month was finally loosening its grip on her too.

Jane was having a hard time getting the gingerbread out of her mind, but everyone else seemed in no hurry to eat.

"Fine."

Israel helped Jane down, propping her up against the broad tree trunk, then went off to tend to the horses. Thelma read while 'Ili and Dot lay back in the grass and watched the clouds swiftly pass overhead. Within minutes, 'Ili was snoring, and Jane quickly lost interest in the book, as it instantly produced a sense of melancholy, the precise sentiment she had been trying to elude.

"Enough of that, Thelma. Unpack the lunch, will you, ladies?" she asked.

'Ili remained on her back, chest rising and falling, deep in slumber. She looked so peaceful, Jane suggested they let her rest, remembering how tired her eyes looked earlier. They tiptoed around her, speaking in hushed tones, but Israel came over and said, "Rise and shine, princess," nudging 'Ili with his boot.

Her eyes shot open, and she leaped to her feet, hair now untamed. "My apologies for nodding off. My younger brother, Max, got a fishhook through his hand yesterday, and I was tending him last night to prevent infection."

"I have something for that in my medicine box if you need it. Thelma, remind me when we get back," Jane said, fanning herself.

"That's kind of you, as I cannot lose another family member," 'Ili said.

Dot and Thelma unpacked a bowl of hard-boiled eggs, set out a plate of Swiss cheese and tongue sandwiches, sad-looking oranges, the tin of creme chocolates Jane had brought with her from San Francisco, and the gingerbread. After wolfing down her sandwich with nary a word between chewing, she ate several chocolates and then reached for the gingerbread.

Thelma leveled her eyes on Jane, and it was easy to see the disapproval in them. "Shouldn't we let ourselves digest for a bit?"

"No, we should not."

"I, myself, could eat a whole other sandwich," 'Ili said, "or two."

"That's because you're thin as a twig, and young," Thelma said.

Jane set a piece of gingerbread in her mouth, chewed and swallowed. "Oh, Thelma, don't be so glum."

Though slightly undercooked, the flavors were a perfect blend of spices. Her stomach had begun to swell and bloat, and she would pay for her gluttony this evening, but for now, she would savor every last bite. After finishing the whole thing, she burped. Everyone pretended not to notice. She burped again and felt a little better.

An hour or so later, when they were packing up, she made the announcement. "Next time I come to Hawai'i, I would like Israel and 'Ili to join me back in this very place. It's been such a joy." As if by declaring it, she could make it happen.

When it was time to go, it took Israel and the girls to hoist her to standing. A bit of an embarrassment, but that was the beauty of being old, wasn't it? You no longer cared a nickel what others thought of you.

THE GIFT

Jane

February 28

BACK AT THE MOANA, after a short nap, Jane woke still feeling stuffed as a Thanksgiving turkey. She had clearly overindulged, and would forgo dinner, but knew that a walk on the pier would do her good. The wind had all but died, and the ocean was streaked in gold. Hawaiian music sailed into the room, giving her a nostalgic feeling. Music had a way of grabbing hold of her heart and transporting her back to the past, when life was still in full swing.

As she was washing up, 'Ili arrived at the door, and Dot let her in. She held something behind her back, Jane could see in the mirror, and said, "I have a surprise for you, Mrs. Stanford."

"Well, who doesn't love a surprise. Give me a few minutes and I'll be out," Jane called.

She could hear the three women conversing about themselves as she applied a dash of rouge to her cheeks. Everyone in Hawai'i had a glow to their skin, and Jane wanted to partake, even if it was manufactured. The young people all came in from the beach with toasted shoulders and a shimmer on their faces, and they seemed to radiate vigor from the inside out.

When she walked into the room, 'Ili produced a delicate flower lei strung with cream-colored blossoms. "I made this, and thought you would enjoy it. I picked the flowers myself down the road from our house."

'Ili placed it around her neck and kissed her on the cheek, warmly. The lei carried more sweetness per square inch than a bowl of sugar, and it at once intoxicated, filling the room with notes of jasmine and citrus and lily. 'Ili adjusted it around Jane's neck, and rotated it slightly so a small patch of ferns rested just above her lapel. "There, now it sets off your necklace beautifully."

"Who needs jewelry when you have such divine flowers at your disposal?" Jane said.

An idea struck her then, which at first seemed preposterous, and Thelma would probably not approve. But she wanted to do something special for 'Ili—something beyond leaving her a substantial tip. It had been years since anyone had treated her with such genuine warmth, and she had developed a fondness for the girl.

"I say they look great together," Dot said, stepping back to assess.

Fiery sunlight poured in the window, reminding Jane they were running out of time for sunset. "Say, I have something for you too, but I want to catch the sunset. Meet me back up here at eight o'clock, would you?"

'Ili frowned. "Oh, this lei was a gift. I don't expect anything in return, not at all."

"Nevertheless, I would like to do this."

'Ili half opened her mouth to say something else, then stopped. "As you wish."

AT FIVE THIRTY, Jane fetched Thelma and went downstairs. On the veranda, three Hawaiian musicians played plucky tunes that had lured several couples to dance. After saying hello to several guests she had become friendly with, they sat on the outskirts and enjoyed the calm evening and last remnants of periwinkle in the sky. Mrs. Highton joined them for a bit, and they recounted their day with her.

"What is it you plan on giving to the girl?" Thelma asked once they were alone and had ordered.

Jane did not care for her tone. "One of my bracelets."

"The ruby one?"

"Don't you worry about it, Thelma. Some things are beyond explanation, and I have this feeling—a chemistry of sorts—that she and I are similar souls. The poor dear has had a troubled life."

Thelma frowned. "I feel like it's my duty to warn you. She knows who you are and is trying to get in your good graces, hoping to end up with some crumbs."

"Oh, for heaven's sake."

"Dare I say, all the natives here are not to be trusted. It's in their blood."

The words raked up the back of Jane's neck. "Now, you're starting to sound like Dr. Jordan, and I won't have any more of it."

She and Dr. Jordan had shared heated discussions on the betterment of humanity and forced sterilization, and his *Blood of the Nation* publication was a real embarrassment to the university as it spewed *decay of the races* and *survival of the unfit*.

"I'm merely watching out for you," Thelma said.

Thelma's tone softened, but Jane was done with the conversation. "Sometimes you can be so churlish. I've made up my mind, so not another word about it, and when she comes to the room, I expect you to be pleasant."

ON THE WAY BACK, they took the elevator. It was loud and clunky, but she wasn't feeling up to the stairs after such an exhausting day. She asked Thelma to fetch Dot and return to help prepare her medicine. Namely, cascara and bicarbonate of soda. The cascara would pray help evacuate this lump of congealed food in her bowels, especially combined with the soda, which could also aid her sleep.

Both women entered the room but a minute later and flitted about, readying the medicine and setting it by Jane's bed. 'Ili arrived moments later, with her eyes half-mast. For the first time, Jane realized 'Ili had been there early that morning and was still on duty.

"I hope you didn't stay late just for me, dear," she said.

But she suspected she had. A person in her shoes often did not think about the secret lives of servants. But with 'Ili, she found she was doing so more and more.

"I work when I'm needed. I'm happy to," 'Ili said.

The bracelet was coiled up in a small box that Dot had tied a ribbon onto, and Jane handed it to her. "A token of my appreciation."

'Ili took the box and opened it. Her eyes went wide as silver dollars, glistening. "Oh." Her gaze darted around to Dot and Thelma, who pretended to be busying themselves with other tasks. "I . . . I . . . don't know what to say."

"There is nothing to say, other than thank you. You've extended a kindness to me that touched me, and what does an aging woman like me need with all this jewelry anyway," Jane said, waving her hands as though this was no big deal. "You can wear it, or should the need ever arise, you can sell it. I imagine it would fetch a nice price."

The smile that spread across 'Ili's face made her own eyes water, and before she knew what was happening, the girl had wrapped her wiry arms around Jane and was sobbing. People did not hug Jane Stanford unless Jane Stanford hugged them first.

"There, there."

'Ili tried it on, and the piece hung on her small wrist in a way it never had on Jane's. "I love it! But I'll be afraid to wear it. What if something should happen to it? What if—"

"Nonsense. Jewelry is meant to be worn and admired. Not kept hidden away. And the rubies suit your skin tone and draw out the red in your lips."

A blush swept over her face. "You are too kind."

"Kindness has nothing to do with it. Now, I'm tired from a long day, so we will see you in the morning."

Jane then gave her a small vial of the serum she brought with her on trips in case of an infection and sent her on her way. Dot and Thelma headed to their own rooms shortly thereafter. Jane finally lay down and read for a bit, curious to see if *The Mighty Atom* got any less depressing—it didn't, so she took the cascara capsules and the bicarbonate of soda, drank a glass of water, and turned out the light. The sounds of the ocean, just a light wash, lulled her almost to sleep. But then, a peculiar feeling came over her, and for no reason at all, she felt like climbing under the bed and hiding out like a scared dog.

THE ROOM
Zoe

A SOFT KNOCK comes at the door, and Storm leaps from the chair and crawls under the bed. When Zoe opens the door, Manu stands there, unsmiling.

"Please, come in," Zoe says. The woman steps over the threshold tentatively and glances around. Both notes are on the table, and Zoe motions to the chair. "Would you like to sit?"

"No, I have to get home, but I thought you would want to know that a woman died in this room a long time ago. Early days, just after the hotel opened."

Zoe feels like the air has been sucked from her lungs. "Oh my God, how?"

"That's all I can tell you."

"Is that all you know?"

Manu glances out at the rain falling down. "It's all I can say, but if you want to learn more, there is a woman who lives at the bottom of Diamond Head. Go see her."

Zoe does not have time to hunt down a woman at Diamond Head. "You said you've been here forever. There must be something more that you know."

"It's not something I talk about with guests."

"It should be, if we are being affected by it. And what does it have to do with the notes? This has happened before, hasn't it?" Zoe asks with mounting anger.

"Not the notes, but there have been things reported over the years by guests in 120."

"Like what?"

"That depends."

"On what?"

Manu turns her dark eyes on Zoe. "If you believe in ghosts or not."

Ghosts are not something Zoe is sure she believes in, but she also doesn't *not* believe in them. And now, at this sugges-tion, the back of her neck begins to tingle. There have been times when she's felt Ginger's presence. Out walking in the hills, or in her room late at night listening to INXS songs.

"I think I deserve to at least know what *other things* have been reported, so I can decide whether or not to switch rooms."

At first Zoe thinks Manu isn't going to answer, but she does. "The strong smell of flowers or perfume. A few people have sworn there was a woman sitting on the lanai in the night. Or the strong feeling that there was someone in the room with them. Strange sounds. It's happened enough that the staff started taking notice. Especially with the history of this room."

"Who was the woman, and how did she die? Please," Zoe begs.

Manu folds her fleshy arms. "Better you hear it from Doris, because I have a feeling you're going to have more questions. Her address is 3000 Hibiscus Drive. She lives alone, but her daughter lives nearby and checks in on her."

"Just show up unannounced?"

"She has no phone."

A burning need to find out what happened consumes her, and she knows she will end up going even though she doesn't have the time for it.

"So tell me," Zoe says, "do you believe a ghost wrote these notes and slid them under my door?"

Manu has a toughness to her, a presence. "No, but I think *you* may have written them."

"Me?" Zoe says, voice cracking.

"In your sleep. It happens."

"You mean it's happened before? In this hotel?"

"Not here, no. But I do know that people walk and talk and do things while they're sleeping, so it's possible," Manu says. "Look, I need to get home. But I don't think you have anything to fear."

"That's easy for you to say. These dreams and notes are terrifying."

Manu heads for the door, then turns. "From what I understand, she was a good woman. You will be fine."

And then she's gone. Zoe sends off a short text to Avery.

All going great! Making tremendous progress. It's stormy though, and I seem to have acquired a cat.

The lies just keep piling up on themselves, and Zoe does not feel good about it.

Avery texts back a few minutes later.

Glad to hear it. Wish I was there with you, storm and all. Hawaii is Hawaii. Have you met my agent friend, Jeff Fallon?

ZOE: Not met any agents. Just other writers.

AVERY: Any handsome writers?

Avery knows all about Zoe's personal life. They've become friends over the years, and Zoe confided in her about the semiautobiographical nature of *The Marriage Pact*, even though there was no single best friend in real life. Just Zoe and her big imagination.

ZOE: No comment.

AVERY: Whaaaat?

ZOE: This trip is not about men. It's about books.

AVERY: True. But don't forget to have fun too. Keep me posted.

Zoe sighs and props herself up on the bed to rest and gain her bearings before going down to the open mic readings, which she feels obligated to attend. The fact that a woman died in this very room makes her suddenly feel like a sheet of ice, and she might crack and get pulled under. Even more strange is the idea that she herself may have written the notes.

She opens her laptop and searches for information on people writing in their sleep. Right away, she sees a link on *sleepwriting*, a type of parasomnia or abnormal sleep behavior that most often occurs during REM sleep. It's rare because writing is a rather complex task, and often people write gibberish, though not always. This makes her feel a little better, that there is a name for what she may be doing. It would explain a lot—but not everything. Like, *why*? Is she losing her mind? Cracking under the pressure?

All of this head-spinning has her sapped. She pulls up the blankets and closes her eyes. Soon, Storm comes out of hiding and joins her.

"What do you think about all this weirdness?" she asks.

Light-footed, the cat prances up and down the bed, then crouches as her tail twitches behind her. Soon she's batting at it, rolling around and trying to catch it, but it always stays just out of reach.

"Sometimes I feel like I'm doing just that," Zoe says.

Storm looks at her, eyes flickering, then continues to go after her tail.

Zoe can't help but laugh. "You don't seem too worried. Maybe I shouldn't be either."

Still, there's a heaviness in her heart.

A CROWD HAS gathered outside under the banyan, with a stool and a microphone set up under a large party tent. Several rows of chairs are set up in front, but it's mostly standing room only. Bill, of all people, is about to start reading. The storm has calmed for the time being, but is supposed to kick back up again later, so they have this small window to enjoy the fresh salty air and sea breeze. Zoe looks for Dylan but doesn't see him anywhere. Tara is sitting close to the front, but there are no empty seats around her, so Zoe takes off her sandals and buries her feet in the sand, listening.

Bill has a conversational tone when reading, and his words are heartfelt with a dash of humor added in just the right place. When his allotted three minutes is up, he stops, but Zoe wants to hear more. Some people have a knack for oral storytelling, and Bill is clearly one of them. She is not. Other brave souls get up and read, some with obvious talent, others who need more practice, but Zoe gives them all credit for baring their souls. Because that's exactly what they are doing whether they realize it or not.

From where she's standing, she can see Diamond Head, and it begins to turn purple. When she looks behind her on the horizon, the bottom of the sun hangs below the clouds in a bloody crescent. The colors are almost unearthly. Zoe feels bad for the reader who has to compete with this dazzling display, and then realizes it's Tara. She's made a few minor tweaks to her opening, and as her words pour out, the crowd grows quiet. You can almost taste the suspense. Zoe needs to introduce her to Avery if she doesn't snag an agent in the next day or two here. It would be fun to have her as an "agency sister."

After Tara, Zoe sneaks to the bar and orders a margarita. She's still feeling on edge, especially at the idea of going to sleep again in her room. So she heads down to the water and watches for the lightning, slowly easing away from the hotel. Soon, she finds herself ankle-deep, skirt getting splashed, but she doesn't mind. In the windlessness, there is warmth. With all the buildings around, there is so much ambient light, and she wishes she could step back in time to when the Moana was the only hotel here. It would have been magical.

When raindrops begin to fall, she makes her way back to the banyan. The reading is over, and people are huddled under the tent or awning. This time she sees Dylan and Sam sitting alone at a table off to the side. Sam looks gorgeous in a strapless dress, her hair worn in a low knot, enhancing her long and elegant neck. There are several empty glasses in front of them, and she's laughing. Zoe feels mildly ill. Then Sam sets her hand on Dylan's wrist, and he doesn't move it away.

Zoe's natural instinct is to hang back in the shadows, which is silly, because why should it matter? Dylan and Sam are friends—allegedly. She and Dylan are friends. Even as she tells herself this, she knows it's not true, at least not on her end. A normal person doesn't repeatedly imagine what it would be like to kiss her friend, or wonder how his hands would feel running over the curves of her body. And the proximity of their hotel rooms only makes it harder to not show up there with some excuse for why she needs to speak to him. Why does she do this to herself, she wonders? Her wild imagination is both her best ally and her worst enemy.

Just as she realizes she is staring, something causes Dylan to glance her way, and their eyes catch. She smiles and waves, then hurries toward the veranda, heat spreading across her cheeks. The lobby is almost empty, and she spends some time looking at the old surfing photos and long wooden surfboards they have on display. Killing time. Avoiding going to the room. These old photographs feel familiar, and a strong sense of déjà vu comes over her.

She wants to text Dylan but stops herself. He has other things to worry about, and she doesn't want to make this his problem. Feeling worn, she takes the elevator upstairs. She'll order room service and get to work and hang out with Storm. But when the elevator doors open, Dylan is standing there, leaning against the wall with his legs crossed.

"Hey, what are you doing?" she asks, with a full-body chill.

"I hustled up the steps so I could catch you," he says, out of breath.

Her hand falls over her heart. "Sorry, I think all these weird notes have me on edge."

"When I saw you coming in from the beach, I wanted to ask about your conversation with Manu and if she clued you in on anything. But with Sam . . . well . . . it can be awkward."

She wants to ask what he means but doesn't. He moves closer, and she can smell the alcohol on his breath. Just a hint.

Otherwise, there's that same pine-and-leather scent that makes her feel like she's on a ranch.

"Yes, she did clue me in—a little bit."

Dylan looks left and then right. "Want to come to my room, and you can tell me everything?"

Not a good idea, but she wants to, more than anything.

"I have this cat in my room I want to feed. How about we go there?" she says.

"Right. Sure."

The minute she opens the door, she's hit by the scent of lavender. Sharp and tart and not her own. "Do you smell that?" she asks.

He sniffs. "Ocean and rain?"

She shakes her head. "Lavender. You don't smell it?"

"I don't."

The lavender soon fades, and he walks to the glass sliding door, looking out into the flickering sky. It's still open a crack for Storm, who Zoe discovers is no longer in the room. She hopes the cat comes back, because the rain is now falling heavy as fish.

"The air feels alive tonight, doesn't it? Like it had us fooled into thinking the storm was ending, but it's only just getting started," he says.

Thunder claps, rattling the windows. A moment later, a black shape flies through the crack in the door and goes straight for the bed. So fast it's all a blur.

Dylan leaps. "Jesus. Tell me that was a cat."

She laughs. "That was Storm," she says, gathering some turkey out of the fridge for her and setting it out on a plate she's borrowed from the restaurant. "She's light on her feet."

"I have a thing for black cats," he says.

"A good thing or a bad thing?"

"Love 'em."

"You're in luck, then."

With another human in the room, it suddenly feels tiny, especially since they can't go out on the lanai. Dylan doesn't seem to know where to sit—the miniature table, the lounge chair, the bed—so he continues to stand.

"Can I offer you something?" Zoe says.

The minibar is quite impressive, with bottles of local Kuleana rum and Koʻolau whiskey. There are mixers and glasses and boxes of crackers. There's cheese in the mini-fridge, along with lilikoi butter and macadamia nuts.

"The rum is incredible, not that I'm a big rum drinker. Half a glass?" he says.

She pours them each half a glass and sets out the cheese and crackers on the table. This will have to tide her over until she can order room service. They both sit, and it feels awkwardly intimate.

He holds up his glass. "Cheers. To Hawaiʻi."

"To Hawaiʻi."

When she clinks her glass with his, their eyes meet, and he hangs on to her gaze with an intensity that makes her squirm. "So, tell me," he finally says.

Zoe sips her rum. Strong and smooth and not too sweet. "A woman died in this room soon after it first opened, and Manu gave me the address of someone who would be able to tell me all about it. I get the feeling she thinks it's haunted."

"That's her answer?"

She shrugs. "I know, it says nothing as to who was writing the notes. She even suggested that maybe I had, in my sleep."

"Huh. That's an interesting concept. Have you ever done anything like that before?"

"Never. I'm a dreamer, though, and my dreams have been escalating here, but I can't imagine writing those notes. *I've been poisoned?* Come on."

Just talking about it brings goose bumps to her arms, and she takes another gulp of the rum.

"Have you been under any kind of undue stress before coming here? Or maybe it's bringing back memories of your friend Ginger. Since this was the trip you never took together? *That* would make sense."

She ignores the undue stress part, and her hand goes to her pocket watch as it often does when she's thinking of Ginger. "She's been on my mind a lot, for sure, but she wasn't poisoned. And in my dreams, I'm in this room or some version of it."

"Our minds are capable of orchestrating incredible things in order to protect ourselves. I wouldn't rule out that you've written the notes. But I'd also be curious about the death in the room. Did she say anything else about it?"

Zoe tells him about the strange incidents in between sips of the rum, which has an incredibly warm and relaxing effect on her, spreading out into all her limbs like honey.

"Do you believe in ghosts?" he asks.

"I believe in the possibility of ghosts, but I've never seen one myself. Do you?"

A cold gust blows in through the crack in the door, and she gets up to close it. It seems the wind is changing directions again, blowing the banyan branches around in a stormy dance. An unsettled energy seems to hover around them. Does he feel it too?

"Not in the usual sense of the word. But I do believe there are phenomena happening around us that we can't explain. Psychic intuition, that kind of thing," he says.

"Have you ever used a psychic to help you solve a crime?"

He nods. "There was a woman who used to help us find missing people. More often than not, she got it right, and the families were able to gain some closure. But she couldn't tell us any more than where their bodies were. Not how they died or who killed them."

"Some can do that though, can't they?" she asks, wishing they could have hired a psychic for Ginger's case.

"Some can."

Maybe it's not too late. Maybe she could find someone to tell her how Ginger died and set her mind at ease, one way or another. Going through life always wondering is like having a thorn in her heart. She finishes the rum and runs her tongue along her lips absentmindedly, savoring its taste, then catches Dylan watching her.

"Let's just say there is some kind of spirit or energy here. Does it feel threatening to you?" he asks.

She thinks for a moment. "Not really. If anything, it's like a cry for help."

An explosion of thunder and flash of lightning come a few seconds apart, and they both jump. The lights blink a few times and go dark. Zoe squeals, then feels Dylan's hand on her arm, reaching around for her hand. His is big and rough and comforting, and it sends a line of heat straight to her toes.

"Bad timing," she says.

At first he says nothing, then, "I guess it depends."

He moves close enough so she feels his breath hot on her cheek. Her heart begins hammering against her rib cage, and the backs of her knees weaken. Now would be a good time to mention who she is, but the moment is so electrically charged, all she can do is breathe—and wait to see what happens next.

And then his phone chimes. She thinks he's going to turn it off, but he pulls it out and says, "Sorry," and reads the message. "Shit. I have to go."

"Why?"

A pause, then, "I promise, I'll explain tomorrow."

The mood is shattered and she steps away, feeling like what was about to happen would have been a bad idea anyway. She would most likely end up just being a fling in Hawaiʻi to add to his belt, whereas she may actually be developing feelings for him.

"No worries," she says flippantly.

"Bridget, I'm serious. It's a long story, and I don't want to get into it tonight, but I'll tell you tomorrow after class."

"I'm going to Diamond Head after class," she says.

There are no afternoon sessions tomorrow—the time has been left open for writing, especially for those signed up to pitch agents—so she wants to see Doris as soon as she's done.

"I'll go with you." He places his hands on her arm, leans over and kisses her above the eye. It's dark, so she cuts him some slack. "I'll find you at lunch," he says.

And then he's out the door, and she's now confused and alone with a frightened cat and the sense that there is someone or something else sharing the room with her.

THE END

Jane

February 28

A JIGGLE IN Jane's leg started up and would not quit. Then her foot cramped. A dark shadow seemed to be working its way in from the ends of her limbs. Or maybe it was the other way around. Her stomach felt tight as a plank. She looked to the window and took a few deep breaths, telling herself she was simply having a bad case of indigestion. Then her entire body seized, violently, throwing her from the bed onto the floor.

She lay there for a moment, stunned, groaning. But with her body in such a state of rigidity, it was impossible to rise. More deep breaths. Through all of this, she was acutely aware of the clatter of voices carrying up from the beach, the way her thick tongue pressed against her teeth, the scent of fresh-cut gardenias sitting on the table, as though she were a separate entity watching it happen.

With one final push, Jane rose to all fours and crawled to the door, hanging all of her weight on the door handle. At first she was unable to get herself up, but finally managed to stand as an unearthly sound emerged from her throat. There, before her, a man appeared. She squinted through strained eyes. Mr. Heunisch, from the room across the hall. She waved at him even though he was only three feet away.

He rushed to her side. "Can I help you, Mrs. Stanford?"

She leaned back on the doorframe for support. "Oh, I am so ill. Get me a doctor!"

That she was able to form words seemed a small miracle. Without another question, he turned and bolted toward the stairs. As she stood there, alone in the semidarkness, the reality of her predicament became clear as spring water.

This was not indigestion.

This was poisoning.

"Dot—Thelma—help me!" she yelled.

Nothing happened. No one came.

"Someone, help me!"

Moments later, both Dot and Thelma came rushing down the hallway, both in robes.

Jane pressed her forehead to the cool, hard wood. "I'm so sick. Fetch me a doctor," she moaned.

"Is it your stomach?" Thelma asked.

Jane shook her head weakly. "I was thrown from my bed in spasm. Please, get help."

Earlier in the week, she had made the acquaintance of a doctor living in the hotel. From what she had gathered, he resided upstairs as part of a trade to take care of the Moana's fashionable guests.

Thelma dashed off, while Dot flipped on the light switch, then came and grabbed Jane by the arm, placing a hand on her lower back. "Come, let's get you to the bed."

"No!" Jane said with great difficulty, the hinges of her jaw rusted into place.

Terror salted the blood in her veins, and she felt cold. Icy cold.

Dot kneaded Jane's shoulder, hurting her. "Stop," Jane gasped.

Thelma reappeared, cheeks flushed. "Dr. Humphris is on

his way. Back into the room we go," she said, taking Jane's hand away from Dot.

Jane tried to take a step, but her leg felt like a foreign attachment—a tree trunk of oak or chestnut, dense and heavy. "I can't. Oh, God, what is happening?"

"Then the chair, at least."

With great effort and help from the girls, she somehow ended up in the chair closest to the door. Her back went tight again, and pain clawed at every square inch of her body. "It's poison! Help me get it out," she croaked.

Thelma hurried to fill a glass with water in the bathroom and came back, holding it to Jane's lips. "Drink."

Their eyes met and held. Light swept across Thelma's cheeks, showing a faint trail of freckles. Jane's mind and eyes seemed to be the only parts of her functioning properly. She shook her head, unable now to even open her mouth. Thelma dipped a washcloth into the water and rubbed it over her face, warm and smooth, and slowly the spasms ceased. Jane nodded at the glass, and Thelma held it up again. This time Jane drank down the whole thing. They then helped her up and led her to the washstand.

"The more water the better," Thelma said, voice taut.

By then, another spasm took hold, and Jane's mouth would not open. "My jaw is set," she said between clenched teeth.

Dot began to massage her cheeks with strong pressure, looking frenzied and near tears.

Then a disheveled Dr. Humphris rushed in, and before he could say anything, Jane told him, "I need a stomach pump. I've been poisoned."

He held up her wrist and felt her pulse, face close to hers. "A dramatic conclusion. What leads you to believe this?"

"I was poisoned last month."

He turned to Thelma, who nodded. "Only a month ago,

someone put rat poison in her Poland Spring water. So her concern is legitimate."

"We need to act fast, then. Have you taken any other medicine?"

Jane found her jaw had loosened slightly. "Cascara and bicarbonate of soda."

He walked over to the bedside, opened the bottle of bicarbonate of soda, licked his finger and touched the power, then tasted it. His face puckered. "Bitter," he said, then slid that and the cascara bottle into his pocket.

The sound of footsteps came thumping down the hallway, and 'Ili showed up in the shadows of the hall. She hung in the background, and no one noticed her but Jane.

"I'll need to run to my room for a mustard emetic and call for a stomach pump. Remind her to breathe, deeply," he commanded the girls.

Not only was Jane's body in spasm, it had begun to heat up like a furnace, and her eyes burned and teared. There was little chance this would end well, and she knew it.

"You'll come out of this, Mrs. Stanford, just you wait and see," Dot said.

Damn, the girl was naive. And then another spasm hit, gripping Jane's hands and feet and turning her inside out. Or so it felt. The doctor returned, managed to pry her dentures from her mouth and gave her a foul-tasting emetic. The indignity of it all was almost too much to bear.

"Take this. It should do the job," he said.

She gagged, producing only a small amount of vomit. More rubbing of her limbs, people flying in and out of the room. All the while, Dot held her hand with an iron grip. Dr. Humphris was mixing up some other sharp-smelling concoction.

"It's chloral and bromine," he said, as though any layperson would know what that meant.

A new and stronger wave began in her body, arching her feet and bowing her legs, and she shook her head when he held it to her mouth. "Oh God, forgive me my sins. Is my soul prepared to meet my dear ones?" Across the room, her boys, her Lelands, stood. She felt a loosening of her soul, but her corporeal self was still in agony. "This is a horrible death to die," she groaned.

And in that moment, before she left this world for good, she knew who had done her in. The idea of it burned more strongly than the poison. If only she hadn't been so blind. Then, all at once, the pain faded and the lights went out. A sense of fullness stretched through her, soft and humming. Dragonflies and white long-tailed birds surrounded her, all draped in light. A shark swam past. People were still in the room—she could feel them—but a force pulled at her with a strong, sucking energy.

Let go, Jane, let go.

THE HOUSE
Zoe

SLEEP TAKES A long time to arrive, and when it does, Zoe tosses and turns and is jolted awake several times by thunder and lightning. Storm curls up, warm against her belly, and she cares not whether she wakes up with hives or her face swollen shut. She needs this living, breathing, purring creature next to her to get her through the night. The story of her life, she realizes—love and suffering, hand in hand.

When she wakes in the morning, she's tangled in the sheets, and her skin feels damp and clammy. It smells like sweat. Storm is now up by her head, and Zoe's eyes itch like mad. Gingerly she touches her face, which feels puffy and tight. She knew having the cat in here would be catastrophic, but it beats being alone, and Storm is such a sweet little critter.

"Thanks, friend, for seeing me through the night. But now I'm screwed," she says, rolling out of bed to go rummage for allergy meds in her toiletry bag.

The room feels different somehow, and then she realizes there is actual light coming in from outside. There's a wide crack in the clouds, and sunbeams spill over the ocean like golden islands. On her way to the bathroom, she stops. There's a piece of paper on the table where she and Dylan had been sitting, underneath one of the rum glasses. Maybe he left a note. But really, how could he have, in the dark? There's only one word written on the paper.

strychnine

This one is lowercase, and it's her own handwriting, without a doubt. Damn, Manu had been right. The idea that she's been writing these all along causes her to sink onto the floor, legs folding beneath her. Fear swarms around her, and strangely it feels more like someone else's fear than her own.

"What happened in here?" she whispers, holding the paper in her hands.

If only the walls could talk. Or maybe they are? And then the dream drops into her mind. This one is of a teenage boy standing at the edge of a pond, holding his arms open wide. His expression is one of pure joy, and she runs toward him full of so much love it threatens to break her. But before she reaches him, her legs seize up and she falls to the ground, crying out. Instead of coming for her, the boy dissolves into the pond. She claws at the dirt, pulling herself forward trying to get to him, knowing she is dying.

The dream ends there, or at least that's all she remembers, and it leaves her feeling hollow and haunted. She needs to figure out what went down in this room, and why she of all people is having these dreams. Afternoon cannot come soon enough.

ZOE HAS TO pass the ballroom where Dylan is teaching on her way to the character workshop she's signed up for, and sees him leaning against the doorframe, looking like he's waiting for someone. When he sees her, he waves her over, ignoring all the people filing past him. She has no choice but to stop, despite the fact that her eyes are puffy and her neck is decorated in angry red splotches. She did find pills, but they haven't kicked in yet.

Before he can say anything, she says, "The cat. I'm allergic."

"Damn. Sorry. How'd everything else go last night?"

There's too much to say right now with all the people around, so she tells him, "Later."

"Come to my workshop today. We can talk during the break," he says.

She feels weird about how last night ended, and wonders what, if not an emergency, would have warranted him to leave her so rudely. "Thank you, but I'm already committed to another class."

"I know it's not romance, but maybe it'll spark something. A ghost story, perhaps?"

It's hard to tell if he's serious, but his words shake something loose inside her, and her muse begins to whisper, *what if.* A ghost story in an old hotel in Hawai'i. Or a murder mystery. She wants to give him the cold shoulder and hurry off, but he's hooked her.

"What do you have on tap?" she asks.

"Catching your killer and nailing your ending. I know, not very romantic, but all books need a stellar end to them." He waits for a man to shuffle past him, through the door, then lowers his voice and says, "It would mean a lot to me to have you here."

The words form a crack in her armor. "I suppose I could, if you promise I'll have a fully formed book idea when I walk out of here."

Wishful thinking, but stranger things have happened.

He grins, holds out a hand. "I promise you won't be sorry. That's my best offer."

She takes it, and as he pulls her inside, she can't help but smile.

DYLAN SEEMS MORE relaxed today than he did on Monday, but there are bags under his eyes, and he looks as though he hardly slept. Despite that, he speaks eloquently about how to set up your novel so the villain isn't revealed until the end, and readers don't guess who it is early on. It's all about knowing your character inside and out, and slowly and deliberately layering your narrative with detail. He gives examples about real clues and false clues, inserting the clue before it has context, misinterpreted clues, and emphasizing the wrong information. Zoe is captivated. She forgets all about last night and is entirely caught up in how for Dylan, it's a true art form.

Every now and then, he catches her eye, and when he does, his look is probing, as if he's searching her face for answers. She finds it slightly unnerving, but it also makes her want raise her hand and ask him questions. Questions like, *Excuse me, but what do you do when you might be falling for the teacher of your writing workshop?* And then she remembers her swollen eyes and blotchy neck and wonders if maybe that's why he keeps looking at her. She pulls her sweater higher and fluffs her hair so it falls over her face.

During the break, some people exit, others chat with their neighbors and a handful walk up to Dylan, forming a line. They ask him questions and gather advice, just wanting to get close to a real live author. Zoe watches from her chair. He's gracious and thoughtful and gives them his full attention. There is nothing pretentious in his mannerisms, and just seeing how he interacts with people makes her hope against hope that he has a good reason for walking out last night. Because for some unknowable reason, Dylan Winters feels different than all the other men in her past.

When they break for lunch, people line up again, and Zoe heads outside. She texts Dylan to meet her in the lobby in half an hour if he still wants to come with her to meet Doris. At the buffet, picking up a sandwich, she runs into Tara.

"I missed you this morning in Jenni Chan's class," Tara says, then squints at her. "What happened to your face?"

"The cat—she slept by my head. How was it?"

"Awesome, just like we expected it would be. Where were you?"

"Dylan Winters," was all she said.

A smile. "I wondered about that. How's it going?"

"There's somewhere I need to be, but I want to talk to you and fill you in on everything. Can you meet me later?" Zoe asks.

She wants to get Tara's take on things—both the notes and the Dylan dilemma.

"I promised Bill I would go to Pearl Harbor with him and a few others. Want to join us?"

"I wish I could, but I found out that a woman died in my room a long time ago, and I'm meeting a lady who knows the whole story. It's been bizarre to say the least."

Tara turns white. "What?"

"I know. Meet me for coffee at seven thirty in the morning, the veranda? We can catch up."

"I'm dying to hear," Tara says.

"Trust me, so am I."

ZOE WAITS AND WAITS, but Dylan does not show up. Finally, she decides to head off without him. The skies threaten rain, so she borrows an umbrella from the front desk and heads up Kalakaua Avenue, passing surfboard racks and what must be the best-located police station in the world. When she walks by the Duke Kahanamoku statue, still feeling disappointed, she hears someone calling out.

"Bridget! Wait up!"

It takes a moment to register who it is. Then she turns and waits for Dylan to catch up. He's changed into khaki walking shorts and a black T-shirt. He looks like an Abercrombie model.

"Sorry, everyone had questions, and then I had to check on Sammy."

At the mention of Sam, she feels her body tighten. "What's wrong with Sam?"

He runs his hand through his hair and says, "Let's walk as we talk." And so they do. "She swore me to secrecy, but I asked if I could tell you because of how it affected you—us— last night. And she said I could."

"That was nice of her," Zoe says.

"Soon after college, Sam married a guy named Willie who moved from Wall Street to Jackson Hole to try and turn his life around. He was older and threw his money around and I never entirely trusted the guy, but Sam was all in. A big house, two kids, Newfoundlands, the whole nine yards. Everything was fine until about a couple months ago, when he told her he was leaving her and moving back to New York. No explanation other than he wasn't happy in Wyoming anymore, and he knew she wouldn't want to be in the city."

He pauses as they skirt a large puddle, and Zoe is now anxious to hear how this ends.

"Needless to say, she begged him to stay and suggested counseling, but he said his mind was made up. She thinks he was having an affair, but he won't fess up. So I talked her into coming to this conference—she's a great writer and I knew she needed to just get out of there for a while. But she started feeling sick the day after we got here, nauseated, throwing up. She kept chalking it up to emotional stress, but last night, she took a pregnancy test, and it was positive. That's when she texted me."

Zoe's whole body relaxes because Dylan has actually presented a noble reason for running off, but she feels awful for Sam. "Oh my gosh, that complicates things, doesn't it?"

"Sam is kicking herself because Willie left for a few weeks, and when he came back to visit the kids, she slept with him against her better judgment. Now this."

"It happens all the time," Zoe says. He shoots her a sideways glance. "From what I hear," she adds.

"I know it was incredibly lame to run out on you in the dark, but I hope you can see why now. It was the last thing I wanted to do," he says, his voice softening.

Neither have acknowledged what is happening here, but whatever it is, it feels real. If you don't count the fact that he has no idea who she really is.

"You did the right thing."

And when he smiles at her, she knows she's a goner. She'll come clean tonight about her big white lie that she's let go on much too long. Is it even white? It feels more dark gray.

THEY ARRIVE AT the door of a gray clapboard house with chipped paint and a yard full of bushy trees and unruly vines. Dead leaves blanket the ground, and the smell of decay floats around them. Blinds are drawn. It almost feels abandoned, but there are several pairs of slippers on the doorstep. Zoe walks up and knocks while Dylan peers around the side of the house.

She thinks she hears stirring, and then the door opens. An old woman looks at her with foggy blue eyes behind thick spectacles. She's in a white eyelet muʻumuʻu and a woven hat.

"I don't need any more eggs," the woman says.

"Doris?" Zoe asks.

Dylan is suddenly standing beside her and in a friendly voice says, "I'm Dylan Winters, and this is Bridget, and we aren't selling eggs. We're guests at the Moana Hotel, and Manu, who works there, told us you might be able to shed some light on a death there some years back."

Her wrinkled face pinches together. "What business do you have with that?"

"I'm staying in the room where the woman died," Zoe says.

Doris pushes up her glasses and looks Zoe up and down. "And?"

"And I need to know what happened, mainly for my own peace of mind."

"Come in, then. I'll tell you what I know. But my brain is not what it used to be, so I'm not to be entirely trusted."

They walk into a small living room, walls lined with oversized framed black-and-white photos. In fact, everything in the house is black and white. The floor is white, the furniture various shades of gray and black, and the tile in the kitchen is black-and-white checkered. Doris turns off the television, and Zoe and Dylan sit around a small table backed by a wall-to-wall bookshelf.

"I used to be a photographer," Doris says, sweeping her arm around. "I captured old Hawai'i."

"Beautifully, I might add," Dylan says.

"Oh, yes. It was beautiful back then, hard to take a bad photo. I was here through it all and carried my camera everywhere. But my aunt 'Ili, she was the lucky one. One generation back. She worked at the Moana."

And here it is. The link Zoe has been waiting for. "What years was she there?"

Doris thinks for a moment. "Early nineteen hundreds? She was hired when she was eighteen or nineteen, and not long after she started was when that woman you want to know about died there. It was a big scandal and the talk of the town for quite a while, from what I recall."

"How did the woman die?"

"She was poisoned."

The room tilts on its axis at the word *poisoned*, and Zoe steadies herself, even though she's already sitting down.

"My aunt was there, witnessed the whole thing," Doris says. Then her face turns cloudy as though trying to remember. "Wait, maybe she didn't, but she knew the woman. They had become friends. Aunty 'Ili was like that. She drew people in."

Doris pauses and looks up toward the ceiling, fiddling with her short silver hair. Zoe has so many questions she wants to pepper her with, but she follows Dylan's lead and remains quiet. A lizard climbs up the wall, and Zoe watches its tiny, delicate toes. The collective feeling in the room is almost as though the walls are breathing.

And then Doris continues. "This woman. She was high *maka maka*—a big deal. Jen, I think her name was? No, maybe it was Jane." Her voice falls away, and she stares at a photo on the wall for a while. "Her last name eludes me, but she had something to do with a big university. My aunt was certain she was poisoned, but in the end, I don't think everyone agreed. The cause of death became muddled."

"What do you mean?" Zoe asks.

Doris shrugs her hunched shoulders. "She was old. And old people die."

Zoe figures if it was an important person, they should be able to find something on the internet.

"What else can you tell us about your aunt?" Dylan says.

"You know, I've just realized how rude I am to not have offered you anything. My manners are slipping," Doris says, getting up.

"Please, we don't expect anything."

Regardless, she rummages around in the pantry, returning with a tin of macadamia shortbread cookies and setting one on a china plate for each of them.

Only then does she answer. "'Ili married my dad's brother, Sarge, so we weren't blood related, but she loved me like a daughter. They never had kids of their own. She went on to become a nurse—I think watching someone die in such a bad way affected her deeply." A light went on in her eyes. "So yes, I guess there's your answer. She did witness the death. And then when Pearl Harbor was attacked, you can bet she was one of the first to arrive at Tripler, medical bag in hand. She was headstrong and talented—beautiful voice, graceful hula dancer—and not a day goes by that I don't think about her," she says, eyes tearing up.

"Can we see a photograph?" Zoe asks.

Doris points to the wall behind them, where a slender woman with long, thick hair and dark lips stands on the beach in front of a tall wooden surfboard. "That's her."

"She's gorgeous," Zoe says.

"I have a box of photos somewhere, and some of her belongings. Mementos, letters, that kind of thing," Doris says, staring at the photo.

Dylan and Zoe share a look.

"Would there be anything in there about the poisoning?" Dylan asks.

"You know, I can't remember. It went up into the attic years ago, and that's where it's stayed. When you get old, it gets harder to keep track of a lifetime of your own memories, let alone someone else's."

Doris offers them each another cookie, and chews hers slowly with her eyes closed. Dylan swallows his in one bite.

Zoe isn't quite ready to leave. "Is there any chance we could look through her stuff? With you, of course."

"Oh, you'll never find it up there."

"I'm an expert at finding lost things," Dylan says, flashing her a smile.

Is he actually flirting with a ninety-year-old lady?

"There are rats and lizards up there and God knows what else. Let me talk to my daughter tonight. She may know where to find it." She searches both their faces for a moment. "What was it you needed it for, again?"

"If a woman died at the Moana, and there was wrongdoing, it would be nice to learn the truth," Zoe says, feeling a sudden *need* to get to the bottom of this.

"Facts don't cease to exist because they are ignored, do they?" Doris says.

Dylan looks impressed. "You've read Aldous Huxley, I see."

Her eyes dart to the books. "It's a peculiar thing, you know, how their wisdom still sneaks out of me when I least expect it," she says with a chuckle.

"We hold on to what matters most," Dylan said.

For the first time, Zoe notices the book titles on the shelves. Classics, big books—important books. Doris was clearly an intellectual of some kind. "Were you a teacher?"

"My husband was. I just read for fun."

"It's an impressive collection," Dylan says.

"I won't be reading any of these again in my lifetime, but here they sit, collecting dust. Words and worms. Books are one of the hardest things to let go of."

Zoe has the same problem. Her shelves are overflowing.

With that, Doris stands and collects the plates. "If you'll excuse me, it's time for my afternoon nap."

They thank her, and Dylan leaves his card on the table in case she remembers anything else, or her daughter knows where 'Ili's stuff is. They say their goodbyes and the door is halfway shut when Doris opens it again and pokes her wrinkly face out.

"You know, now that I think about it, Aunty 'Ili always kept a journal."

Zoe turns. "Oh?"

"Come back tomorrow and we'll see if we can find it."

THE RESEARCH
Zoe

BACK IN THE room and after a hot shower, Zoe sits on her bed with a bag of taro chips and a ginger brew, and sets her laptop on a pillow. Chilled to the bone from their walk back to the hotel, with spitting rain and sideways wind, huddled with Dylan under the umbrella, she now is swaddled in a thick terry cloth Moana robe. The swelling in her eyes has calmed a little, though they still itch, and thank God the maid has replaced all of her bedding, as requested.

According to Dylan, the Kona low should move off in the next day or two, just in time for them to head home. It's rare for storms to last this long here, but every so often, the winds align and keep the moisture hovering. He's having dinner with his agent tonight, who has just flown in for the author/agent panel tomorrow. She forgot to ask which literary agency he's with. Probably a big one.

The first words she types in are *moana hotel murder* and then almost chokes on her chips when she sees what comes up. *Jane Stanford, co-founder of Stanford University, died at the Moana Hotel from strychnine poisoning.* And below that, another article titled *Murder at the Moana: The Death of Jane Stanford.* Every hair on her body stands on end. How is it that she's never heard of this?

Zoe's father went to Stanford and was a die-hard Cardinal, but in all his stories about the university, he's never mentioned Jane.

She clicks on the second link, an article that sums up the story in two paragraphs and includes a photograph of an old newspaper clipping titled *Mrs. Stanford is dead in Honolulu.* Subtitles read *During her final minutes, she states she was poisoned* and *Police confirm strychnine in her medicine.* The rest of the page contains other columns with equally splashy heads. *Agonizing convulsions affect benefactress* and *Contents of recent will are being kept private.*

Zoe feels her whole body tighten, and fragments of the dreams she's had this past week roll through her mind. It is simply too much to be a coincidence. She reads on to glean more details, all the while wondering how any of this can be real. The sketch of Jane shows her profile, hair in a loose bun, strong, almost masculine features, and wearing a high-necked dress. Zoe feels a sudden wave of compassion for the poor woman, and she reads the top story.

On the night of February 28, 1905, Jane Stanford, the widow of the late Leland Stanford, California senator and president of Central Pacific Railroad Co., unexpectedly perished in her room at the Moana Hotel. Circumstances are questionable and have aroused suspicion of murder by way of strychnine poisoning. Stanford's longtime secretary Thelma Bellingham and maid Dot Hale are both under police surveillance though no charges have been brought. Strychnine was reportedly found in the bicarbonate of soda she imbibed before retiring, and a coroner's jury of medical experts is in agreement that Mrs. Stanford's death was at the hand of some person or persons, presently undetermined. In a shocking twist, a similar attempt on her life had been made on January 14 in her Nob Hill mansion, involving rat poison in her Poland Spring water. What had previously been considered an accidental tainting of her water is now being called into question. Suspects are adding up left and right in this most sinister case.

When she finishes reading, Zoe holds back a sob. It seems inconceivable that she knows nothing of this woman, yet has felt her fear and pain so palpably over the past week. She pulls the blanket up around her. Something has remained in this space over the past century, and Zoe has for some reason been chosen to receive messages. An actual ghost? Or just the residue of a heinous crime. She rereads the article again, this time noting the date. One hundred years ago, almost to the day. A new wave of goose bumps covers her entire body.

Closing her eyes, she relives the dream in which her body had gone rigid and her throat burned with the bitter taste of what she now knows is strychnine. It's almost too much to bear.

"A horrible death to die," she says, but the voice is not her own and is strained and strangled and frightens her to the point that she questions if perhaps she is losing her mind.

The world is full of weird happenings. She knows this. There are books and movies and documentaries and countless stories of this kind of thing. But until this very moment, she has never stood so close to the edge of the unexplainable, ready to tumble into the abyss. She wishes Dylan were here to hold her back. Storm, who had been on the chair grooming herself, looks over at Zoe with what feels like concern.

Zoe pats the bed next to her. "Come over here, sweets."

The cat assesses the distance between the chair and the bed and takes a flying leap, just making it onto the edge of the bed.

It's an amazing feat of acrobatics, and Zoe is impressed. While Storm makes biscuits on her leg, Zoe reads on and on about Jane's incredible and tragic life, then pulls up more recent stories about her mysterious death.

The description from Dr. Humphris, the first doctor on the scene, nearly causes her own heart to stop. *Whereupon she was seized by a tetanic spasm that progressed relentlessly to a state of severe rigidity: her jaws clamped shut, her thighs opened widely, her feet twisted inwards, her fingers and thumbs clenched into tight fists, and her head drew back. Finally, her respiration ceased.*

Many people have theories, but no one was ever convicted of the crime, despite private investigators and police in both Hawai'i and California looking into the matter. The more Zoe reads, the more incensed she becomes. Because though there were not one but two doctors who came to her aid as she was dying, and both affirmed that the manner in which she died was consistent with strychnine poisoning, and everyone involved in Hawai'i—including four of Honolulu's most respected physicians, the Hawai'i high sheriff, the toxicologist and even the mortician who also witnessed the autopsy—asserted that she was murdered, the official cause of death was ruled natural causes. *Heart attack.*

A familiar anger claws at her. How the hell can this be, when poison was found twice in her drinks? Zoe carefully moves Storm to the side, gets up and pours herself a glass of rum. Hungering for fresh air, she stands out on the lanai and lets the salty breeze whip her hair into a frenzy. Leftover sunlight tints the cloud-lined horizon orange, but other than that, the sky has gone to sleep for the evening.

It feels only too convenient that Jane Stanford, lone female player in a very male world, knew she had been poisoned— even told the doctors, for fuck's sake—but was ultimately silenced. That's what power does, Zoe thinks. It still happens all the time, though maybe a little less blatantly. If the murder had happened a hundred years later, would the facts surrounding it have been so malleable? She drains the glass of rum, which runs through her veins and cuts the sharp edge of her rage.

Numbed, she goes back in and reads on about David Starr Jordan, president of the university. According to many sources, Jane was planning on removing Jordan from the presidency due to recent controversies he'd been involved in—faculty issues and political leanings and general differences in opinion. But most agree he was not involved in the actual poisonings, which seems curious to Zoe, because as an ichthyologist, he would have had a very good handle on the chemistry of strychnine.

Rather than Jordan, most fingers point to Thelma, her longtime secretary, as the likely culprit. But did she work alone? That is the million-dollar question. Zoe is rapt, and her mind begins threading together fragments of this unfathomable story. It happens on its own, but by the time she's done reading about Jane Stanford, the tragic loss of her son, her key role in the founding of the university, and her unsolved murder, she has a book sketched out in her mind.

The furthest thing possible from a romance, but the pull is so strong, it feels like someone has tied a rope around her and is leading her to water. Now she just needs to drink.

THE BEACH

Zoe

LATER THAT EVENING, the wind dies down, and Zoe decides she needs to get out of the room and clear her head. Her pocket watch says it's nine o'clock. Perfect, the beach will be empty and the bar quiet. She heads toward Diamond Head as she watches for any sign of moon or stars. None appear, but the sound of the water lapping on the shore lulls her and brings her back down to earth.

Feet in the cool sand, she remembers the summer before graduation, when she and Ginger went to the Oregon coast to stay with Ginger's aunt Maxine for a week. Maxine was usually down a bottle or two of wine by mid-afternoon, and the two girls went feral—baking in the sun topless, blasting Nirvana and Guns N' Roses and dancing in the moonlight, and getting high with Johnny, the neighborhood chronic. They existed the entire time without showering, salt from the ocean coating their bronzed skin and sun-streaked hair. One night, just after the sun went down, Ginger got the bright idea to go skinny-dipping, and Zoe ended up hypothermic. Her teeth chatter now just thinking about it.

Skinny-dipping here would be an entirely different experience. Ginger would have insisted they do it every single night, rain or shine, and God, how she misses her friend. How is it that Zoe gets to be here on the shores of Waikiki, while Gin had the life knocked out of her as she was just on the brink of womanhood? Fairness, it seems, has no rhyme or reason, and chooses favorites at whim.

The water, though not warm, feels silky on the skin of her ankles and calves as she wades in up to her knees, broken-hearted all over again. As she stands there facing a dark sea, the image of the white tip shark swims back into her consciousness. For a brief moment, she almost sees a shadow of the old pier jutting out into the ocean. She shivers, but not from the cold.

She makes it to the end of the beach, then heads back to the hotel as rain falls, feeling prickly and frightened to go to sleep. A part of her wishes Dylan had called or texted, but he hasn't. Her phone has been in her pocket, though, just in case. Back in the room, she takes a steaming shower, then pours another glass of rum in the hopes that maybe it will help her fall asleep. The gold liquid burns as it goes down her throat. Storm watches her and lets out a soft meow.

"I'm okay. I think," Zoe says to the cat. "But why do people have to be such assholes?"

But she's not okay, not really. Dressed in leggings and a long T-shirt, she considers going to Dylan's room and knocking on his door. The pull is strong, and she leans her forehead on her own door, hand on the knob. What is it with the two of them? Why, even now, can she not stop thinking about him?

Then, a light knock comes. Zoe startles, and Storm flies under the bed. It comes again, a little louder.

"Bridget?" a voice says.

It's Dylan. Surprised, she opens the door a crack. "Hey."

"I hope you don't mind my stopping by so late," he says, voice low.

Seeing him breaks something loose inside her. "Not at all. I was just . . . well, struggling."

He steps closer and pushes the door so it opens all the way. "What's going on?"

Zoe leans back on the door as he passes, then closes it behind her. He turns and faces her so they are only inches away from each other, close enough that she can feel his heat. His jaw flexes. Tonight, backlit by her bedside lamp, he looks as though he's glowing. Neither says anything. Neither looks away. Gently, he reaches out and runs the side of his hand from her cheekbone to her jaw.

"Because whatever it is, I want to make it right," he says.

Zoe feels herself sway. "There's so much to tell you."

She watches in slow motion as he moves in for a kiss. It's so light, she wonders if she's imagining this moment. In another dream state. But the fire between her thighs is real, no doubt about that. He pulls back and looks at her, as if wanting permission, so Zoe stands on her tippy toes and presses her lips against his, featherlight. His tongue reaches out and meets hers, and he tastes like sugarcane and rum. One of his fingers traces up along her wrist and forearm. There is no hurry to his movements, and she feels as though she's suspended in time and space.

Pretty soon, one of his hands works its way down her back and presses her into him. At the same time, his kisses grow harder and deeper, and she aches to feel every inch of his body against hers. Avoiding men for so long has created this longing that now threatens to unravel her. His mouth moves down her throat ever so lightly, and a gasp escapes her lips. She's aware that he's slowly backing her toward the bed.

"You are so damn . . . sexy," he says, face buried in her hair.

THE GUEST IN ROOM 120

He's the sexy one, but she can't say a word because he starts kissing her again. His thigh moves between her legs, and she rests on it, heat gathering up her middle. Wind has kicked up again and lashes furiously on the glass door, and the wildness of night makes her feel reckless. Tomorrow, they say, will be sunny.

Tell him, her inner voice says. But she doesn't listen because of his mouth and his hands and his taste. She wants to disappear into him, if only for the night. He kisses down one side of her neck, across her collarbone, then up the other side before coming up for air.

"Remember that first morning? When you showed up in my class?" he says.

How could she forget. "No, remind me."

He grins. "Well, here I was, trying to pull myself together—I'm always nervous on day one—when the door opened and this woman walked in late. I recognized her from the elevator. She was trying not to be noticed, but how could anyone not notice her? Tall, wild-haired, stunning."

Zoe laughs. "Oh, come on."

He takes her by the shoulders. "Let me finish. Then you came up front and completely threw me off balance. It was like my mind kept short-circuiting and I was forgetting what I wanted to say."

She thinks back and remembers how a few of his looks felt hot on her skin, but other than that, she was too self-conscious of her own bumbling intrusion into the class to notice much. "Absolutely not. You were smooth as butter."

He takes her by the hand and sits her down at the table, not the bed, and she's a little disappointed. He pours them both a splash of run. "Now tell me everything you've found out. We'll have time for other stuff . . . later."

So she does. She talks until her throat is raw. And he listens like a champ, hangs on every word as though his life depends on it.

DYLAN STAYS THE night and she falls asleep in his arms, fully clothed, exhausted, happy. But in the middle of the night, she lies awake, wondering how he will react when she tells him in the morning. Because no matter how awkward and painful and weird it is, she *will* set the record straight. *So, I need to tell you something, but first, promise you won't hate me?*

When she wakes, he's already gone. There's a note on the table, and she's terrified to look in case it isn't from him. But she does.

Wish I was still in bed with you. Ð

The thought of his kisses sends little sparks down her spine, and she plops back down on the bed, trying to piece together last night's dream. This one feels different. More detached somehow, like Zoe was there as a spectator, not the one *in* the dream.

She remembers two men talking to a distressed woman. Her face is red and blotchy, and she keeps repeating, *It's just too dreadful!* One of the men tries to console her and offers her a sedative, and they are all so caught up in the drama that no one notices Zoe standing there in the doorway. She's calling out to them, but no one hears. There is someone standing next to her, but when she turns, she only sees a shadow running down the hallway, away.

The dream is easily explainable, based on everything she read last night, but she wonders about this person next to her. There had been no mention of a Moana maid or local woman in anything she'd read. But that doesn't mean she wasn't there. When she picks up her phone, she sees a message from Tara.

I can't make it for coffee, but I'll find you at lunchtime before my agent meeting.

Zoe texts Dylan. We need to go back and look for the journal.

DYLAN: This afternoon. Join me for lunch under the banyan?

ZOE: I'd love to. There's something I need to tell you.

DYLAN: Sounds good. PS You're cute when you dream.

ZOE: Thank you for staying . . . see you soon.

That last comment makes her smile, even though her dreams lately are nothing to smile about, and their lunch is likely to be the end of things. He might be over the bad review, but misleading him is another story.

SUN POURS IN through the banyan branches, and birds chirp and flitter and swoop around after one another. The beach is packed with sunbathers and swimmers and surfers, and the smell of suntan lotion slams into her, reminding her that yes, this actually is Waikiki Beach. Zoe is wearing a minidress because it feels like spring after a long winter, and she's emerging out of hibernation. She is lighter as she walks around, looking for Dylan. Finally, she spots him at a far table, closest to the ocean, a bald man in mirrored aviators sitting across from him.

When she approaches, Dylan lights up and stands and pulls out a chair for her. "Bridget, I'd love for you to meet my new agent, Jeff Fallon. He's just switched over to Author House."

Author House? Shit! Zoe wants to turn and run, but it's too late, and she is going to do it anyway. Avery is with Author House. One of the top New York literary agencies.

Jeff is already standing. He holds out a hand, looking puzzled. "Wait, aren't you Zoe Finch, Avery's author? *The Marriage Pact?*"

Dylan frowns. "Wrong person—"

At the same time, she says, "Bridget is my middle name, but yes, I'm Zoe."

Jeff has no idea what he's just fallen into. "Ah, makes sense. Avery told me to look for you when she found out I was coming."

Dylan sits there staring at the two of them like he can't figure out what is happening. "Wait, I don't get it."

Zoe sits down. "I know this is really awkward, but I can explain."

He assesses her more closely now. "You're Zoe Finch? *Monotonous, depressing and full of cliches* Zoe Finch?"

A direct quote from her review of his book, and it makes her feel queasy.

She nods. "I was going to tell you, Dylan, but the timing was never right, and then this morning I had my little speech planned out, but you were gone. When I signed up for the conference, I used my middle name—"

"What about White?"

"My mom's maiden name. I just thought it would be easier to fly under the radar, so I didn't have to explain to anyone why I'm here, which is a whole other story, and then I met you and it got . . . complicated."

Dylan throws out another ending to her sentence. "Weird."

He gets up without a word, but she can tell by the dark expression on his face he's upset and probably in shock. Who could blame him.

"Please, I swear, it was not supposed to go this far. I didn't expect to—"

He cuts her off. "I have a lot to do. You two enjoy yourselves."

His tone sears.

"Dylan, wait."

He holds up a hand, then walks away. Her heart is on the ground, under his shoe. Jeff looks shocked and still has a mouthful of food that he starts chewing again.

"Sorry to put you in the middle of this. I know I should have told him sooner . . . and it's a long story that I'm sure you don't care about." She takes several long slow breaths, trying to ward off the palpitations. "I really fucked up."

"Sounds like it. But tell me, now I'm curious."

"It's not just about me using a fake name." She tells him the bad review story as Jeff sips his iced tea, which smells like it's spiked. Or maybe it's a mai tai. She has half a mind to poach it from him and then order several more.

"Do you think he cares about one bad review eight years in the past? Look how far he's come since then. The man has sold millions of books."

"*Monotonous, depressing and full of cliches.* He still remembers my words. You know how it is with bad reviews. They stick."

Jeff shakes his head. "I can almost guarantee you he's over that. But I can see why he's pissed. No one likes being lied to."

She's lost her appetite and wants to chase after Dylan, but knows it would do no good. His expression keeps playing over in her mind. The shock and disgust she can live with. It's the hurt she can't.

She stands. "I'm sorry, Jeff, but I have to go. If you talk to Avery, tell her I have a killer idea—a new one."

Avery is going to lose it when she hears Zoe's plan.

THE ATTIC
Zoe

T ARA IS SITTING on a big chair in a nook off the lobby, typing away on her laptop, deep in thought. Zoe can tell that she is in some faraway fictional world, untethered to the here and now. She doesn't want to interrupt her, but does anyway.

"Here you are," she says.

Tara's fingers dance across the keyboard for a few strokes, and then she looks up. "Sorry I didn't come look for you. I am so close to nailing my ending and want to have it perfect before meeting the agents."

Zoe slides down so her head is against the back of the big, comfy chair. "It's okay. Writing takes precedence."

Tara studies her. "Did something happen?"

"I did something really, really dumb. Incredibly, mind-bendingly stupid, and now I'm paying for it. It started off perfectly innocent, but now Dylan thinks I'm a weirdo, and you probably will too," she says.

"Tell me," Tara says, looking concerned.

So she does, and when she finishes, Tara reaches out her hand and rests it on Zoe's. "I can totally see why you did that, and as your friend, I have to admit I wish you had told me sooner, but I'll get over it. It might be harder for Dylan, who clearly has a thing for you, so who knows what to expect there."

"I knew you would understand. It seemed like such an innocent thing, and then suddenly it wasn't," Zoe says.

A slow grin spreads across Tara's face. "Aside from all of that, I can't believe you're Zoe Finch."

"In the flesh. Not as impressive as you'd think, huh?"

"Stop. I adored every word of your book. Whip-smart and funny as hell. And I know your next one, whatever it is, will be just as good."

Zoe feels thankful for this sweet new friend. "Look, I know you are meeting with agents today, and I don't want to take up any more of your time, but I wanted to get your permission to also share your work with Avery Silver, my agent. I think she would love your writing."

The space between them grows quiet. "Are you serious?"

"Absolutely."

Tara leaps up and throws her arms around Zoe. "She would be my first choice over any of these agents here. Do you think she would really be interested?"

"No guarantees. But I have a good feeling."

"Oh, Bridget—or Zoe? That would be the best thing *ever*. I have so many rejections under my belt, and I won't be surprised if she says—"

"Don't even go there. You've put in the work and it shows. Your writing shines."

"Thank you," Tara whispers.

"It's the least I can do. And you can call me Bridget, or Bridge. Some of my oldest friends still do."

"Zoe Bridget White Finch. Maybe a pen name in there somewhere?"

Zoe wishes she could laugh. "Maybe."

IN HER ROOM, she changes out of her summery dress and into her leggings and T-shirt, ready to brave centipedes in Doris's attic if she needs to. She jogs down Kalakaua at a fast clip, melting under the early afternoon sun and trying to block the incident with Dylan and Jeff from her mind. That look on his face kills her. She knows what it feels like to be lied to, and that sense of your heart being scraped across the rocks. For now, she forces herself not to think about it.

Along with the rest of the world, the whole feeling of Doris's house has changed now that the sun is out, and it feels less overgrown and run-down, and more whimsical and wild. She wipes the sweat from her forehead with her T-shirt and knocks on the door.

"Doris, it's me, Bridget, from the Moana," she calls.

This time, a young, brown-haired version of Doris opens the door. Long-lashed eyes, fine-boned face. "My mom is napping. How can I help you?"

Zoe smiles. "We spoke with your mom yesterday about her aunt 'Ili and her time at the Moana Hotel. Did she tell you?"

"Oh, yeah."

But she makes no move to let Zoe in.

"Doris mentioned a journal 'Ili kept, and I was hoping to have a look at it. She thought you might know where to find it."

"*If* there is one, it would be in the attic. But I wouldn't count on it. My mom is confusing fact and fantasy more and more lately."

"Can I at least look?"

A voice comes from inside. "'Ili?"

"I'm here, Mom. Your friend is back from yesterday. Do you want to see her?"

A stretch of silence, and then her wrinkled face appears behind 'Ili. She stares at Zoe for a few moments, then says, "Where is your husband?"

At least she remembers. "Dylan is back at the hotel. He's teaching at the writers conference we're attending, and he couldn't get away."

"Herb was the one who went into the attic. I never did. You should wait for your husband," Doris says.

"Are you sure you want someone up there, Mom?" 'Ili says.

"Why not?"

Zoe interjects. "Unfortunately, I can't wait for him, and I promise I'll be careful. But I'm wondering, are things labeled?"

'Ili nods. "That would be a yes. My father was fastidious about that kind of thing. But really, I think you're wasting your time."

It's my time to waste, Zoe wants to say, but instead smiles graciously. "I'm hoping to write a book about Jane Stanford's poisoning, and I just want to make sure I've covered all bases. I'm sure you understand how important following all leads is?"

A bit of wishful thinking, but she hopes against hope she can turn it into the truth.

"Fine, I'll get the ladder. And a flashlight."

The ladder is barely tall enough, and wobbles, so Zoe has to pull herself up and into the hole in the hall ceiling. Once she's in, a foul smell hits her. 'Ili hands her the flashlight.

"There should be a string for the light bulb," 'Ili says.

The minute Zoe pulls the string, she wishes she hadn't. There is lizard shit everywhere, and the sound of tiny scurrying feet. Lizards she can deal with, but rats are another story. It's obvious no one has been up here in years.

"Do you have something I can tie over my nose and mouth?" she asks.

A minute later, 'Ili hands up an old T-shirt. "All I got."

Thankfully, there is a plywood plank running down the middle, with boxes of all shapes and sizes piled on both sides. The light only goes so far, and she begins to crawl and read the labeled boxes. Photo albums, trains, paddling medals and trophies, books, and all kinds of old files and documents, but nothing that mentions 'Ili. When she hits the edge of darkness, she switches on the flashlight. It's creepy as hell up here, and she fights an overwhelming urge to turn around. The journal, if there is one, is probably a dead end anyway.

On the right, the beam catches on something wrapped in a dusty blanket that looks remarkably like a dead body. That's it. She's done. But as she shuffles around on her hands and knees so she can head back down, she sees a box marked *Aunty Stuff*. All concern about creatures falls away, and she yanks the cardboard box toward her. There is no way to open it up here, so she slides it to the attic opening, scraping and smearing dust and gecko poop. The stench intensifies.

"I found something that says *Aunty Stuff*. Would that be it?" she calls down, hoping there are no other aunties.

"Could be," 'Ili says.

"Okay, get ready, I'm going to hand it down. It's dirty, so beware."

They set the box on a towel that 'Ili has laid out in the middle of the living room. Doris stands by, fiddling with her gold bangle bracelets, which Zoe has learned are a common Hawaiian tradition.

"I don't know that I ever opened this box. When Sarge died, which was much later than 'Iliahi, Herb packed away his stuff in the attic. And when things go into the attic, they have a tendency to never come out again," Doris says.

Aside from fraying along the edges, the box looks intact. With permission, Zoe cuts the crusty tape and peels it open. There are several fragile-looking photo albums, a rusted metal box, a smaller ornately carved jewelry box and a wooden bowl with smaller ones inside of it. No journal. She takes everything out and sets it all on the table, which Doris has cleared.

"None of this looks familiar?" Zoe asks.

"My aunt was a talented surfer. Those bowls are trophies, I believe."

'Ili shrugs. "Dad had cancer when uncle Sarge died, so they probably intended to look through this at some point but never got around to it."

"Open the metal box," Doris says, staring at it with a strange expression on her face.

Zoe does. In it is a large tiger cowrie, and two velvet pouches resting on a thick leather-bound notebook or journal. She sets the pouches on the table, pulls out the book and glances over at Doris. "Do you want to look first?"

"Yes, please."

Doris's hand shakes slightly, and she lifts the leather cover. "'Iliahi Baldwin—that was her maiden name, so this was from before she married Sarge Kekai. Yep, she told me she kept a journal of the Moana years, and here it is. I wasn't imagining it," she says, shooting a look at her daughter.

"I never said you were. I just had no idea if it still existed," 'Ili answers back.

Doris looks back at Zoe and whispers, "She doesn't trust me."

"Mom, I'm right here. I can hear you. And I do trust you, but sometimes you get confused is all. It happens to the best of us."

"Do you get confused?" Doris asks Zoe.

Zoe nods. "All the time. I'm confused about a lot of things." Which is more true than she wishes it to be.

Doris leafs through the pages, then holds up the book. "Look at this handwriting. No one writes like this anymore."

"Impressive," Zoe says, but what she really wants to focus on are the words, not the perfect curly handwriting. "Can you tell what years it is?"

"It says 1904 and 1905. Early years."

A couple of the pages stick together, and Doris carefully separates them. Zoe sits on her hands to keep from grabbing the book from Doris and devouring it. In the meantime, 'Ili opens the smaller of the two pouches and pulls out a small blue box.

"Whoa, look at this." She holds up a bracelet of red stones that seem to shine from within.

Doris's eyes go wide. "Oh dear. Could those be real?"

"I'm no jeweler, but the look and feel and velvet box tell me they are," 'Ili says.

"I never saw her wear such a thing. She only wore lei and her small collection of Ni'ihau shell necklaces, which she left to me," Doris says.

Zoe asks 'Ili, "Did you know your great-aunt at all?"

"I was young when she died, so I have memories of going to their house for holidays and barbecues—they had this huge yard in Waimanalo—but not much else."

Doris holds up a photograph. "This was stuck in the pages. Aunty and another woman standing on the old pier. She looks so young—so thin."

Even with the poor quality of the photo, Zoe can tell that 'Iliahi was a beautiful woman. Thin, yes, and with a mass of hair, but those almond-shaped eyes staring directly into the camera and full lips give her a sultry look. Her expression holds just a hint of a smile. Beside her is a straight-faced Jane Stanford.

Zoe wants to take the journal back to her room, where she can read through it uninterrupted, but she's afraid to ask, so she sits and tries not to bite her nails as Doris leafs through it slowly. The old woman wears no glasses, and Zoe isn't sure if she can actually read or is just going through the motions, though she *had* read the dates.

Then 'Ili checks the clock and says, "Mom has a dentist appointment at four, so we need to get going. Do you want to take this and bring it back tomorrow?"

"That would be wonderful. I promise I'll take good care of it," Zoe says, then remembers the other pouch and points to it. "Can we just see what's in that before I go?"

"Sure." 'Ili opens it and pulls out a gold-plated name tag, tarnished with age. She holds the pouch up again, shaking it, but nothing else comes out. "That's it."

But finding the journal feels like fate.

THE JOURNAL
Zoe

SOMETIMES, LIFE HAS a way of hurling everything at you all at once, as though time got jackknifed and now everything is piling up at your feet. Tonight feels like one of those nights. Zoe only has tonight and tomorrow to get her proposal done. The only problem is, she wants to scrap the current proposal, start from scratch and figure out a way to tell Jane's story. There's a ninety-five percent chance that Avery will nix it, but she shoots her a text anyway.

> Can you talk? I have an idea I want to run by you. Sorry to text so late, but it's important.
>
> AVERY: I'll call you in the morning. 6 your time.

It's not the answer she wants to hear, and now she has to decide whether to spend precious time on this new idea or forge ahead on the romance story she's not in love with. She ends up doing neither. Instead, she composes a message to Dylan that she rewrites at least fifty times. She's surprised by how much her heart weighs right now.

Can we meet tonight? Please? All I ask is that you hear
me out. xx

He doesn't respond right away, and her morale tanks. She
knows he has so much going on, but she can't help but feel
that she blew her one and only shot with him. And who could
blame him, really?

The journal calls her name, and she can't wait to read it.
But first, she orders a beet and goat cheese salad from room
service, along with lilikoi cheesecake—why not?—and pours
herself a half glass of Kuleana rum. It goes down smoothly,
and she sinks a little deeper into the chair.

Curious what the word *kuleana* means, she looks it up online. To the Hawaiians, the word embodies both a right and a
privilege when one assumes responsibility for something. This
notion resonates deeply in the seat of her belly. Strangely, it
feels as though it is her *kuleana* to do justice to Jane Stanford, a
woman she has only just learned of.

Before handling the journal, she washes and thoroughly dries
her hands, then lays it out on the table, which she has also cleaned.
The paper is in surprisingly good condition, having been squir-
reled away in the attic for who knows how long. It smells musty
but also has a sharp, chemical odor to it. Entries begin in Novem-
ber 1904, and Zoe resigns herself to reading through the whole
thing. Slanted and graceful, the writing is meticulous.

December 6.
I am happy to report that my brothers and I will no longer
be living on taro and fish day after day! Miracle of miracles,
I was hired today to work at the stylish beachfront Moana
Hotel. I owe everything to Mr. Price. I begin day after

tomorrow, and I am a bundle of nerves. Liko says I should take some of that tonic Uncle Mel gave us when they first took Mother away. But I rather enjoy the thrill of it. I have a feeling our luck is about to change, and this long period of darkness will lift.

Some words are indecipherable or maybe in Hawaiian, and some Zoe has to look up, but she reads on, taking in the thoughts of an obviously bright young woman a hundred years ago. It feels like time travel, and she's so absorbed that when room service knocks on the door, she nearly falls off her chair. Taking a break to eat, she brings the food to the table outside and enjoys the balmy air and a sky full of stars. Soon she sees a black shape moving up the banyan branch, and Storm leaps across the divide.

"Enjoying the sunshine today too, were you?"

Storm does a figure eight around her legs, rubbing her cheeks against Zoe's ankles, and Zoe realizes it's not just Dylan she's fallen for. For the first time, she considers taking the cat back to Oregon with her. Storm is young enough that she would probably adjust, but adopting a cat was not on her list of things to accomplish. The idea stresses her out, and she shifts her focus back to Jane and 'Iliahi and the poisoning.

Zoe reads on, and by the time she gets to the part where Jane Stanford and her entourage arrive, she has to fight to keep her eyes open. 'Iliahi seems genuinely taken with Jane and speaks highly of her, which chafes against some of the things Zoe has read online about Jane. Descriptions like *iron-willed, duplicitous, demanding, entitled, unpleasant* and *unlikeable* were but a few of the adjectives she'd come across.

She's about to stop for the night when 'Iliahi mentions a ruby bracelet on Jane's wrist. *Today, Mrs. Stanford was wearing a bracelet the color of Mr. Kinoshita's beets. Her fleshy arms puffed out around it like she had outgrown it years ago but refuses to accept the changes in her aging body. Thelma caught me eyeing the jewels, and I know she doesn't trust me, but I don't trust her.*

Zoe sits up straight. Since a ruby bracelet was in the box with the Moana journal, Zoe theorized it might have come from Jane. Now here's her proof.

Unfortunately, the entry ends there, though she can see some pages have been torn out. She's also curious about Jane's jewels and searches online, discovering that a library endowment was created out of funds from the sale of her jewelry. This fund is now worth upward of twenty million dollars. She scrolls through, looking at images of elaborate diamond necklaces, emerald brooches and ruby tiaras. 'Iliahi was not kidding when she said Jane had more jewels than the queen of England.

Several pages in, an article titled *Jane Stanford's Jewelry and Pocket Watch* catches her eye. She clicks the link and scrolls down until she gets to a photo of a gold pocket watch. *Her* pocket watch—or an exact replica. Same gold weave, same rose-cut diamonds outlined in black enamel. The photo below it shows the inside of the watch, and if she wasn't already sitting, she would have dropped to the floor.

N249421, JW Tucker & Co, San Francisco is etched into the gold, and beneath it, *For my beloved J, From L, Jan 1st, 1868.*

The mystery inscription in the timepiece that Ginger gave her all those years ago has just been solved. A lifetime of wondering who *J* and *L* are is over. This pocket watch once belonged to Jane Stanford, a gift from her robber baron husband. Her skin pricks with goose bumps, and her mind jumps back to the day Ginger presented her with the box.

Zoe now wonders where Uncle Leo had picked up the watch. And even weirder, she traces the sequence of events that brought the watch to the very location of Jane's death a hundred years later. It really does feel like Jane is speaking to her from beyond the grave, begging for the real story to be told.

Iron will is right.

FROM THE JOURNAL OF 'ILIAHI BALDWIN, 1905

Last night, I watched a woman die, and I can say with certainty it will never leave me. I am still quite shaken, but I will record this as best I can for posterity's sake. Yesterday morning started off on the wrong foot when Mrs. Stanford's gingerbread would not rise, but we managed to have a fine picnic on the Pali once she calmed down. Aside from overeating, dare I say gorging herself like Mrs. Hayashi's hogs, everything went smoothly. On the way back, she complained a couple times of indigestion, but other than that, we chatted and sang and enjoyed the views.

I was tired, absolutely drained, but Mrs. Stanford asked if I would meet her in her room at eight, and I had no choice but to remain at work. These are the kinds of things Mrs. Akina expects of her employees. The hotel and its guests come before all else. Anyway, when I arrived at her room, she presented me with a ruby bracelet as a gift for my kindness to her. Bloodred and beautiful, the bracelet now sits in a box under my mattress. I did not want to accept something so extravagant, but she insisted. Thelma was in the room with us, and disapproval oozed out from her pores. I realized then what a horrible burden it must be to have so much wealth, since it causes people around you to behave bizarrely. Everyone wants a piece of your kalo.

Again, Mrs. Stanford seemed fine. After leaving the room and returning downstairs, I realized I had left my office key on the table in Jane's room, so I went back up and knocked on the door, announcing I had forgotten something. There was a long pause before the door opened, and it was Thelma who opened the door just a crack. Jane must have been in the bathroom, because I heard water running. I assured Thelma I was just there to retrieve my keys, and rather than ushering me in, she shut the door in my face. I noted that she was wearing gloves, but didn't think too much of it until what transpired later.

I left, figuring I would try again later to retrieve my keys, and went downstairs to help finish closing up for the night. After helping clean up on the veranda, I heard loud voices coming from the floor above. I don't know what came over me, but I had an intense knowing that something had happened to Mrs. Stanford. I left the veranda and ran up the stairs, not bothering to wait for an elevator. When I arrived, Dr. Humphris was already there, and he had Jane sitting in a chair. She did not look well and was groaning, her body tensed in unnatural ways.

Jane kept repeating that she had been poisoned, and the goal seemed to be to get her to vomit. Humphris asked for the bottles that Jane had taken medicine from. As soon as he tasted the bicarbonate, his face contorted. Another doctor arrived, and they both stated that this was classic strychnine poisoning. All the while, I stood by the door, quiet as a mouse. My mind went back to the gloves Thelma was wearing, and I looked around the room for any sign of them, doubtful they would still be there. Nor did I see them.

Between spasms, Jane seemed coherent, and for a moment our eyes met. By this point, her jaw was clenched tight, and I could tell by the vacancy in her look that she was close to leaving this world. I wanted to go to her and help usher her out, but I knew my presence would not be welcome since I am no doctor. I am merely a hotel employee. Ma always said a hand to hold is more valuable than a whole pot of gold, and I believe that. Weak with distress, and feeling useless, I stepped away.

At the top of the stairs, I came upon the wastebasket. I almost walked on by, but seeing that Thelma's room was across the hall, I took a chance and looked inside. And wouldn't you know it, but there were two white gloves, wadded up in a burlap sack. Carefully, I took the sack and tucked it in the folds of my skirt. I was on the verge of hyperventilating, unsure of what to do with this knowledge and probably evidence of a murder. It now sits under my mattress, along with the ruby bracelet.

It's early morning now, I am deprived of sleep, and yet I must leave for work again soon. I am an absolute shipwreck.

THE VISIT
Zoe

AVERY CALLS AT five to six, and Zoe is shaken out of a dream where sharks are circling all around her, brushing their sandpaper skin upon her legs.

"Morning," she says, mouth dry and cottony, but happy to be plucked out of the dangerous water.

"I have church this morning, so we need to make this quick. What's up?" Avery says, all business.

It takes a moment to gather her thoughts. "I have an incredible story for you, but it's not romance, and I'm not even sure it's fiction."

Pure silence.

"Hello? Avery?" Zoe says.

"What happened to the proposal you've been promising me? The one that's going so well?"

Zoe groans. "It feels flat, and my heart isn't in it. But this one—the one I'm obsessed with—it could be a big book. I know we'd be genre swapping, and we'd have to run it by Melinda—"

"Absolutely not. Your contract says *romance*, and time is up," Avery says, speaking fast, as though she's had three cups of coffee already.

"I have until Monday."

"To get me a whole proposal and at least ten pages, preferably more. This leaves me in a tough position, Zoe. You know how badly Melinda wants a follow-up to your last book. It would be another story if *The Marriage Pact* hadn't been such a big success."

Zoe rubs her eyes, puffy from Storm's dander. "I'm sorry, Avery. I came here fully intending to finish my proposal, and I have it mostly done. But I don't think it even comes close to my last book. And aren't you at least curious what my idea is?"

She hears Avery sip something, then she says, "Fine, tell me."

Zoe sums it up as best she can. "This is a story that needs to be told. There are books hypothesizing about the case, but none that actually nail the real murderer and get to the heart of Jane Stanford."

"How did you find out about this?"

"I'm staying in the room where she died."

Something slams down. "Holy shit."

"Not only that, but I've found a journal that belonged to a maid who knows things, and may even have a piece of evidence—if I can find it. I have to write this. As it stands, the official cause of death for Jane Stanford, mother of Leland Stanford Junior University, is natural causes."

She leaves out the nightmares and notes and the pocket watch and Storm, because she doesn't want to seem unhinged.

"So you're telling me you want to switch from fiction to nonfiction for your sophomore book."

"I am. Yes."

Avery sighs. "I'll see if I can reach Melinda. But have that other proposal shiny and ready, because I already know what the answer will be."

IT'S HARD TO think about anything other than the journal and the pocket watch and those gloves that 'Iliahi says she kept. Why wouldn't they be in the metal box with the other things? Perhaps Zoe overlooked something in the main box, but more likely they were thrown away over the years. Who needs an old pair of gloves, especially in Hawai'i? But damn, they are the final and critical piece in this mystery, and she needs them for her story. Maybe Doris knows.

She heads down for the final half day of the conference, grabbing a malasada and a few hunks of pineapple at the continental breakfast bar. She's hoping to see Dylan and tell him what she learned in the journal—she can't stop it from looping around in her mind—but instead runs into Sam, who looks more bleary-eyed than Zoe. Up close, and now knowing what she knows, Sam seems less intimidating and more human. Fragile, almost. And it reminds her that everyone is hiding some pain or hurt, no matter how put together they may appear.

"Hey there," Sam says, holding a mug of tea.

"Good morning," Zoe says.

"How are you doing?" Sam asks, her eyes sweeping the room as though making sure the coast is clear. "Dylan told me what happened—who you are and all that. And I get why he's not happy, but I thought it might help you to know that his wife had a real tendency to lie. It was at the heart of why they split. I won't go into detail, because that's his story to tell, but it's probably why he reacted so harshly."

The information hits Zoe hard. "Thank you for telling me. I feel like such a bad person. It was not my intention at all and a stupid thing to do. I intended to fess up sooner. It just never seemed like the right time."

"It never is for the difficult conversations."

"And of course I had no idea that anything would happen between us—I mean, not that it did. But . . . almost."

Sam shakes her head. "It did, Zoe, trust me. He's pretty shaken up about it, and Dylan rarely gets shaken up. Just give him some time."

"You two are really close, huh?"

"We are."

Zoe loves that Dylan is still such good friends with a girl from high school. It says a lot.

"I have to go talk to Andy Burns right now, but promise me you won't give up on him, okay?" Sam says.

"None of this is really up to me, but I promise. And did you sign with Andy?"

Sam smiles, and even with the dark circles under her eyes, she's gorgeous. "He likes my first pages, but we'll see about the rest. I gave him my full manuscript yesterday."

"Good for you. It only takes one."

ZOE FEELS LOST and has no idea which workshop to attend. At this moment, she has no interest in romance, nor is she in any mood to listen and critique, which is what they're doing in plot. What she really needs is *Think Like a Detective* and to see Dylan and beg for forgiveness, but she does not want to disrupt his class. She passes the door and sees that everyone is still milling about, but there's no sign of him. She keeps walking and slows about ten feet past the door. It wouldn't be too late. Unable to stop herself, she turns around and goes in and slides into a far side, back corner chair. She opens her laptop so she can be as unobtrusive as possible until class starts.

Only when the room quiets, and Dylan says, "Good morning," does she look up.

There's Always More to the Story is written on the whiteboard, and he's standing there looking hot in a pair of worn jeans and a teal-colored aloha shirt. She swears she can smell his leathery scent from this far away, and it causes a swish in her heart.

He seems a little less energetic, less enthusiastic than on day one, but the information he delivers is still precise and engaging. He talks about how there are many layers to a story, and it's often those layers simmering just beneath the surface that give a story its power.

"And one thing I can't stress enough is that oftentimes, your subconscious mind is doing the work for you, and sometimes you have to get out of the way and let it do its work. Trust and faith are a huge part of the process. So on your first draft, don't worry too much about all of this. Just write. The revision phase is when you'll glimpse layers of the story you didn't even know existed, and you will want to find those and flesh them out. Has anyone experienced this?"

Zoe wants to raise her hand but doesn't. A dozen or so others do, and Dylan scans the room to see who knows the feeling. Before she can look back down at her computer, his eyes stop on her for but a second, then move on. His complete lack of acknowledgment makes it hard to breathe. If only she could crawl out of here on her hands and knees and not be noticed, she would. Coming to his workshop was a bad idea, and she should have had more self-control.

Not missing a beat, he then talks about how to connect seemingly unrelated threads to create that emotionally satisfying ending that readers crave. And leave no loose ends. Readers are infuriated by loose ends, he says.

"And remember . . ." He pauses and lowers his voice for effect. Everyone leans in. "Oftentimes the killer or the guilty party has been the most obvious person all along, but there is one thing that keeps people from suspecting them. That's what you want to push for. Follow every lead, and interview everyone in the room, no matter how insignificant they may seem. Your hero is the one who wouldn't give up when everyone else already had."

His words resonate. For unknown reasons, Jane did not have someone doing this for her. There were plenty of people who thought she was murdered, but no one to push all the way into the end zone. Zoe is no detective, but she is good at following leads. And she knows just what she needs to do next.

SHE STAYS UNTIL the break. A few times, she can feel Dylan's gaze brushing up against the people next to her. Like he wants to look at her but forces himself not to. It's an awful place to be, for both of them. So at the break, when people have crowded around him like pigeons, she leaves and makes the twenty-minute walk to Hibiscus Drive.

Doris is outside today, sitting at a small wrought-iron table in the yard, reading a book. Sun crisscrosses down on her through the branches of a bushy tree. Zoe counts three lounging cats. One belly-up on the warm brick, one in Doris's lap and another lying on a small concrete bench. All black with white paws or chests.

"Hey, Doris, it's Bridget from the Moana," she says, leaning up against the peeling picket fence.

Doris waves. "Bridget from the Moana, it's lovely to see you. Come join me."

The hinge sticks, but eventually she manages to open it and enters what could be a Hawaiian version of the Secret Garden. A small brick courtyard surrounded with half-dead rosebushes ten feet high, clumps of rosemary and scrawny gardenias covered in some kind of black mold. At one time it probably was charming, but now it just needs tending.

"Come, sit," Doris says.

Zoe wipes a layer of damp leaves from the other chair. "Lovely morning, isn't it?"

"When you get to be my age, every morning is a lovely morning."

A tangy smell wafts over from a tangerine tree, where the ground is blanketed in orange fruit.

"So, I read the journal, and it's incredible. Your aunt was a real character, and extremely observant. I wanted to ask if I could keep the journal another day or two because I've found something in there that could possibly prove who poisoned Jane Stanford at the Moana."

Doris's face pinches. "Really?"

"Really. 'Iliahi mentions seeing Jane's secretary, Thelma, wearing a pair of gloves, and then she took them off. Do you know anything about that? Have you seen any old gloves?"

"A regular Sherlock Holmes, are you?"

Zoe laughs. "Not at all, but I'm trying, and I feel a sense of duty since this whole mystery kind of fell in my lap."

"Nothing about gloves rings a bell. I'm so sorry."

"That's fine, I know it was ages ago. Did your aunt ever talk about why she never went to the police with what she saw?"

Doris's forehead creases, and she looks up at the tree. Zoe waits in silence, listening to the birds chattering, not wanting to pressure her.

Eventually Doris says, "Nope, I don't recall anything about that either. Say, where is that husband of yours?"

"Dylan? He's not my husband. He's just a friend."

"Just a friend? No, that can't be right. I saw the love, bright as day."

Love?

Zoe nearly chokes. "Not quite. We've only just met. But I do like him . . . a lot."

"And he likes you. It's easy to tell if you know what to look for," Doris says, a smile shining in her eyes.

Something rustles in the bushes behind them, and Zoe checks to make sure there's nothing dangerous, then remembers they are in Hawai'i. Doris doesn't seem to notice the sound.

"Oh? What do you look for?" Zoe asks.

"It's all in the eyes. The way they sneak glances and hold eye contact, and their gaze follows you around the room like a puppy dog. Sometimes it's easier for someone else around to tell, someone who notices these things—"

From the bushes, a cat emerges. It's small and black and looks remarkably like Storm. The dainty animal saunters toward them and comes straight up to Zoe, who has stopped listening to Doris.

"Storm?"

Meow.

"Did you follow me here?" Zoe asks, leaning down to pet her as she rubs up against Zoe's shins.

Doris looks confused. "This little thing? Follow you from where?"

"My hotel room. She's been holed up with me during the storm. I would recognize her anywhere."

"Well, now that I think about it, I haven't seen her in a while. She isn't one of mine, but she showed up about a month ago, hungry and covered in stickers. 'Ili got them out for her, and I guess she decided we were okay, so she hung around."

Would a cat walk all the way down the beach to the Moana? And from the very house where Zoe has ended up?

Nothing makes sense and there are too many strange connections, but after everything that's gone on in the past week, it hardly surprises her. Zoe reaches down and scoops her up. Storm doesn't resist.

"What is going on here?" she says aloud.

Storm hunkers down in her lap, purring.

Doris rests a hand on Zoe's knee. "Maybe she planned on luring you here. Animals know things, dear."

"I've thought about taking her home with me because she seemed like a stray."

"She sought you out. You belong to each other now."

"You wouldn't mind?"

Not that she actually will, but she just wants to be sure.

"Not one bit," Doris says.

They chat for a while as sun pools around them. Doris seems to enjoy the company, and Zoe wishes she could stay longer but has to get back so she can change her flight. She can't leave without those gloves.

"Would you mind if I come back tomorrow and have one more look through your attic?"

"Whatever you need."

FROM THE JOURNAL OF
'ILIAHI BALDWIN, 1905

WHEN I ARRIVED for work, Mr. Price, with a twitch in his eye and liquor on his breath, took me into the back office and filled me in on the tragedy, despite me telling him I had witnessed a portion of it. It turns out that after I left last night, Dr. Humphris took a carriage to the sheriff's house and reported the murder of Mrs. Stanford. Deputy High Sheriff Rawlins made it to the hotel soon after midnight to investigate. Seeing that Dr. Humphris had the bottle of bicarbonate, he rounded that up, then tried to talk to Thelma and Dot, who Price says were both incoherent with grief.

This, dear diary, is where I beg to differ. Dot might have been, but if you ask me, the cause for Thelma's incoherence was not grief but guilt. I informed Price that since there had been nothing I could do, I left. I did not bring up my theory and what I know about Thelma, because I could see that I needed to tread carefully, and boy was I right.

Both women were said to be holed up in their rooms, and I decided to pay a visit to Thelma. When she saw it was me, I thought she might turn me away, but instead she invited me in. Her well-groomed hair had turned into a nest for a flock of birds, and her eyes were rimmed in red and swollen. She appeared possessed, and I wondered if I was endangering myself by being here, since she was, in my opinion, a murderer.

When she asked what I wanted, I wasn't even sure I knew myself. Did I have the nerve to accuse her to her face? No, I think I merely wanted to get a sense of whether or not her grief seemed genuine. Because even though I saw her wearing the gloves, and I dislike the woman, I did not see her scooping the poison into Mrs. Stanford's water. To answer her question, I said I was merely checking in on her to see if there was anything she needed. Surely, the police will come for her, and then I can tell them what I saw.

Thelma turned on me then, most wickedly, telling me she knows that I was plotting to steal Mrs. Stanford's jewelry, and that I was a low-down scheming heathen. The veins in her neck bulged blue, and she said something that turned my blood cold. "I know what you're thinking. You think I killed her, don't you?" My feet grew roots, and though I wanted to run from the room and the venom spilling out from her, all I could do was stand there.

With an eerie calm, she said, "What I need from you is to keep quiet about anything you *think* you may have seen. Because if you don't, I will gladly tell the police that I caught you in the room last night, and that this morning, I discovered that Mrs. Stanford's ruby bracelet is missing. Also, I found it very peculiar that you were wearing gloves, and only after Mrs. Stanford ingested the poison did I put two and two together."

We stared each other down like feral cats, and I felt a sob welling up in my throat because we both knew who the police would believe. They would believe the longtime secretary of Jane Stanford before they believed a young kanaka maid whose brother has been caught stealing and dragged home by the sheriff more than once. My mind tried to find a solution but came up only more distraught. Any hope for justice for Jane had just gone out the window.

I backed out of the room, feeling like someone had pressed a hot iron to my cheeks, and ran down the hall, down the stairs and into the guest bathroom, shutting myself in a stall and trying to catch my breath. If I'd had any speck of doubt of Thelma's guilt, the last of it evaporated in that toilet stall.

THE SURPRISE
Zoe

ZOE GETS BACK halfway through the goodbye luncheon, hoping to find Dylan. She knows he wants nothing to do with her, but she has no one else to turn to. As a detective, surely he will understand her need for advice on how to proceed. The journal is one thing, and wouldn't likely stand up in court as any kind of evidence, especially because 'Iliahi did not see Thelma putting the strychnine in the glass. But she did see her wearing gloves, and then taking them off.

When Tara sees Zoe, she waves her over to a table with Bill and two other women. "Guess what?"

"You got an offer?"

Tara beams. "Two offers. I can't believe it!"

Zoe high-fives her. "I can. From who?"

"Jennifer Lockhart and Rudy Stein."

"Incredible! But you didn't accept yet, did you?"

"I told them each I need a week to think about it." She laughs. "Can you believe that? Me telling agents I need some time?"

"Get used to it. I emailed Avery your stuff, so you should hear within the next few days."

Tara points to an empty chair. "Sit?"

"I would love to, but my book proposal and pages are due

tomorrow, so I'm on borrowed time," she says, keeping an eye out for Dylan.

"He's not here," Tara says, picking up on what Zoe isn't saying.

"Who's not here?"

"I saw Dylan in the lobby checking out about half an hour ago."

"Are you sure?"

"Bags and all. And he had a jacket over his shoulder that looked far too warm for Hawai'i." Tara drops her voice. "I'm sorry, hon."

A lump forms in her throat, and her eyes water, and there's not a thing she can do to stop it.

Tara hops up and gives her a hug. "You're gonna be okay, Bridge."

"I know I screwed up, but I thought I would at least see him again."

"Forget about him for now and focus on yourself and your work. If you two are meant to be, you will. Trust me."

The ache is all too familiar, though. Of things not working out. Every single time. Though this one is on her. It's her fault.

"I'm leaving soon too, but we'll be in touch," Tara says. "What about you? When do you leave?"

"I'm extending my trip another day or two. I have to get this done."

They say their goodbyes, and after a long hug, Zoe heads to the lobby on the off chance that Dylan might still be there. But he's not, and she feels gut-punched all over again.

GOODMAN INVESTIGATIONS CLAIMS to be the oldest detective agency in Hawai'i. Full-service with an impressive résumé of backgrounds—law enforcement, legal, finance, even intelligence. She decides to call them rather than the police so she can avoid any bureaucracy, and to be discreet. She'll write off the expense, assuming she can sell this idea.

"Hello, I'm looking for a private investigator as soon as possible to help me on an unsolved case from 1905," she tells the secretary.

"1905, did you say?"

"Correct."

"I'm not sure—"

"Please, I just need a consult, and I'm happy to pay. Do you have an ex-cop, preferably? The older the better," she squeaks in.

The woman sounds annoyed. "We have a two-month waitlist, ma'am. But . . . hang on, let me check something."

Zoe's heart sinks. Two months is not going to cut it. She crosses her fingers and says a little prayer, even hoping Jane can pull some strings. She waits and waits. And waits.

The woman comes back on. "We do have someone. A brand-new hire who starts tomorrow. If you give me your name and contact information, I'll have him give you a call."

"Ah, perfect, thank you."

THAT EVENING, AFTER A long beach walk and a dinner on the veranda alone, Zoe sits down and forces out words that don't excite her at all, so why would they excite anyone else? She fluffs up her five-page proposal, which should really be ten pages, and falls asleep with her computer on her lap. Storm has not returned, but the door is open a crack, just in case. Now that the weather is nice, maybe the cat doesn't need Zoe anymore.

Her alarm is set for four, but she wakes before it goes off, creating a new document titled *The Poison Theory*. Publishers love to change titles, but she likes this for its simplicity, and it works for now. The whole story is already there in her head, but she highlights the main points and creates an outline. She likes it as nonfiction because in this case, truth really is stranger than fiction, and she wants people to know every unbelievable detail. But it's still missing a definitive ending.

Twenty minutes later, from the darkness, a scrappy figure leaps onto the bed and curls up as though she never left. She's the perfect writing partner, cat dander and all. Even after just a week, Zoe feels less allergic. Maybe there's some truth to the belief that over time, people can lose their sensitivity to a particular cat.

At eight o'clock, while she's rearranging and finessing words to get things just right, the phone rings. She almost lets it go to voicemail, but sees it's a Hawai'i number.

"Hello?"

"Aloha, this is Detective Santos. I hear you lookin' for some help with a case," says the man.

"You're from Goodman Investigations?"

"That's right."

"Thank you for getting back to me so soon. I know this is a lot to ask, but I'm visiting from the mainland and staying at the Moana. I don't have a car. Is there any way you could come to my hotel room today?"

"First half hour free consultation, and if you want to hire me, you gotta fill out a contract," he says.

"Of course. Would noon work?" she asks, holding her breath.

"What room are you in?"

"120."

She swears she feels something shift in him, but he says, "I'll be there."

A BIG BALL of fish swims around in her stomach as she waits to hear if Avery has spoken to Melinda. A part of her wants to just call Melinda herself and make the plea for this story, but that's not how it works. Everyone in publishing is slammed with a hundred different tasks and projects, while you, the author, have only your precious book to focus on. So you wait and you wait and you wait. And try not to gnaw your foot off in the meantime.

That she hasn't heard from Avery by now is strange, though. The day is almost over—Eastern time, but it's still early in Hawai'i, so whose EOD are they going by? The more she thinks about writing the romance novel, the more she wants to just erase the whole file. The story is fine, the characters are fine, but it feels formulaic and like she would be settling and writing the book just to write it. As much as she wants it to be, *fine* is not good enough. She holds her finger over the trackpad and gets ready to drag the file into the trash, but in the end, she can't go through with it.

At a point where she can no longer concentrate, she goes back to the leather-bound journal on the table, holds it up and smells the musty leather, admiring the hand-stitched edges and the craftsmanship. The front and back covers are thick and heavy and have warped in the humid weather. She runs her fingers over the cover. It almost feels as though it's padded, and the front padding is old and coming apart. The back one too. Curious, she opens the journal and runs her finger along the inside. At the bottom, her fingertip slips between two pieces of leather.

There's something soft in there, and she tries to work it out, but it's wedged. She comes at it from the top and feels the material peel away from the cover. Pinching and pulling, she gets it out. Every inch of her body goes still when she sees that it's a glove, once white, but now yellowed with age. She

runs to the bathroom and grabs a couple of towels and wash-
cloths. The other glove is in the back cover of the journal. She
handles them carefully and lays them out on the table.

FRANK SANTOS SHOWS up five minutes early. Tan with shallow-
water-blue eyes and receding hair, he looks more like an aging
movie star than a detective. He shows his badge, and Zoe lets
him in.

He goes straight to the glass door and looks out. "I know
what happened in this room," he says.

"You do?"

"Our old police chief used the case to teach us back when
we were rookies—about a thousand years ago. He thought it
was a prime example of a good case gone bad."

This is the best news she's heard in a while. "So you know
the whole sequence of events?"

He shrugs. "Been a minute, but I remember a lot. What's
your interest in it?"

Storm peeks out from under the bed and eyes Frank with
suspicion, and when he spots her, he does the same, but says
nothing.

"I believe I have new evidence that Jane Stanford was
murdered."

His eyebrows shoot up. "That would be something, but
from what I gather, no stone was left unturned back then by
our guys."

"People always have their reasons for not coming forward,
don't they?" Zoe asks.

"Sure. Happens all the time. I'm curious, Miss Finch.
How did you come upon this new evidence?"

Zoe tells her story again, saying she learned of Jane from

the hotel staff and that started her down a rabbit hole—which is not entirely untrue.

"I have the journal of 'Iliahi Baldwin, and in it she states that she witnessed Thelma wearing gloves earlier in the night in Mrs. Stanford's room. I found these gloves hidden in the cover of the journal. Tell me, Mr. Santos, do you know how long strychnine can be detected on a surface?" she says.

He looks unsure. "A long time."

"A hundred years?"

"Not sure about that."

"I couldn't find anything online, so I'm hoping you can help me find out, and maybe get these analyzed for any trace of poison as soon as possible. Also, I'd like to find out if there was any mention of 'Iliahi in the official records? In the articles I've seen online, her name never appears, which seems strange to me."

"What are you gonna do with the results?" he asks.

"What should have been done in 1905, or actually was done, but then changed by university cronies. Let the world know what really happened to Jane Stanford. That she didn't die of natural causes but was killed in cold blood by a woman she trusted. It blows my mind that there was a failed murder attempt at her mansion in San Francisco, and then here, the job gets finished. How could anyone see that as natural causes?"

He studies her, then scratches his head. "I can get these analyzed, but don't hold your breath. And sure, I can poke around too, but so much time has passed. Don't get me wrong, I agree with you that Mrs. Stanford was poisoned. Most Hawaiians who still remember the story do. But without proof, it's gonna be hard to make a case," he says.

"Murder has no statute of limitations, does it?"

"No, but your alleged perpetrator is no longer among the living," he points out.

"Obviously, but that doesn't mean the truth shouldn't be told. We're talking about a huge cover-up, a huge scandal, a huge injustice."

Frank comes over to the table and runs his hands over the leather-bound journal. "What I don't get is why this maid, 'Iliahi, never came forward, if she knew what happened and even took the gloves. Have you thought about that?"

"It's the one thing I don't know. But I would guess she was afraid. There were a lot of powerful people involved, and money, and secrets people didn't want to get out. 'Ili was a young girl from Hawai'i, just trying to support herself and her young brothers."

"She never alludes?" he asks.

"The journal ends. But . . . " Zoe turns the pages to the back of the book. "It looks like there were pages torn out."

He catches her eye. "Your *kuleana*, then, is to find those pages."

"So you'll take the case?"

"I will."

THE LAST SEARCH
Zoe

THE BIGGEST QUESTION Zoe has is whether or not the pages were torn out for a reason—because maybe there was something important on them—or whether they were empty and just ripped away. As she approaches Doris's house, a sweet and buttery scent wafts out from the windows and fills the air. Salivating, she knocks on the now familiar door.

"I'm so glad you came back," Doris says with a bright smile.

Zoe is touched that Doris remembers. "It's lovely to see you again, and I wish I had more time to visit, but would it be okay if I have one more quick look in your attic?"

Doris steps aside. "Certainly. But you can't leave without a lilikoi muffin."

"I wouldn't dream of it."

After rummaging through the boxes again for missing pages or another journal, Zoe is sorely disappointed when she comes down without anything but cobwebs in her hair and gecko poop on her pants. The need to find these pages sears through her, and she feels helpless trying to reach back in time and search for such old answers.

"Is there anywhere else here in the house that might hold more of your aunt's stuff? Or anything she might have told you?" Zoe asks.

Doris gives her a sad smile. "Time swallows things, and most times, there is nothing we can do about it."

"Well, if something should pop into your head, please have your daughter call me," Zoe says, leaving her card and a note on the table in case Doris forgets. "I'll be heading back to Oregon tomorrow morning."

"In that case, here's a little edible souvenir. Something to remember us by," Doris says, handing her a muffin wrapped in a napkin.

Cut in half and slathered in butter, it's sweet and tart, with crunchy black seeds. But a muffin is not what Zoe came here for, and she needs to get back to the hotel room and figure out her next move. She checks her phone again; still no word from Avery.

ZOE LIES ON the beach under a coconut tree, making up for the past week of rain and wind. The fronds rustle lightly above her, shifting the shade. So much has happened since she arrived, she almost feels like she's been living someone else's life. Except she hasn't. It's her own. She begins to doubt herself. Doubt that anything really happened with Dylan, question taking Storm home, doubt this new book idea. What authority does she have, telling such a complicated and controversial story?

The doubt builds into a panic, and she hurries back to the room. Time to quit the wishful thinking and send the weak romance book proposal. It's the professional and mature thing to do, and it might save her contract. Storm looks up at Zoe, whiskers twitching. Zoe runs her hand down the cat's back, and Storm actually bites her. It's hard to tell if it's a love bite or a real bite, and Zoe yanks her arm away. Storm glares at her.

"What was that for?"

The cat settles back into her cocoon in the blankets and begins licking her tail, apparently not interested in discussing the matter. Zoe wonders, what is the message here? There must be one. *There always is if you look close enough*, she can hear her mom say. She goes and sits on the lanai, quieting her mind and staring at the ocean. In time, thoughts begin to arise. *You are here. You are doing the work. This is the part where you struggle and then come away stronger. Storms stir things up, but eventually they settle and the sun comes out again. Trust yourself.*

Still in her bikini, she drags the romance proposal and the pages into the trash and composes an email to Avery and Melinda. She feels numb for a moment, then hot and cold, then excited and relieved and free as a seabird. So what if they don't want it? She'll find a way.

Greetings from Waikiki,

I hate to let you both down, but in the end, I do not have a second romance novel proposal for you. I came to Hawaii with the intention of getting it done, but what I ended up with would not have been a decent follow-up to The Marriage Pact, and people would have noticed. In the end, it's my name on these books, and I can't live with a mediocre book going out onto shelves, one that I feel lukewarm about. But hear me out. This Jane Stanford story, what I'm calling The Poison Theory, is the book of my heart, the one I need to write right now. It's a story the world needs to hear. I have a feeling that another romance novel is in my future, but it's not in my present. I hope you

will consider switching gears and picking this one up,
Melinda. I can promise you one thing: You won't be
sorry.

Aloha,
Zoe

It feels like she's just leaped from a cliff, but once she hits
Send, there is no turning back.

AFTER TAKING A cab to a nearby cat clinic and picking up a
cat carrier for the flight tomorrow, Zoe takes one last swim
just as a honey-gold sun dips below the horizon. She follows
the sand channels leading out to where the waves break on a
shallower patch of reef. The water feels silky on her skin, and
it wraps her in its warmth as she floats on her back, arms and
legs spread wide. The trip hasn't been what she expected—it's
been so much more.

She thinks of Ginger, and senses her in the salt water that
holds her body, in the bright white puffy clouds that hang over
the ocean, and in the strange events that have led her to this
moment. Gin would have loved Dylan, and she can almost
hear her rooting for him and getting in Zoe's face, demanding
to know what she was thinking when she led him on under
false pretenses for so long. Gin put up with no bullshit, and
that was one of the things Zoe loved most about her.

"Friend, I miss you more than you will ever know," she
says to the sky and a white, long-tailed bird riding the wind
currents overhead.

It strikes her that Dylan reminds her of their senior year
art teacher, Mr. Wolf. Gin and Zoe both had crushes on him,
as probably did most girls in their class. He had a lovely wife,

twin boys and a cabin in the woods that he brought the class to on a field trip to paint *en plein air*. He felt like a mix between a teacher, a father and a good friend, and Gin used to say, "We need to hold out for our own Mr. Wolf."

Maybe in a roundabout way, Zoe had been holding out. She just hadn't realized it yet.

It's twilight now, and she finds herself farther out than she realized, and no one else is near. The waves are tiny, and two surfers sit on longboards in the distance toward Diamond Head. Zoe turns to head in when a torpedo-shaped figure darts in front of her, just beneath the surface save for the white tip of a fin. She has no idea what you're supposed to do when approached by a shark, so she goes completely still.

The small shark comes around again, this time more leisurely. Somewhere between three and four feet long, the creature looks to be mostly tail, and there is nothing aggressive in its movement. *Fish. It's just a fish*, she tells herself. Through the clear water, she sees a dark eye and swears it's watching her. There is an awareness and intelligence there that surprises her.

Her whole system seems to be tuning in to things on a different frequency, and she wonders if it has to do with Hawai'i or is just a result of allowing herself to be vulnerable.

"Is that you, Gin? Because it would be just like you to turn yourself into a shark," Zoe says, filled with a powerful knowing that the animal means her no harm.

She watches the small fin slice through the water, meandering out toward open ocean, leaving her with a sense that maybe things will work out after all.

IN THE MORNING, a knock comes on the door. It's early yet, and she cracks it, expecting housekeeping, but instead, a young dark-haired woman, all made up and in a blue Hawaiian-print uniform, stands there. It takes a moment for it to register that this is not a ghost but the living, breathing 'Iliahi. 'Ili. Doris's daughter.

"Can I come in?" 'Ili asks.

Zoe steps out of the way. "Of course."

She's holding a Ziploc bag, and in it, a book. "I know it's early, but I have to get to work."

"No worries. I have to catch a flight anyway," Zoe says, eyeing the bag.

"My mom said you came by yesterday, asking if there were any more journals, and it got me thinking—all those book-shelves. Could it somehow have ended up there? So I looked over every square inch of them, and I found this on the top shelf, lying under an old photo album."

She holds out the book in the bag, and Zoe carefully takes it. This one is different—it's a Victorian-style hardback note-book. "Have you read it?"

"I have. And I think you'll find what you're looking for. I have to go or I'll be late, but I ask that you hand-deliver it back to us once you are done, and the other one too. I'm a flight attendant with Hawaiian, so I can get you a buddy pass if you need it. These journals are too important to send in the mail."

"Absolutely," Zoe says, breathless.

There's no time to read it now, but the journal burns a hole in her carry-on as she takes a hotel shuttle to the airport with one very unhappy cat.

FROM THE JOURNAL OF
'ILIAHI BALDWIN, 1905
March 1

THE PRESS IS having a field day with the story, and the entire front page is dedicated to Mrs. Stanford. And though I was interviewed by the sheriff, there is no mention of me, not even when they retraced our carriage ride to the Pali. When we spoke, my tongue burned with the need to tell him what I saw, but Thelma's threat was stamped in my mind. Telling would not bring back Jane, and I have two young brothers to take care of. I worry the decision may haunt me, but my hands are tied. The woman is shrewd, I'll give her that.

In the newspaper, the sheriff goes so far as telling of Jane's previous poisoning, and that the bottle of bicarbonate is said to contain strychnine, but he's waiting on the chemist results on the bottle of bicarbonate, the glass she drank from and the spoon that was used to scoop it in. There was also a theory mentioned that Mrs. Stanford may have committed suicide, and that she was a spiritualist and plagued with hallucinations. Just because a person consults mediums does not mean they are insane.

A coroner's jury has been called, consisting of Mr. Price, Mr. Hersche, Mr. Hayes, Mr. Jeffrey, Mr. Harvey and Mr. Cunha. No females, of course. Dr. Humphris has refused to make a public statement until the inquest, which they say will be held tomorrow, though he did go as far as saying the contents of the vial were bitter. *The Hawaiian Gazette* does go so far as having a box that states the circumstances surrounding her death strongly suggest poisoning.

There are also photos of Dot and Thelma, and Thelma found it in herself to speak to a *Hawaiian Star* reporter. The way she gave minute details immediately caught my attention. I know from living with Liko, who often lies, that when people are not truthful, they tend to go overboard, spewing mounds of irrelevant information in the hopes of appearing cooperative. I can always tell when Liko is lying and have developed a knack for it in others too.

Interestingly, there is also a small box at the bottom of the front page that says, "A friend of the late Mrs. Stanford said last night, 'Did someone want to profit by her death? Not all her fortune was turned over to the University. A million or so was withheld for private bequest. Perhaps some of the heirs got in a hurry.'"

That makes me curious.

THE ANSWER
Zoe

PORTLAND IS FOGGY, and the plane shudders a few times on the descent. Zoe closes the journal, which she has studied word by word for the past four and a half hours, and thinks to herself, *this is it.* Her whole body hums with tension at this new information. Though all accounts paint a picture of a distraught, hysterical woman agonizing over the death of her employer and friend, Thelma was actually cool and calculating. Bold and daring with a touch of evil. To have all those around her fooled must have taken some special skill.

And poor 'Iliahi—what a heavy burden to carry all those years. But her family came first, and she was savvy enough to know that no one would believe a young Hawaiian maid who lied about her age in order to get hired. Thelma held all the cards, and she used them cunningly. Zoe can't help but admire 'Ili, forced to make an impossible choice. And yet chasing the truth would not have brought back Jane, and would likely have drawn all eyes to herself as a possible suspect.

Zoe leans back, closing her eyes and saying a silent prayer that the lab results back up what she already knows. She can ask Frank to take what they have to the police. The Hawai'i police, not the California police. This thought brings her some peace, but her soul still feels restless.

STORM HOWLS THE whole way to the house, and by the time they pull into the towering Douglas-fir-lined driveway, her little voice is hoarse and scratchy. Nothing that Zoe can say comforts the frightened animal. The minute they get inside the house, she sets out bowls of water and tuna fish and opens the carrier door in front of them. Storm sniffs, then tentatively steps out and surveys her new surroundings.

Zoe lets her be, turns on the heat and flops down on the couch, looking out the high chalet-style windows at the cluster of trees that surround her. The house is tiny but perfect, and far enough out of town where she has space to dream and wander. Six acres of mostly wooded bliss, and she knows that Storm is going to eventually love it.

Avery has been ghosting her, which isn't entirely unusual. Every now and then she goes radio silent, but this feels weird for even Avery. She feels sure that she's blown it. Avery will drop her, and no publisher will ever want to work with her again. And then over on the table, the phone rings. Finally. But it's not Avery, or even Dylan. It's Melinda.

Zoe picks up, pulse spiking and trying to sound casual. "Hey, Melinda."

Melinda never calls her. "Zoe. It's late here, so I'm going to make this quick. Avery and I finally spoke this morning. I was in meetings all day, and I need to run this by the team before I come back with an answer. But before I take it to them, I need to ask you one thing."

She swallows hard. "Okay."

"Are you prepared for the backlash this could stir when the book comes out?"

Hell yes. "I am if you are."

"That's all I wanted to know."

Wingbeats of hope. "So, what are you saying? That I can write it?"

"If the team gives us the green light, I'm all for it. But I need to warn you, it's going to be a tough sell. This is a big jump from your last book."

"What about the ending? I just found even more proof in a journal, but I haven't heard back yet on the lab results of the gloves."

"It sounds to me like you know enough. I should know Friday what the team decides."

That's the thing about books, though—they present the facts and let readers decide for themselves.

FRIDAY FEELS LIKE a decade away, and Zoe keeps herself busy getting Storm acclimated. All day long, the cat sits under a chair by the picture windows, peering out at meadowlarks and sparrows and woodpeckers. When a hawk floats past overhead, her whiskers twitch. She's taken to the litter box well, but Zoe can tell she wants to go outside and explore these strange new surroundings. From what she's read about moving cats, Storm should stay inside for two weeks before they begin venturing out. Let her settle.

Zoe could go out if she wanted to, but the weather is dreary and cold and depressing, so when she's not thinking about Dylan and trying to coax Storm out from under the chair, she spends her time delving into David Starr Jordan's past. Not only was he a university president and prominent ichthyologist, he was a highly influential eugenicist and is considered to have spawned its rise in the States. He wove eugenics into his talks, wrote papers on it and took leadership roles on boards that promoted the movement.

Her eyes sting when she reads how California passed a law in 1909 that legalized forced sterilizations on anyone deemed *unfit*. In one of his texts, she sees that he supported education for women solely for the purpose of them being able to raise intelligent and worthy children. As she weeds through the information, one thing becomes clear: David Starr Jordan answered only to David Starr Jordan. Under his thumb, Stanford became an old boys' network of professors who Jordan deemed fit—often white men with similar beliefs, regardless of their moral character. No wonder he and Jane clashed.

But questionable ethics do not a murderer make, and no amount of searching gives her any proof that he was directly related to Jane's death. Zoe so desperately wants to nab him but realizes she might have to settle for Thelma, present Jordan's actions and let the readers decide for themselves. If, of course, she gets to write the book.

ON THURSDAY, IT SNOWS. Zoe lies in bed, Storm by her feet, watching snowflakes fall and fighting the urge to pick up the phone and call Dylan. To beg and plead her case, and tell him everything she's learned. It hasn't even been a week since she last saw him, but she misses him badly. Maybe she'll just stay in bed all day and watch the floating snow and snuggle with Storm, let the world outside do what it wants. Everything feels so out of her hands.

Eventually, though, she has to get up to make coffee. A steaming mug of strong brew jump-starts her into cleaning mode, and she scours the house from floor to ceiling. Then later, when the snow stops falling and the temperature climbs to a reasonable twenty-eight degrees, she takes a long walk in the squeaky fresh snow, ending up at the trailhead that leads up the mountains to the network of trails where she and Gin used to hike. Zoe pushes out the darkness by holding on to her gold pocket watch and imagining the shark in Hawai'i.

Black clouds slide down the mountain, so she has to turn around and hurry home, but she feels an urgent pull to visit the place where her friend took her last breath. As soon as the weather clears, she'll go. On the way back, she thinks of the séances Jane Stanford attended and her frequent attempts at communicating with her lost loved ones, and the overwhelming feelings of loneliness in her dreams. The broken heart, it seems, is one of our most human conditions.

AVERY CALLS FRIDAY morning as Zoe is rereading the journal. It's hard to answer, knowing that so much hangs in the words that Avery has to say.

"I have good news for you!" Avery almost sings into the phone.

This is how she always delivers the good news. Right up front. For which Zoe is thankful.

Zoe squeals. "No!"

"Yessss."

A towering wave of happiness breaks over her. "Any more details?"

"Delivery date is December, ninety thousand words. Same advance, same everything. Have you found out about the gloves?" she says all in one breath.

"Not yet, but I'll let you know as soon as I do."

Zoe dances around the room, and Storm tips her head, watching this strange human.

"I've been reading up on the story, Zoe, and I agree with you. This is a story that needs to be told. I can't believe the university hasn't changed their position."

"They're going to have to, if we can help it."

SATURDAY DAWNS CLEAR and crisp. Zoe drives to the trailhead this time, wearing a wilted yellow plumeria lei around her neck that she purchased at the Honolulu airport. The weather is supposed to hold all day, and she can't wait any longer to go see Gin. Bundled, and carrying a full thermos of coffee in her pack, she sets out at a fast clip. It's been a while since she's hiked all the way to the cliff, and it's a less direct route than from the neighborhood she grew up in. But strenuous hikes often work miracles. They are when her best story ideas usually present themselves.

As she travels the pine-scented trail, all of the worries she's been accumulating slowly peel off of her. So when she reaches the cliff that Gin supposedly tumbled from, her mind is open and attuned to the trees and the rocks and the two hawks that spiral above. The way down is steep, and she carefully descends, holding on to roots and branches. At the bottom, nothing has changed, and it's impossible not to see Gin lying there, crumpled.

If only starts playing in her head. If only Zoe had pushed Gin to let her in on the secret affair. If only Zoe had insisted the police do more. If only Zoe had investigated on her own. Come up with something—anything that Gin's parents or the authorities could not ignore. But she had been so young, and still under the illusion that the adults had it figured out.

There are patches of snow everywhere, same as all those years ago, and she takes off the still-fragrant lei and places it on the flat sheet of rock. Her hand is trembling, and she sits under an ice-blue sky, mourning a friendship that ended too soon. But Gin will always live on in Zoe, their souls intertwined.

After a time, she says out loud, "Turns out Hawai'i was where I was meant to be. I know you were with me every step of the way. And the pocket watch you gave me, that was the connection, wasn't it?"

A tickle of wind blows across her skin, and above, one of the hawks screeches. She has no idea how long she's been here, but her whole body shivers, and her fingers have gone numb. It's time to leave and get her blood pumping before the rock claims her too.

Zoe stands. "Ready to shake things up a little? Because I certainly am."

FROM THE JOURNAL OF
ʻILIAHI BALDWIN, 1905
March 5

M Y DREAMS AND waking hours alike have been tormented by the vivid memory of my poor friend Mrs. Stanford in the throes of death. Those unearthly noises coming out of her sounded like hell itself. I keep reliving the look of fear in her gray and swollen eyes, and my sad inability to save her. That someone would purposefully kill another is unfathomable to me, but it happens all the time. What kind of cruel creatures are we humans?

In the past few days, rumors are running wild and accusations flying. It turns out that Thelma is not the only suspect in the San Francisco poisoning case. Fingers are also pointing at Ah Wing, Mrs. Stanford's house servant; Wong Toy Wong, a man with ties to Ah Wing, who maintained that he'd been defrauded by the Stanford University Trust Bank; Eliza Sutton, the maid who Dot replaced; and a British butler named Albert Beverly, who was reportedly in cahoots with Miss Sutton and siphoning off money on the side. It is said that the two were also having an affair. It would be hard to know what to believe, unless you were me. I know what I saw.

Though I have been steering clear of Thelma, who hides in her room half the time despairing, and then parades around like a princess the other half, I have been paying close attention to what the papers say, and, diary, believe me when I tell you not all of her statements add up. Several times she has changed her story. One minute she says she last used the bottle of bicarbonate January 1, and the next, that Jane never went more than a few weeks without it. Also, it's been announced in the papers that the president of Stanford University, a fish scientist of all things, is on his way here on the *Alameda* to retrieve Jane's body and bring it back to California. I should like to see this man myself, and determine what it was that Mrs. Stanford did not like about him.

March 7

THE CORONER'S JURY was begun this morning, with the attorney general here and many men of importance. Mr. Price has asked me to help out in fetching anything required, which allows me to be a fly on the wall. Today, Dot and Thelma were both interviewed. Dot was red in the face and weepy, but her answers were straightforward. Thelma played dumb as a doornail and then smart as a cat. When asked what prompted Mrs. Stanford to come to Hawai'i, she flapped her eyelashes at the judge and said, "How will I begin to answer?" The judge had no patience and asked her if it was a simple trip for pleasure and if she understood the question. I cheered to myself.

Thelma tried to appear upright and composed, but the twitch in her eye and the way her left hand clutched her skirt made it clear she was anything but. She was put through the wringer up there, with one hundred questions about where and when the bottle of bicarbonate had come from. She also described in strange detail how on the night of Jane's death, she put in the spoon, tilted the bottle and tapped out the soda, then tipped the bottle again this way and that, taking care not to let the soda pile up on one side. This elaborate description went on for some time. You ask me, it was bizarre.

I imagine she has her feathers up because yesterday it came out in the papers that she stands to inherit fifteen thousand dollars from Mrs. Stanford's estate. The sum is a large one and no doubt offers motive. It seems to me like the elephant in the room, and yet no real progress seemed to be made in finding any guilt on her part. The doctors also took the stand, announcing in no uncertain terms that everything they witnessed pointed to strychnine poisoning.

Meanwhile, I sat in the back biting my tongue until it bled. I feel like a coward for not stepping up, but in my heart, I know that it would come down to my word against hers, and who would believe me? Maybe Jane herself would have, but she is in another realm. These blasted men know nothing of my substance.

THE VISIT
Zoe

WHEN SHE PULLS into her driveway, Zoe almost slams into a vintage Blazer backing out. Whoever it is is hauling ass, and she honks to make sure the driver sees her. Then she pulls off to the side so they can pass, rolling down her window so she can tell them to slow down and see what they're doing here. The other car's window is up, and she can make out the silhouette of a man. Instead of rolling down his window, he gets out of the car and walks around to her side. Chilled to the bone, Zoe just wants to get back and warm up by the fire, and then she realizes the guy looks remarkably like Dylan.

Oh my God. It *is* Dylan.

"Sorry about that. I have a tendency toward having a lead foot," he says, a smile visible only in his eyes.

"What are you doing here?" she asks.

He leans down and says, "I wanted to talk to you—geez, Bridget, your lips are purple. Can we go back to the house?"

"Follow me," she says, teeth chattering.

She had run the whole way back to the car from the cliff, trying to warm herself up. But maybe being in Hawai'i had thinned her blood, because she still feels numb. When she parks, Dylan pulls up behind her and hops out lightning-fast, coming to open her door.

"You came," she says.

He nods. "I did."

"This is a surprise," she says, climbing out. "A good one—I hope."

She doesn't want to read too much into his showing up here, but oh, he looks good. Same jeans and boots, but now in a fleece-lined flannel jacket and a wool beanie, all mountainous and rugged.

"I hope so too," he says, breathing out a cloud of warm air.

Something has shifted in his voice, and the way he says it causes a warm current under her ribs. At the door, she fumbles for the key, and she feels him next to her like a heater. She steps inside, and his hand lightly touches her lower back.

"Go, sit by the fireplace," he orders, then surveys the room and grabs the fuzzy throw on the couch and brings it to her. "Can I start some hot water?"

She nods. "In the kitchen. You need to light it with a match. They're on the counter."

Storm keeps herself hidden and will come up on her own time, Zoe knows. With numb hands, she grabs some old newspaper, pine cones and firewood, and barely manages to get it all in place. Dylan comes out a minute later, adds dried bark, and lights it.

"Where were you?" he asks.

"Ginger," is all she has to say.

He nods. "How long were you out there?"

"I'm not sure. The hike was about an hour and a half—one way."

"You of all people should know that this is dangerous cold, the kind that sneaks up on you."

"I had to go," she says, "and I have so much to tell you, and I'm so, so sorry. What I did was awful and shitty and preposterous."

Dylan sits down next to her, their backs to the flames. When his knees splay out, his thigh rests against hers. "*Preposterous* is a good word for it. But I owe you an apology too. I'm sorry for being such an ass in Hawai'i and completely shutting you out. It was a knee-jerk reaction after dealing with my ex for so long. With her, it got to the point that I couldn't believe anything she said, and that really messed with my sanity. Because if you don't have trust, what do you have?"

She knows it's a rhetorical question, but she answers anyway. "Nothing."

"I had no time to process anything at the conference, and I was tired and running on fumes, and when Jeff called you Zoe, it was like a flip just switched. I went on autopilot, and I just wanted to get away."

She glances at him, then at the snowflakes drifting down outside. "Believe it or not, I had no idea that you were you when I signed up for your class. Somehow I missed the pen name part. And I would give anything to take that review back. I was young and clueless and did not realize the impact my words could have."

"You were honest. The book was everything you said it was. You actually did me a favor," Dylan says, putting a hand on her leg. "Made me hell-bent on writing a page-turner. I loaded up on writing books and got down and dirty with them until I knew I could nail the next one."

"Still, I could have done better."

One shoulder lifts. "Hindsight."

"I know, I know."

"So, why were you at the conference? Really," he asks.

There are so many reasons she could give, but in the end, she tells him the simple truth. "Because I had lost faith in myself."

"Have you gotten it back? If not, I think I can help."

She smiles. "Working on it. But yeah, I think I have."

Because the truth is, she is not an imposter. She's an imperfectly perfect human being.

"All of this, it's not why I came," Dylan says, pausing and glancing down at his scuffed boots.

"Oh?"

"Yeah, well, on the flight back, and over the past week, I haven't been able to stop thinking about you. Not one bit."

The words hang between them, and Zoe feels suddenly warmer.

"What I realized was that I really don't care if your name is Zoe or Bridget. What I care about is seeing more of you."

The heat from his hand now drops into her leg, and those light-catching eyes hold her gaze. Zoe can't look away.

"So, what do you say? Will you give me another shot?" he says tenderly.

"I should be asking you that."

"The answer is yes."

She laughs. "Did you really believe you had to ask?"

He leans close, pressing his forehead against hers. "Not really, but I wanted to be a gentleman."

Zoe inhales his scent, which is now mountain air and pine cone. "I'm glad you came, DS Wilder."

Now he laughs. "Call me whatever you want. I really don't care." A whistle comes from the kitchen, and he jumps up. "Stay here."

"The hot cocoa is on the shelf next to the fridge," she calls, marveling that Dylan Winters is in her kitchen, making her a cup of hot chocolate.

From under the couch, Storm pokes her head out, then moseys on over to Zoe. With each day that passes, she's become more emboldened. When Dylan comes out, holding a steaming mug, he and the cat both look at each other, surprised. Storm hunches her back slightly.

"Hey, little thing, I'm not going to hurt you," he says, approaching slowly. Then to Zoe, "Don't tell me—"

"It is. I brought her back with me. It's a long and convoluted story, but it feels like we were meant to find each other, and I couldn't leave her."

"I want to hear everything. Don't leave a thing out."

And so she tells him. The gloves, how Storm appeared in Doris's garden, the pocket watch, the second journal, Frank Santos, Melinda's earlier call. So much has happened in a matter of days, it's hard to keep it all straight. "Now we're just waiting to hear back from the lab."

"Your physical evidence."

"I really don't know what to expect. From what I've been able to gather, it's unlikely any residue would still be there. *If she used them to handle the strychnine, which is speculation.*"

"Possible, but not probable. Based on everything you've told me," he says.

Storm comes up and weaves her way through their legs, and Dylan leans down to scratch her behind the ears, and she lets him. Petting the cat seems so second nature, and she loves that about him. *You can tell a lot about a person by how they treat animals,* her mom always says. Zoe sips the cocoa, and he reaches behind her and gently rubs his hand up and down her back for warmth.

"I'm thinking you might need someone to keep an eye on you so you don't go and get yourself frozen to death out in the wilderness," Dylan says.

"I have this cat to keep watch over me."

"I was thinking more along the lines of a man. Someone to supervise your writing too, make sure you keep up with your word count."

"Would this someone also happen to be an ex-detective and a cowboy?"

And that's when he does it. He leans and kisses her, and every inch of her skin heats up—lips, chest, back of the knees, toes. He wraps his arms around her and they hold on to each other, fire crackling in the background.

DYLAN IS STILL there the next morning, and they watch the sunrise from the small table under the windows, where she writes. The temperature is fourteen degrees, too cold to sit on her porch, so they talk about writing and next books, and every chance he gets, he touches her. She shares her outline with him, and he offers a few suggestions. It feels so natural and yet so new and exciting, as though she has an expert at her disposal. An expert who also happens to have chafed her chin raw and kissed her in places she'd never been kissed before.

"I have to get back to the ranch and the animals. They're spoiled," he says.

She's not ready for him to leave, and already misses him, if that's possible.

But he asks, "Want to come?"

After a quick breakfast of oatmeal and berries, Zoe follows him the half hour to Sisters, then onto a winding road, wooded with towering conifers. They travel into the sticks, following a narrow stream with evidence of beaver dams. When they hit a break in the trees, she catches a glimpse of a wide-open field where several horses stand at the fence expectantly. Up ahead, Dylan turns into a driveway with two wooden posts and a sign that says LONESOME CAT RANCH.

His driveway is long, and the horses trot alongside his truck, whinnying. A black one, three chestnuts and a painted horse that resembles a dalmatian. They are beautiful, just like the property. As they drive, they pass several other fenced pastures with more horses, a giant barn and stables that remind her of a dude ranch she went to with Ginger one summer. The house sits on a bluff overlooking it all, and you could fit several of her cabins inside it.

Dylan gets out and holds his arms open wide, facing the view. "Welcome to this beautiful land that we get to call home."

Zoe spots two black cats lounging on the sun-warmed deck, one short-haired, one long. They look plump and lazy and blissfully happy.

"Lonesome Cat Ranch?" Zoe asks.

Truly a man after her own heart.

"I told you, I love black cats."

She grins. "I guess you did. But these two don't look very lonesome."

"I'm a McMurtry fan. What can I say?"

"You can take the boy out of Texas, but I guess you can't take Texas out of the boy. Isn't that what they say?"

"Something like that. Oh, and did I tell you most black cats are male? So Storm is a really special little feline."

"No, you have not."

He comes up and grabs her hand, pulling her toward the house. "Yeah, well, there's a lot I haven't told you. We haven't had the time, but I hope that's about to change."

And right now, there is nowhere else in the world she would rather be than at this ranch with this man, surrounded by trees and mountains and green as far as the eye can see.

FROM THE JOURNAL OF
'ILIAHI BALDWIN, 1905
March 10

T ODAY WAS A big day. The coroner's jury wound up announcing to the world their findings, which did not surprise me one bit, obviously. "Jane Lathrop Stanford came to her death at Honolulu, Island of O'ahu, Territory of Hawai'i, on the twenty-eighth day of February, AD 1905 from strychnine poisoning, said strychnine having been introduced into a bottle of bicarbonate of soda with felonious intent by some person or persons to this jury unknown and of the contents of which bottle Jane Lathrop Stanford had partaken."

I feel a sense of relief that this panel of experts, if you consider Mr. Price an expert, were all in agreement, but also worry that if they hone in on Thelma, she may in turn point the finger at me.

I feel so alone in this, and long for my Ma and Pa.

David Starr Jordan arrived later in the day, and I did not like the way he smelled, much like rank leather and dead fish. As a person who might consume too much meat and rich food. Nor am I sure why he is called David Starr Jordan, and not just David Jordan. He came along with three other men—a trustee named Hopkins, a detective named Callundan and a cop named Harry Reynolds—who are here to take charge of the investigation. Dr. Jordan has informed Mr. Price that he does not trust the Hawaiians, and at that I laugh. Never trust a man who will not look you in the eye, Pa always said, and Jordan has gazed at my hair, studied my breasts, inspected my hands and looked at my feet, but never once met my eyes with his.

I have decided to make myself indispensable to him, not because I like the man, but because I want to keep tabs on what he's really doing here. I get the sense he has an agenda. I overheard the two of them talking to Mr. Price in his office, and there was some heated discussion about the verdict. Dr. Jordan seemed to be fixated on the idea that Jane died of natural causes, and he kept trying to persuade Price that this was the case. Peacock tried to appease him, but remained firm in defending his jury. Good for him for standing up to such a thunderous man.

March 12

THERE HAVE BEEN meetings held here in the past couple days that have incensed me. A Dr. Waterhouse, who Jordan pulled out of the woodwork, is helping call into question every aspect of the investigation here in Hawai'i. It took me by surprise until I learned from a guest also visiting from California that a murder trial would dredge up all kinds of unsavory information about Mrs. Stanford and the university and therefore threaten its very foundation. Even worse would be a ruling that Jane committed suicide, because no document signed by an insane woman can be legally binding.

Detectives Callundan and Reynolds come and go as though they own the place, and I've seen them interviewing the doctors all over again, Thelma and Dot, and a host of others too. It was announced in the papers that the Honolulu police are no longer involved in the case, heathens that they are. What I think is that these Californians have decided it will be easier to bend the truth to whatever they need it to be without our island police force watching over their shoulders.

My invisibility has allowed me to eavesdrop, and I pick up tidbits of information in the hallways, while cleaning rooms, while serving food, while making deliveries. Though all I can do is write it down here and hope there will be an opportunity to present it at some future date.

I witnessed Thelma entering into Dr. Jordan's room, and against my better judgment I pressed my ear to the door but heard nothing through the thick and dense wood. Disappointed, but not despairing, I later found her and Jordan in a small room off the lobby with Dr. Waterhouse, and I stood at the edge of the cracked door, listening. I nearly dropped dead myself when Thelma told him Jane only had one spasm, and then seized up and died. No mention of those terrible whole-body seizures, and no mention of any of the utterances Jane made as the life leaked out of her.

I then heard Jordan asking Thelma if she thought Jane could have died from angina pectoris, spurred on by over-eating on the picnic and distention. She said yes. My blood began to curdle then, listening to the ichthyologist asking the secretary for her medical opinion. As if she would know! It does not take a genius to understand that Thelma also stands to benefit from a death from natural causes verdict, and they appear to be teaming up to somehow make this happen. I had heard enough and went back to my regular duties, which of late seem very irregular.

THE NEWS
Zoe

FRANK CALLS ON Wednesday morning with news. "I hope you are sitting down, young lady."

Zoe is outside, walking Storm on a leash, which she feels silly about doing, but she doesn't want her to bolt. At his words, she sinks onto a big boulder nearby.

"Sitting," she says.

"The gloves are laced in pure strychnine. And not just a little. Thelma must have spilled some in her palm when handling the poison."

The news hits her with the force of an avalanche, and she's glad to be supported by the rock. "So there's no question?" she says.

"No question. I have the analysis in front of me, and Mr. Yee is top-notch. Studied at—get this—Stanford University."

She's not sure whether to laugh or cry, but manages to eke out, "Thank you, Frank. I owe you big-time. Now we go to the police. I need to bring back the journals too, so I'll arrange a flight to Honolulu as soon as I can."

FROM THE JOURNAL OF 'ILIAHI BALDWIN, 1905

March 15

MR. PRICE, BLESS HIS HEART, allowed me to attend the early morning funeral of Jane Stanford at Central Union Church today. The arrival of her coffin, pulled by four black stallions, was quite a spectacle, and throngs of people crowded the street hoping for a glimpse. I got all choked up the minute I saw them, and pushed my way into the back of the church where I could at least hear the sermon. It was not lost on me that I was one of the few here who had actually met Jane, and even more rare, that I cared for the woman.

The pallbearers all wore double-breasted long coats and walked solemnly alongside the coffin. Rather than Dr. Jordan, Governor Carter, Judge Smith and Timothy Hopkins, I felt like it should have been me and Charlie and Israel from the hotel ushering her along. Not a group of men who either hardly knew her or secretly despised her. Thelma and Dot were there, all covered in veils and making a big fuss of behaving like grieving widows. Poor Dot. I wonder if she has any inkling of Thelma's true nature.

The service was simple, with the reverend droning on about how Mrs. Stanford fought the good fight, and we sang hymns that Thelma picked out on account of them being some of Jane's favorite. *Nearer, My God, to Thee* and *Beneath the Cross of Jesus*. Who really knows, though. I just hope Jane gets a better service in California. At least she still has family there. A brother and a niece who she spoke of. Beneath my breath, I hummed *Aloha 'Oe*, our song of goodbye.

March 17

THAT WORM-FACED BASTARD! Dr. Jordan has hit the high seas, and in his wake left a written statement that Jane died of natural causes and that the doctors and police and witnesses here had it all wrong. Mainly that she was old, unfit, and overate on our picnic. He claimed to have some kind of new evidence—and I know he will cite Dr. Waterhouse when questioned—that shows Jane did not die of poisoning. From the moment he arrived at the hotel, he had it out to discredit Dr. Humphris and the others as incompetent, and now I see why. Also, to add insult to injury, he had the nerve to say that Thelma took the same bicarbonate and the same cascara capsule along with Jane and experienced no ill effects. A bald-faced lie if I ever heard one, contradicting her own testimony.

High Sheriff Henry is my new hero, because he wasn't buying any of it. He even told the papers that the Californians came here not to solve the murder but to erase the fact that it ever happened, and that Jordan's statement goes against what Thelma herself had told the jury. Everyone knows that Jane came here to escape another poisoning, but the poisoner traveled alongside her like a wolf in sheep's clothing and found an unlikely ally in Dr. Jordan. I can't help but wonder if he knew ahead of time what was coming down the pike. That we may never know.

THE BOOK

Zoe

Sixteen Months Later

A COOL MORNING in June finds three black cats lounging on the bed with Zoe, soaking in the heat from the fire that Dylan lit before he went out. Zoe had fallen back asleep after he left, and the house is quiet, so she assumes he's still out feeding the horses. She pinches herself that she gets to wake up in this bed every morning, in this house. Most importantly, with this man. The scents of coffee and sweet firewood infuse the room with coziness, and she wants nothing more than to curl up and snuggle with the cats and avoid her computer all day.

But today is the big day. Release day. A day she's been waiting for since that moment in Hawai'i. Release day has always been surreal for her. With so much buildup on the way to publication—waiting to hear if the editor loves the book, hoping for a dream cover, biting your nails as those first trade reviews come out, and then hoping against hope that people buy the book and better yet, love it. The starred trade reviews and the glowing write-up in *The New York Times* have helped.

As a ghostwriter, the anticipation was nothing compared to how it was when her own book came out, and this one feels even more meaningful. More real. Writing it has quite possibly been the toughest thing she's ever done. It split her open and exposed every raw emotion in her body, but most of all sorrow and anger in equal measure. She shed more tears than on any book she's written. And when she sheds tears, she knows she's tapped in to the heart and soul of the story. One of her favorite quotes: *No tears in the writer, no tears in the reader.*

The poisoning of Jane Stanford is a kind of history that she never wants to see repeated, and yet it was an all too common occurrence in those days. A time when a woman, by chromosomal chance, was valued less than a man. And as if death by murder was not enough, to then have it brushed under the rug so blatantly.

Eventually she sits up and rubs Storm and Lulu, running her fingers through their soft fur, while Manoa sleeps by her feet. It makes her happy to see how well Storm has adjusted to moving not once, but twice. They've been here seven months now, but it feels like forever. Zoe still has dreams of Waikiki, but they are trailing off in their frequency.

Now she remembers she had another dream last night. She sees herself sitting at the edge of a wooden pier, feet dangling in the warm blue ocean below. Hawaiian music lifts off the shore, adding to the relaxed and easy feeling. The white tip shark passes below, and a gray-haired woman next to her picks up her hand and holds it tight. Someone else sits down next to them, dark hair, dark eyes. She too picks up Zoe's hand, and they all sit there in silence, watching the sun go down.

It isn't until Zoe gets out of bed that she sees the paper on the floor. Strange, it's a piece of Moana stationery. Dylan brought back a pad of it, and she's seen it sitting on the bookshelf, but he never uses it. As though it's some kind of memorabilia of where they first met. He's sweet like that. She reaches down and picks up the paper, curious. There are two words written on it, in her handwriting, not Dylan's.

Thank you.

Zoe clutches the paper to her heart, feeling like she's done something substantial—and magical. With a little help from her friends, somewhere on the other side.

'ILIAHI BALDWIN
1945

I T HAS BEEN forty years since the death of Jane Stanford, and yet I still think about her often. Her large gray eyes, the force of her character and the way she bore her sadness like an albatross. She came into my life but for a fleeting moment, and yet left me with a deep imprint of how strong a woman can be, even when all seems lost. I carry this with me still, and it has served me well over the years—when I was not able to conceive, when Max fell ill with pneumonia, when Ma finally succumbed to her illness.

This morning, word came that Thelma Bellingham at long last died. I've kept tabs on her over the years, as she lived out her life in a house in the Palo Alto foothills called Monte Blanca. Jane Stanford gave her the house, imagine that. Rather than leave the Stanford world behind, which I thought she might do, she boldly embraced a comfortable and privileged life.

Ten years ago, she published a book that was full of crap. It was as though she believed enough time had passed that people forgot what really happened and she could craft things as she wished in a strange and twisted tale.

I have not forgotten, yet I write this while knowing that in my lifetime, I am not going to the authorities with my story. I have told Sarge, and we have both decided that now is not the time to bring the truth to light. It would surely be ill received. I still believe we have a long way to go before anyone would believe me.

But if there is one thing that I've learned, it's that everything has a season, and as with nature, you cannot rush these things. One day, when the sun is at just the right angle and a storm washes in, all will be revealed. I know it in my bones, and so does Jane, who visits me in the moonlight now and again.

THE END

A NOTE FROM THE AUTHOR

While this book is a work of fiction, much of what I've written about Jane Stanford is based on accounts that I've read of her life, as well as her death and the investigation that followed. I've also changed the names of some of those involved and took some liberties with the setting at the Moana. Most scholars agree that the Hawai'i authorities and the doctors who attended her death believed she was poisoned, and that the cause of death was changed to *death from natural causes* (presumably a heart ailment) once David Starr Jordan (then president of Stanford University) arrived in Hawai'i and hired a local doctor to give an outside opinion. Robert W.P. Cutler, MD, a prior professor at Stanford who later studied the case in depth, wrote in his book *The Mysterious Death of Jane Stanford* that there "is ample evidence that Mrs. Stanford was poisoned, that she was given good care, and that Jordan went over there to hush it up." Another professor emeritus at Stanford, Richard White, who wrote a more recent book called *Who Killed Jane Stanford: A Gilded Age Tale of Murder, Deceit, Spirits and the Birth of a University,* points a finger at Jane's secretary Bertha Berner as the likely killer.

Sadly, we will never know for sure what really happened, but based on the information out there, I decided to write an ending to the story in which we do find out the truth of what really happened to Jane. This meant I would have to invent a character, 'Iliahi Baldwin, who witnessed something at the Moana Hotel to implicate the killer. Because, to me, it is entirely likely that a housekeeper or hotel employee may have seen something suspicious, but for reasons of their own never came forward. When you think about it, to challenge the president of a prestigious university would have been intimidating for most people, especially a young woman of that time period. I also changed Jane's secretary's name to Thelma and created a scenario that to me felt very plausible. For story's sake, I thought it would be intriguing to have a woman staying at the Moana in the same room as Jane one hundred years later (though Room 120 no longer exists after a remodel) and because of Jane's interest in spiritualism, to connect the two on that level.

I've always had an interest in Stanford University because my father and many of his friends attended school there. He was on the swim team and those friendships and memories he made while at The Farm lasted a lifetime. So, when I stumbled upon this story while researching for another book, I was shocked that I had never heard this story prior to that moment. The more I looked into what happened, the more I knew I had to write about it. It really was a case of truth is stranger than fiction. I've also attended many writers conferences over the years, so the 2005 storyline was a delight to write.

My own love of Waikiki formed early, as I grew up going to the beach there, surfing out front at Canoes, and paddling in the 4th of July Walter J. Macfarlane regatta every year directly in front of the Moana Hotel. I have watched countless sunsets from these very shores, so it felt very special to write about the setting and include a bit of Waikiki history, especially in 1905. The result is three strong women across time and space, whose lives intersect in both haunting and life-altering ways. I hope these characters came to life for you the same way they did for me!

If you are interested in reading more about Jane Stanford, here are several other books I found interesting and helpful in my research: *Mrs. Leland Stanford, An Intimate Account* by Bertha Berner, *Jane Lathrop Stanford, Mother of a University* by Catherine Pyke, and *Iron Will, The Life and Letters of Jane Stanford* by Gunther W. Nagel.

ACKNOWLEDGMENTS

As always, I am ever so grateful to my agent Elaine Spencer, who goes above and beyond with every one of my books. Her wisdom and suggestions always make me dig so much deeper, and I don't know what I would do without her as my first reader. Also, I am so thankful for my editor Meredith Clark and her guidance and keen insight, as well as her kindness and enthusiasm for my book. I owe so much to everyone at my publisher MIRA who has helped work on my books along the way—marketing, sales, publicity, cover designers, copy-editors, proofreaders and every single person involved. I have so much appreciation for my TEAM!

And to the book-loving community and all of my readers, none of this would be possible without YOU, so thank you! All of your messages, posts, letters, reviews and emails mean the world to me, truly. I appreciate each and every one. Getting to do something I love so much is one of the greatest gifts in life and I don't take any of it for granted. I am also thankful for my love Todd, who holds me up and makes me laugh and is always there for me (including making me hard-boiled eggs with cute notes written on them). He also makes sure I don't sit in the house all day writing and editing, and that I get out and walk or swim or paddle. And of course, a huge mahalo to my friends and family and kitty, who are my biggest cheerleaders and supporters. Each time I get to publish a book, my heart is full. It never gets old.

DISCUSSION QUESTIONS FOR
THE GUEST IN ROOM 120
(Warning: Contains Spoilers)

1. Had you heard the story of Jane Stanford's death at the Moana Hotel before reading this novel?

2. Jane, Zoe, and 'Iliahi are all so different, and yet there is an undeniable connection between the three. Which of the characters do you identify with the most and why?

3. Jane Stanford was a complicated woman and was known for her iron will, yet she was also a doting mother and a loving wife. How did you feel about her character?

4. Have you ever been to the Moana Hotel? Waikiki Beach? Would you rather visit in 1905 or 2005?

5. 'Iliahi's mother contracted leprosy (Hansen's Disease). Are you familiar with the story of people in Hawai'i with the disease being sent to a remote peninsula on Moloka'i to live out their lives?

6. Jane was quoted as saying her late husband and son would visit her often from the afterlife, and she was known to

attend seances. What are your thoughts on the spiritualism of those times? Fact or fiction?

7. Zoe has nightmares that feel hauntingly real. Have you ever had exceptionally vivid dreams or episodes of sleepwalking or sleeptalking. Or even sleepwriting?

8. How did Zoe grow and change while in Hawai'i at the Writers Conference?

9. Did you think Zoe should have told Dylan sooner about who she was? Would you have come clean?

10. Did you have suspicions about who poisoned Jane as you were reading?

11. What do you think Storm represented in the story?

12. In real life, we do not have any proof of who killed Jane, though there has been much speculation. Did you feel that what happened in the novel is plausible? That there may have been an employee at the hotel who knew what really happened?